HOW SHE ESCAPED

MARTINA MONROE BOOK 10

H.K. CHRISTIE

KEEKSTAR
MEDIA

Cover design by Odile Stamanne

www.authorhkchristie.com

First edition: October 2023

ISBN: 978-1-953268-17-4

012725h

For Mr. Founders

1

VICTORIA

THIRTY-FIVE YEARS EARLIER

My courage was in full force. This new fortitude came to me the week before as I was healing from a punishment. I guess I couldn't take all the credit for it. If I had the money to give him, I wouldn't have been laid up and had a few sober moments to think about my life and daughter. My family. What did they think of me? Did they still love me?

All I knew was that if I was going to start over and be there for my baby girl, I was going to need some money. That was a problem, considering I didn't have any. The moment I earned some cash, Blade took it. That was when I had come up with my plan. I would break free and go out on my own—just for a bit until I could save enough money to get a place of my own. The social worker said I had to if I wanted to regain custody of Shannon.

Full of confidence, I faked being too sick to work when really, I'd gone out on my own a few streets over. I wanted so badly to tell someone I was going to make it out, but I couldn't risk Blade learning the truth. He'd stop at nothing to find me, and I needed my girls to have deniability.

The plan worked for a few days. But I'd been a straight fool to think he wouldn't find out and come for me. I hadn't realized he hadn't believed my story for more than a minute. He had been following me. And when he found me, he wasn't happy.

After a jab to my ribs and a right hook to my jaw, he found my stash and took all of my money—everything I'd been saving to get away from him. He'd beat and tortured me for days. A lesson for me and the others. Nobody crossed Blade.

To be honest, I was surprised he hadn't killed me.

And I used that new development for a new plan.

I wasn't always like this—broken, battered, bruised, and shamefully addicted. But I didn't want to be like that anymore, and I knew my time on this earth was limited if I didn't get away.

When he left, certain I was too injured to leave, I made my escape. I was shocked to have made it all the way down Market Street before he spotted me. It must have been my black-and-blue face that stuck out in the crowd.

Our eyes locked, and I sprinted down the nearest alley and zigzagged across the bustling street. I made it two blocks over and down another side street. With my back up against the concrete wall, I took a moment to catch my breath and ignore the pain radiating through my body. Shaking with fear and exhaustion, I found some more of that courage and inched forward to peek around the corner, then gasped and stood back.

He was less than a block away, his face red and angry. Who would have known, with the size of his gut and the amount of alcohol he consumed, he could run so fast? I was pretty trim, and on a good day—not having been beaten for three days straight—with the right dosage, I was fast and had energy.

Realizing I didn't have anywhere to go, it occurred to me my plan was flawed. Could I do anything right? Maybe. Maybe not. But I knew what my fate would be if he caught me.

Despite my waning energy, I sprinted down the alleyway. It felt like an eternity, but then I heard him yell out, "You can run, but you can't hide."

Fairly certain it was him and not just the voices in my head, I looked both ways and made a left. I wasn't familiar with this part of the city, with gentrification making things look nice and distant from all the sex shops and peep shows—it was the new San Francisco.

I spotted a man—a young man, good-looking. Would he help? Or would he see me as an old rag and think I wasn't worth his time? That's how most of society felt about me and the other girls, like we were less than human, unworthy of being in the same places as the "clean, friendly folks." Johns, on the other hand—pillars of the community.

Explain that one to me.

But I'd come too far not to try. With every bit of gusto I had left, I hobbled toward the young man. Just a few feet away from safety, a force from behind pushed me. I tripped, my face hitting the pavement. My head screamed and my neck arched backward as he pulled my hair. Blade, with his knee on my back, growled, "Now, you get to meet the real Blade." I'd heard the stories of how he'd gotten his street name. It was his weapon of choice.

At that moment, I squeezed my eyes shut and offered a prayer to God. The one who I was sure had forgotten me a long time ago. But the cut didn't come, and I heard a scuffle and the pressure on my back removed. I wondered if I was dead.

My eyes sprang open to see Blade and the young man fighting. Blood was spurting from the young man. It was a lot of blood. Too much blood. That man had sacrificed himself for me, perhaps unknowingly. All I knew was I couldn't take that window of opportunity for granted.

I ran across the street as fast as I could, dodging cars with horns blaring, knowing the only way I was going to live was if I ran and never stopped.

2

MARTINA

WITH EXTRA PEP in my step, I made my way over to Stavros's office. "Hey," I greeted.

He looked up with inquisitive brown eyes. "You look happy. I'm assuming it went well?"

It had. We'd successfully extracted a woman from an abusive relationship she'd been trapped in for nearly seven years. She had tried to leave several times on her own, but each time he tracked her down. He had even filed motions in the courts, claiming she had tried to abduct their children, which, technically, she had. That was when her lawyer told her about our firm.

We created a safe and legal plan to extract her and the children. Once we extracted them and placed them into a safe house, the lawyer initiated proceedings to gain emergency custody of the children and an order of protection. That way, she wouldn't be imprisoned for child abduction if her husband found her. The plan had gone off without a hitch, and they were safe until their next move. Helen faced a long journey ahead, but she was strong. She was determined to start a new life, away from a husband who not only abused her physically and mentally, but had also turned his violence toward the young children. Helen explained that in the moment he hit their eldest child, she knew she had to leave.

"Yep," I said to Stavros. "All paperwork is in order, and the family is in a safe house."

"Nice job. Are you heading out?"

With a smile, I said, "Just about."

"Pizza night?"

Friday movie and pizza nights seemed like a distant memory. Zoey was almost seventeen years old and often had plans on Friday nights. Time changes things, and I found myself having other plans too. Wilder and I had been dating for eight months, and it was going really well. Dating was so different from what I remembered, and I hadn't really dated since Jared. I was in my early twenties when I met him. We got married, and then, a few years later, I'd become a single parent. Life changes, and all you can do is change with it. But I had no complaints. Wilder was funny, smart, and handsome. He made me see the world in a new light.

"Not unless Wilder's taking me to a pizzeria tonight."

"A date?" Stavros hesitated, choosing his words carefully. "I know I shouldn't say this in the workplace, but you look genuinely happy. I think Wilder deserves partial credit for that."

It wasn't that I wasn't happy before I met Wilder, but he added an extra zest to my life. I never would have imagined I'd be dating into my forties, but I wondered if that dating chapter was going to end soon too. Wilder said he had an important conversation he wanted to have with me. Marriage? Was it too soon?

Working on the family extraction and all the paperwork associated with helping Helen leave with her children legally and safely had distracted me from that night's conversation. But now, butterflies fluttered in my belly, wondering about the nature of the impending conversation.

Did I want him to propose? Would he do it on a Friday night, after both of us had endured long workdays? He'd surprised me before, so I couldn't rule it out just yet.

My mind raced, trying to discern my own feelings. Would I say yes if he proposed? I knew Zoey adored him, and honestly, I did too. But wasn't it too soon for marriage? Or maybe he just wanted to move in together? But even that felt like a leap, with Zoey still at home. She and I had our routine. Our life was quiet, and we had Barney, our furry pup, to provide extra love and laughter.

Introducing another person into our household felt strange. I certainly wouldn't consider it without discussing it with Zoey first. In fact, I thought I'd prefer marriage, or at least a longer courtship before moving in together. Knowing all the signs of a bad relationship, I was cautious, but I hadn't seen any red flags with Wilder.

"Well," I replied. "I am happy."

"I'm glad. You know, it's what Jared would've wanted. He'd never want you to be alone or to think you couldn't move on in a new relationship because of him."

Stavros had worked with, and served alongside, Jared in the Army, what now seemed like a lifetime ago.

"I know," I whispered. "And I believe he'd want me to be happy."

He nodded. "Well, have a good time tonight. I'll see you on Monday."

I waved and headed back toward my office, ready to pack up. My cell phone buzzed; it was my darling daughter. "Hey, Zoey, what's up?"

"Just a reminder that I have plans tonight. I know you do too, so Grandma said she'd come over and take care of Barney."

"That's great. I'm sure he'll love that." Although I had planned to stop at home to feed and walk Barney, I knew he'd enjoy the company instead of being alone for a few hours.

"Have fun tonight, Mom."

"You too, sweetheart."

I hung up the phone and finished packing my bag. Zoey would graduate this year, and she had been eagerly awaiting her college acceptance letters. Would she stay on the West Coast? I certainly hoped so. The thought of her being far away unnerved me, but there were airplanes. Wherever she went, I would be sure to visit—frequently.

Confident and prepared for the big night ahead, I walked to the lobby and stopped. I was surprised to see Mrs. Pearson at the office at this hour. I suspected it was because of her visitor. The woman, probably in her late fifties or maybe early sixties, was standing close and talking low. I waved discreetly, not wanting to interrupt their discussion. But when Mrs. Pearson noticed me, she said, "Oh, Martina, do you have a minute?"

Considering that my mom was taking care of Barney, the spoiled pup, I figured I didn't need to rush home before meeting Wilder. "Sure, what's up?"

Mrs. Pearson gestured to the woman next to her. "I want to introduce you to a dear friend of mine. This is Nancy Galloway. She's hoping you can help her find an old friend."

I raised an eyebrow. "Oh?"

Nancy had kind eyes, and while she was dressed conservatively, I noticed old tattoos on her arms and chest. Had she led a different life before she became friends with Mrs. Pearson?

"Is she missing?"

Nancy hesitated a moment. "Not exactly. I haven't seen her in thirty-five years, but I'd like to find her if you can. Patrice and I had spoken over the holidays about all the work you did during your time with the Cold Case Squad. She said if anyone could find her, you could."

"That's very kind. But I should say, thirty-five years is a long time." I wondered if I had the time or inclination to delve into the story of Nancy's old friend, but then again, it could be exciting to go out pounding the pavement searching for the woman.

Mrs. Pearson interjected, "It's a special case, Martina. Nancy can explain. But it's a tough one. She doesn't have her last name, just a description of what she looked like and some details about her life and family from all those years ago."

That certainly piqued my interest.

Over the past eight months, I'd worked on a few mildly challenging cases, including one with the CoCo County Sheriff's Department. It was exhilarating to be back in action with them. I loved my work, but I hadn't had many truly tough cases lately. If I were a betting woman, I'd bet this one would be. Glancing at my new sparkly wristwatch—a recent birthday gift from Zoey—I figured I had a little time if I headed straight to dinner from the office. "Do you have time to discuss the details now?" I asked Nancy.

Her eyes brightened. "Yes, if you do. I mean, it looks like you were about to leave."

"I've got a little time."

Mrs. Pearson placed a comforting hand on Nancy's shoulder, her voice full of confidence. "I knew Martina would help. She's our best. If anybody can find Victoria, it's her."

I felt a surge of gratitude for Mrs. Pearson's faith in me. My gut was telling me this was going to be an interesting case.

3

MARTINA

AFTER LEADING Nancy into a small conference room, I sat my bag down. "I have to admit, I only have about forty-five minutes," I said. "But anything you can tell me will be useful. I promise, first thing tomorrow, I'm on it."

"You're so kind to talk to me now. I really appreciate it."

If I were being truthful, it was a relief to have forty-five minutes less of wondering what Wilder wanted to talk about. Could he be breaking up with me? I mean, things were going great. It could only be a proposal. I wasn't sure I was ready.

"What can you tell me about your friend Victoria?"

"Well, it might be easier if I tell you my story and how it connects with Victoria, how we met. It'll give it context, I believe."

"Sounds great."

She placed her hands in her lap and took a deep breath. Whatever she was about to tell me, it was evidently difficult for her. "About forty years ago..." She paused, shaking her head as if she couldn't believe that much time had passed. "Things weren't very good for me. I didn't come from a solid background or a stable family, and I got mixed up with drugs and the wrong people. When I was seventeen, I met a man who I thought was going to show me the world and everything else he promised. But that illusion crumbled pretty fast. You see, he was first my dealer, heroin, and then my boyfriend, and then... my pimp."

She paused, and I gave her an assuring nod. It was a little surprising to learn that Nancy had once participated in sex work. She must've gotten out a long time ago. She didn't have that look of someone still working the streets. But the tattoos were likely permanent reminders of that time.

"I'm sorry you had to go through that."

She raised her brows. "It wasn't great. At first, he just asked me to do it as a favor for a friend. I didn't want to, obviously. But he said it was the only way he could get more drugs. Little did I know, I was just one of many. That was the beginning."

Lifting my laptop, I said, "Let me just take some notes." As a blank project opened, I asked, "What was your boyfriend's name?"

"I think his name was Anthony. I didn't know his last name. He went by the name Blade."

Charming, I thought as I entered the notes. "Okay, what else?"

"Well, I was in it for a few long years. It was a hard time. I completely lost myself, you know, and I was high all the time. It was the only way to get through my days."

"Where were you living?"

"Oh, sorry, yeah, this was in San Francisco. I was staying at Blade's apartment. A lot of girls were. At first, he told me they were just friends, but I soon learned they were other sex workers. He sold them and took most of their money."

Blade sounded like a real peach, but unfortunately, it was a tale as old as time. An awful tale.

"Where in San Francisco was the apartment?"

"It's in the Tenderloin," she replied.

"Do you remember the exact address?"

"I do. I actually typed up all this information just in case I started to forget. You know, as much as a part of me would like to." She fished into her purse and handed me a piece of paper. It had an address in San Francisco and details about her and her friend Victoria.

"This will be really helpful," I said, scanning the paper. I would have to find property records from forty years ago. That was a long time ago. But there were archives, and I'd do my best.

Nancy nodded appreciatively. "Anyway, I was doing that for a few years before I met Victoria. She met him a different way. She was looking for work. Like the rest of us, she had a habit, but she was trying to get money for her little girl. We became really good friends. I wanted to help her, and she wanted to help me."

"What can you tell me about Victoria?"

"She had blonde hair, blue eyes, and freckles. She was about 5′5″ and thin, at least she was back then. Age can change that, as I've learned," she said with a bittersweet smile. "Oh, I can't believe I nearly forgot." She went back into the handbag and pulled out an envelope. She removed a faded photograph of two young women. "That is Vicky on the left, and that's me on the right."

Two young, beautiful women. Sold to men. One's fate unknown. "Is this the only photo you have?"

She nodded.

"And you don't know Victoria's last name?"

"No."

"And you're sure Victoria was her legal first name?"

"It was. She told me and when it was just us, I called her Vicky. Her street name was Jade, which was what everyone else called her. They called me Kitty. I'm not sure if you'll need that information or not."

It could come in handy. "What else did she tell you about herself?"

"She was originally from Concord, and her mother kept her little girl after the state took her away. She didn't have any siblings."

That might actually help to find her. "Do you remember how old her daughter was?"

"The last time I saw her, which was about thirty-five years ago when I got out of the business, her daughter was two years old and living with her mom in Concord. Her daughter's name was Shannon. I remember she affectionately called her 'Little Shandy'."

"Did she ever mention her mother's name?"

She shook her head. "No, she said she didn't want to talk too much about her other life. What she was doing was temporary. She was hoping to get out eventually. Once she saved enough money."

"This is really good information. It might help, but it'll take me some time. A lot of the records from thirty-five years ago are on paper, if they still exist, so you'll have to have patience with me. But I promise I will help you find her."

"I understand."

"When was the last time you saw Victoria?"

"The day I left the business. I was one of the lucky ones. I met a woman who was putting together a rights group for sex workers. They provided legal help and medical care. They were trying to protect us and get the public to stop demonizing women. They knew that the pimps were bad—taking most of our money, beating us, keeping us addicted, ensuring we were still profitable for them. This one woman who helped start the program picked me up. She arranged it to look like I was going with a john, but really, they took me to safety and helped me get sober." A tear fell from her eye as she added, "I've been clean for thirty-four years."

"Congratulations," I responded and pulled out my own token from my pocket, adding, "Nine years for me."

"So, you understand?" Nancy questioned, her eyes probing mine.

"Not everything you've been through," I replied. "But I understand addiction and what it can do to you. How hard it is to stay clean. I, too, have a daughter who I know I have to be here for."

"That was a lot like Victoria. Anyhow, I was able to get clean and start a whole new life, thanks to this organization. But I couldn't tell anybody about it because I knew that Blade would try to hurt anyone who knew of my plan to escape. My plan was, after they got me and I was all set up, to go back for her. To approach her, tell her how to get out, how to get clean, help her get her daughter back, and find a legit job. But when they went to approach her, the organization said they couldn't find her. Then they heard she got into trouble with Blade and nobody ever saw her again. I fear he killed her, but part of me thinks—*hopes*—she's still out there."

"What was the name of the woman and organization that helped you?"

"They called it COYOTE. Call Off Your Old Tired Ethics." She chuckled. "The woman who helped me was named Gloria, but I couldn't get a hold of her to ask her about Vicky—see if she remembered anything special about that time and to thank her. But COYOTE's not around anymore."

"And now you want to find Vicky?"

"It's taken me a long time to face all of this without shame. Without judging myself or anybody else in that life. Now I have a family and my very first grandchild. When I look into that little baby girl's eyes, I think of Victoria and her own daughter.

If she's out there, I want her to know that I care about her. Whether she's still in that life or if she's gone... I feel guilty for leaving her behind."

"Sounds like she meant a lot to you."

"Oh, she did. She's the only one who made me feel normal during that time working for Blade. We would talk about movies and our favorite candy and just normal stuff. It was like we were sisters from another mother. Having Victoria was the only way I got through those last couple of years. I want to thank her. I want to help her. I want her to know how much she meant to me. I just pray that she's still with us."

If she hadn't gotten out of that life, it wasn't likely. Drug addiction, sex work; both high risk and dangerous. "Well, like I said, with records this old, it'll take me some time. I'll see if I can pull some other members of the team in on this, if necessary. I promise, I'll help you find her."

"Thank you so much," she said, looking close to tears. Just as I was about to speak, she added, "My goodness, I've been talking your ear off. You said you needed to go." I stared down at my watch, and my heart rate sped up.

"Yes, I do have to go. It was wonderful to meet you, Nancy." I handed her my business card and said, "Like I promised, first thing tomorrow morning, I'll start working on it."

"Isn't it Saturday?" she asked with a soft chuckle.

Right. "Well, sometimes I lose track of days. But no later than Monday, I'll get working on the case."

"Thank you, Martina. I've waited thirty-five years; you can take a weekend, or longer. I appreciate you helping me find her."

After walking her out, I bravely headed toward my car, my stomach a ball of nerves. What would the night hold?

4

MARTINA

THE NEWS HIT ME HARD. Like a kick to the chest. It was a proposal all right, but not one I was expecting. How could he think I would move across the country with him?

"I hear what you're saying, but my life and business is here. Zoey's here," I said, struggling to keep my composure.

How could Wilder think I would just up and leave? To follow him to a new position with the ACLU in Washington DC? Things were good between us, but move across the country? Leave my business and Zoey behind?

"I thought about that," Wilder began, looking earnest. "Zoey graduates in six months. My new job with the DC office doesn't start until March. We'd be apart for a few months, but then after Zoey graduates, I figured you could move out there. Maybe even start up a new branch of Drakos Monroe in DC. There's plenty of work."

It took a lot to shock me, but this had done it. I had always thought Wilder's spontaneity and constant surprises were good things. They brought so much joy and excitement to my life. But there was no way I would move across the country, leaving everything I had here—my mother, Zoey, my business. I was beside myself, wondering how Wilder and I had gotten this far into our relationship and he thought I wouldn't object to the idea.

"These are all nice thoughts, but you're asking me to pick up my entire life and move across the country. We haven't even been dating that long. And even if we had, you took the job! You didn't even discuss it with me beforehand. I just don't even know what to say."

Wilder's face fell. His rugged good looks and that smile I couldn't resist—until now—was gone. He looked almost like a stranger. "I guess it was wishful thinking, hoping for miracles."

I thought he was only thinking of himself, which wasn't fair to me. In my mind, if we were really a couple—a couple that would move across the country with each other—it would've been a discussion. Not just, "I'm going. Do you want to come too?"

I could see the regret in his eyes. "Say something. You're killing me, Martina."

"Well, I guess I'm feeling a bit like an afterthought. In a healthy relationship—one that's solid and committed enough to move across the country together—you would've talked to me about the job before you accepted it. I'm not saying you should have, just that if we were that kind of couple, you would have."

Wilder shut his eyes and nodded. He knew he'd made a mistake. Just then, the waiter approached. "Can I interest the two of you in some dessert?"

I shook my head. Usually, my instincts were fight, not flight, but now, I just wanted to get out of there, away from Wilder, away from my fantasies about a marriage proposal.

"Not tonight. Just the check, thank you," Wilder said, clearly sensing my distress. "Can we talk about this more?"

"No. Honestly, I just want to go home. It's been a long day, and I'm just really surprised by all of this."

"This doesn't have to be the end of us. We can do long distance."

I met his gaze, and in that silence, he knew my answer. More than anything, I wanted to retreat, maybe shed some tears in solitude, cuddle with Barney. The thought of Mom waiting for me at home was a comfort. Maybe she'd baked something, and that warmth would heal a bit of the hurt. "I need to go home. I just need some time by myself," I whispered.

"I understand." He quickly took care of the check and nodded.

Summoning all the composure I had left, I murmured, "I'll talk to you later," and hurried to my car. Every fiber of my being wanted to run, to escape, to let out the sobs building up within. How had I not seen this coming?

Tears streamed down my face the entire drive home. By the time I reached home, my face was red and swollen. I was grateful Zoey wasn't home to witness this mess. Not that showing vulnerability in front of my daughter was wrong, but I didn't want to burden her, especially since she had grown fond of Wilder. The realization stung. I'd allowed her to become attached, and now she'd have to navigate the aftermath of this too.

As I inserted the key, the familiar sound of claws tapping on hardwood greeted me. The tiny, tail-wagging blur of Barney always managed to brighten the gloomiest moments. I knelt, giving him the scratches he eagerly asked for, feeling a little bit of the weight lifting. Mom appeared, a puzzled look on her face. "That was a short evening..." Her voice faded as she noticed my swollen eyes.

Swallowing hard, I stood and shut the door, quickly briefing her on the evening's events, culminating with the painful admission, "I think it's over for us."

"Oh, dear." She sighed, a hint of sympathy in her voice. "I made cupcakes—chocolate with peanut butter frosting."

I nodded, appreciating her comforting presence.

We settled onto the couch, Barney snuggled beside me. Mom handed me a cupcake on a plate. "You know, you don't have to stay. I'll be okay."

"Do you want to talk about it?" she asked gently.

I shrugged, taking a bite of the cupcake. Eating my feelings wasn't the healthiest coping mechanism, but we all needed indulgences sometimes. After explaining the night's discussion, I said, "I feel blindsided. He had to have known I wouldn't move across the country, right?"

Mom nodded thoughtfully. "One would think. But he's so dedicated to his work, just as you are. It sounds like a fantastic opportunity for him."

"He did say he was hoping," I mumbled.

"And he suggested long distance?" She wrinkled her nose.

"It's better to have a clean break."

"I hear you. You know, before Ted, I dated quite a few men who weren't the right one."

"I guess I was naïve to think I'd find the second love of my life just like that." Wilder was the first man I'd really dated after Jared's death. I should have known better.

"It'll be okay, Martina. If this is how it's ending with Wilder, perhaps he wasn't the right one for you after all."

"He obviously wasn't."

My cell phone buzzed. I hesitated, fearing it would be Wilder asking to talk. But seeing Hirsch's name on the screen was a pleasant surprise. Why was he texting late on a Friday?

"I got a text from Hirsch. He's asking if I'm up for a call."

"Are you?"

"Talking to Hirsch might be just the distraction I need right now." Considering it was likely work related.

"Of course."

I dialed him up.

"Hey. Are you still in the office?" he asked.

"No. Just got home. It's been a night."

"What's wrong?"

I hesitated but eventually shared. "Let's just say my day didn't pan out as expected. Wilder's moving across the country. He took a job at the DC office of the ACLU, heading up a new division."

"I'm so sorry, Martina. You probably don't want to talk about work, then."

"Actually, please talk to me about work. What's up?" Mom gave me a knowing smile, patted my shoulder, and retreated to the kitchen.

"Well, I have some good news and wanted to share it with you."

My heart fluttered. I knew Hirsch and Kim had been trying for a second child for some time without luck. My mind drifted to little toes and onesies, but Hirsch quickly broke my train of thought. "I just got approval for a new cold case squad."

I straightened, interest piqued. "Are you serious?"

"Not a big one like before, but I had a chat with the sheriff. I explained how all the departments were thriving, and how I found enough budget for two investigators. It's not much, but I'm thrilled because it means I will be working active cases again —well, cold cases—and splitting my time with admin duties."

"That's incredible, Hirsch! Honestly, this is the best news I've heard in a while."

"Well, the reason I'm calling is not just to share the good news. We have a budget for a consultant, just part-time though. If you have any time in your schedule, we could pick a case together. It'd be the inaugural case for the second coming of the Cold Case Squad."

I'd just taken on a thirty-five-year-old cold case. Could I manage another one with Hirsch? "I'm not sure. As I was leaving the office tonight, Mrs. Pearson approached me about a case. A friend of hers is trying to find an old friend she hasn't seen in three and a half decades. I don't even have a last name to work with."

"Sounds tough," Hirsch said sympathetically. "So, maybe you won't have time for the first case with the new mini squad." A hint of disappointment tinged his voice.

Could I do it? "Maybe I could find a few hours a week, maybe just to help advise or direct."

He chuckled. "Well, I know how much you like to take control of a case and tell everyone what to do. We'd be happy to have you, any time you can spare."

That brought a smile to my face. While I was feeling down over my boyfriend moving across the country, it seemed God was intervening, reminding me of where I truly belonged. I wouldn't be crossing the country for anyone; this was my home. "I could meet Monday."

"Perfect. We can have lunch and talk, see how much time you can commit to us," Hirsch suggested.

"Do you have any idea which case you want to open first?"

"Not yet. But let's talk about it on Monday. Kim's texting to know when I'll be home."

"Okay."

"Did that at least cheer you up?"

I nodded, momentarily forgetting he couldn't see me. "You have no idea, Hirsch. This is exactly what I needed. It's affirmation that I'm right where I belong."

"I'm inclined to agree. It's Wilder's loss, but I still think there's someone out there for you, Martina, assuming you want someone."

"Thanks, Hirsch," I replied with a smile in my voice. "Give my love to Kim and Audrey."

"Will do. I'll see you on Monday."

"Can't wait," I said, ending the call. I waved over to Mom. "Guess what? Hirsch got approval for a mini squad. He'll have resources to work on cold cases again. And even a few hours a week for a consultant."

She smiled warmly. "Well, there you have it."

A tingle of excitement coursed through me. Though I was sad about Wilder's likely exit from my life, I concurred with Hirsch's sentiment. If there was someone out there for me, he was still out there, waiting to be found when the time was right. But for now, solving cold cases alongside my best friend was exactly what I was meant to do. And to find Victoria.

5

PRISCILLA

THIRTY-FIVE YEARS EARLIER

THE CARPET WAS FILTHY. The air carried an unpleasant mix of mold, dirt, and sweat. The pungency of the room was unbearable. He needed to get with the new ways, or he'd find himself out of work. Warnings had been given about his deteriorating situation and he'd been told to clean up his act, to go to a more upscale model like the rest of the organization. He swore he would. Said he was just waiting on a few of his girls to straighten up.

Studying his slovenly appearance, I said, "How many do you have here?"

"Two."

"That's all?"

"Yeah, two went missing."

How did he lose two women? If his father wasn't the boss, he would be dead or out. "Tell me about them."

"Kitty. She's been with me a long time. I thought I could trust her, but she's been gone three days."

"And you have no idea where she went?"

"No. I never had a single problem with her. She's always been a good worker, a good earner. Obedient, most of the time.

In the beginning, she was more hesitant, but she adjusted. I don't know what happened. Maybe one of the johns got too rough, and she's dead."

"Anyone find a body?"

He shook his head. "Not that I know of. But I also didn't walk into a police station asking if they found any dead hookers."

It was a fair point, but the entire situation was concerning. How had he let two slip away? Was he that careless?

"And what about the other one?"

"Jade. She's a classic junky. Been with me a couple of years. I found her working the streets on her own, thinking she didn't need any protection. I taught her otherwise."

"Was she obedient like Kitty?"

"No, this one fought me all the time. The only way I could keep her in line was with the dope. But then she got this notion of going on her own. I knew, but I found her. Taught her a lesson, roughed her up good. But then she ran."

"She ran? Thought you roughed her up good?" His nonchalant attitude infuriated me. If it were up to me, he'd be out. We were trying to run a profitable organization with accountability and a defined hierarchy. He was only near the top because of his bloodline.

"I did. She played it up like she hadn't healed much, but I saw her running in the streets like a lunatic. I found her and was about to give her the blade when some dummy wanted to play hero and try to help her. Stupid kid. Had to rough him up too. She saw the whole thing but ran again. She's like a cat—nine lives. Don't know where she went. I ran after the incident with the civilian, not wanting to get busted. I haven't had a chance to look. I want the heat to cool before I go back out. But nobody's seen her."

"So, not only did she witness a crime, but you're also losing money left and right with two of your girls gone."

He shrugged as if it was no big deal.

Observing him, it was clear how far he'd fallen from the tree. It was incomprehensible how the only trait he'd gotten from his father was his taste for violence and the urge to take whatever he wanted.

"Well, this good Samaritan you mentioned, you roughed him up good. What does that mean?"

"He was bleeding bad."

"Bleeding bad? What do you mean?"

"It could have gone 50-50."

Eyes wide, I said, "Like he could have died?"

"I suppose."

How someone could be so callous about potentially facing a murder or attempted murder charge was beyond me. Such indifference seemed to be a luxury men of means held, one which women, unfortunately, did not.

"All right, I have a message from your father. He wants you to clean out this dump. Clean up the girls or cut them loose. We have a new way of operating." I gestured to the mess around the apartment. "It's not like this. We're transitioning into a more sophisticated operation, bringing in more money from higher-end clients."

"So, what do I do with the girls?" he asked, his voice laden with indifference.

I sighed in exasperation. It was exhausting having to explain everything to this dimwit. "If you think they're capable of being cleaned up and fetching a higher price for a more sophisticated clientele, keep them. Otherwise, throw them out. Another pimp can have them."

"I'll see what I can do."

Almost as if on cue, one of the girls stumbled into the living room. "Hey, Blade, I need some more stuff."

A pang of sympathy hit me. I'd once been like her but clawed my way out of that pit. Not that I was ever free of the man who once controlled me. But at least I wasn't selling myself on the streets anymore. It was them or me, and I chose me.

"Sure, sure. Give me a sec. Why don't you take a shower, and I'll get it ready for you."

"Okay." She looked at me with her drug-addled eyes. "Hey, are you new?"

I shook my head in disgust. "I'm just an associate."

She looked puzzled. I guessed it was a look she wore often. "An associate?"

"Go get cleaned up, honey."

When the poor soul left for the shower, I turned back to Blade. Such a stupid name. "Keep looking for Jade. She could be a problem for you if this civilian got really hurt. Your father doesn't need you dirtying the family name."

"First I'll take care of the girls, then I'll look for Jade. I'll make sure she hasn't spoken to anybody about anything and never will."

The guilt of aligning myself with the darker side was slightly lessened by the realization that staying in the business might be a fate worse than death. I didn't wish it upon anyone. Some of these drug-addicted, shameless souls were beyond help. There was little I could do for them now. I couldn't change the fact they didn't have the intelligence to get out or to persuade their men to use them as a partner as opposed to a sex toy, like I had. In that world, it was eat or be eaten. And I was nobody's dinner.

6

MARTINA

SITTING AT THE DINING TABLE, I sipped my cup of coffee while studying the screen. Wilder had already texted me twice, but I'd ignored it. I wasn't ready to talk. Instead of dealing with my disaster of a love life, I dove right in to Victoria's case. And I was thankful for the distraction.

All I had was a photo, a name, the place where she grew up, the name of her daughter, and her pimp—but not likely his real name. With so little to go on, I decided I would start with her last known address in San Francisco, the heart of the Tenderloin —a rough district in San Francisco.

Zoey padded in, holding Barney in her arms, still in her pajamas, even though it was ten o'clock. "How'd you sleep?"

I looked up. "Pretty good. What time did you get in?"

"Around midnight. How about you?"

"It was an early night."

She put Barney down and said, "How come?"

"I think Wilder and I broke up."

Zoey's face fell, and her mouth dropped open. "What? Why? I don't understand. Things were so good! I really liked him."

Dating with kids was complicated. Not only would breakups hurt my feelings, but hers too. "I know. It was surprising to me too. But Wilder's accepted a position in Washington DC. He wanted me to come with him, but I can't. You know that."

"I can't believe he thought you'd move across the country!"

Even my teenage daughter knew that abandoning a relationship for work was not cool. Maybe I dodged a bullet with Wilder. Do we ever really know anybody? We'd only been together eight months. I supposed I wasn't special enough to avoid heartbreak. Nobody is. "I was surprised too."

"Sorry, Mom," she said softly, wrapping her arms around my shoulders. "But you know, there are other fish in the sea."

Smiling at my wise-beyond-her-years teenager, I replied, "I'll be okay. We'll be okay."

Zoey pondered for a moment. "You know, Wilder was a bit full of himself. I mean, he was nice and everything, but he had this vibe."

"What do you mean?"

"You might not have noticed because you're so confident, but I think he can rub people the wrong way."

Did he? "Anyway, that's not great news. But I did get some really good news from Uncle August."

Her eyes lit up. "Really?"

"We'll be working together again, only part-time. But he got funding for another smaller Cold Case Squad."

She gasped, clearly excited. "That's incredible! Maybe this summer, I could intern? Think he'd let me do that? It would be so cool if we all worked together."

My daughter, Zoey, in the field, fighting criminals was a hard no. "Let's wait until the summer, after you're done with school. We'll talk about potential internship opportunities then."

She shrugged it off and grabbed a cup of coffee for herself. "What are you working on?"

"A case. The client is a friend of Mrs. Pearson."

"Oh, is it interesting?"

"Yes, it actually is. It's a thirty-five-year-old missing persons case."

"Intriguing."

Zoey had been fascinated by my cases ever since she was old enough to talk. During her teenage years, she eagerly listened to the details but never seemed to lean toward a career in investigations. She had a soft spot for animals and was pretty set on becoming a veterinarian.

"I'm thinking I might head down to San Francisco to take a look at her last known address, get a sense of what might've happened to her."

"Maybe I could go too." She frowned. "Actually, I can't. I'm supposed to go over to Kaylie's to make posters for the Sadie Hawkins Dance."

"Maybe next time."

I had reservations about my teenage daughter exploring the Tenderloin district of San Francisco. It wasn't the safest of places. Even though I had taught her self-defense from a young age, the idea of her being there, even with me, was unsettling.

One can be snatched or assaulted in a blink. I wanted her safely ensconced in our suburban cocoon, even though the reality was that I couldn't shield her forever.

"Well, I won't spend too much time out there. Maybe I'll see you around lunchtime?"

Zoey hesitated. "Oh, lunch might be tricky."

Being a typical teenager, Zoey's friends were her world. She only had six months left of her high school journey. The inevitable goodbyes loomed as her friends would soon scatter across the country and some even overseas for college. I understood her urge to capture every moment with them.

"Dinner?"

"Dinner, definitely. How about a movie, pizza, ice cream, and Red Vines?"

And then fall into a deep sugar coma. "Sounds perfect."

She walked over, enveloping me in a warm hug and planting a kiss on my cheek. "I love you, Mom."

The emotions from the night had hardly settled, and her words triggered fresh tears. "I love you too, Zoey."

She gave a tight squeeze and retreated toward her bedroom, presumably to prepare for her visit to Kaylie's.

Everything was shifting. Just as I began to adapt to one phase, another change was on the horizon with Zoey heading off to college. I felt a pang at the impending emptiness but found solace as my gaze landed on the fluffy little pup. I thought, *At least I still have Barney.*

THE APARTMENT BUILDING on the corner of Golden Gate Avenue and Jones Street likely looked quite different thirty-five years ago. It was the last known address for Victoria, and from what Nancy told me, it was probably where she had run into trouble with Blade. I wasn't optimistic about finding any tangible evidence inside the apartment, but stranger things had happened. I waited outside for tenants to leave so I could question them.

After an hour, I'd only met a few, and all had lived there less than five years, and none had heard of Blade or Anthony. My guess was the building was no longer housing pimps and drug dealers. As I paced, I spotted an elderly man wearing a newsboy hat and leaning on a cane slowly emerging from the inside.

"Good afternoon, sir," I greeted him.

He glanced at me, a hint of curiosity evident in his eyes. "Good morning. You new around here?"

"Just visiting. Have you lived here long?"

"Oh yeah, forty years," he responded with enthusiasm.

"Wow. The things you must've seen here in San Francisco over the last forty years."

"I could fill a set of encyclopedias," he remarked, grinning.

"I'm actually a private investigator, looking for an old friend for a client. Do you remember any of the tenants from around thirty-five years ago?"

As I sized him up, a wild thought struck me—could this man be Blade, the alleged pimp?

"Oh, yeah," he continued. "We had a different set of folks back then. Now, with rent control, we mostly have older folks."

"Are there any other tenants who lived here around thirty-five or forty years ago?"

"Maybe one or two. Who are you looking for?"

"Her name was Jade back then," I divulged.

The old man raised his wiry eyebrows. "Oh, one of those."

"One of those?"

He nodded. "Back then, there were a bunch of ladies with sweet names and there was Blade—the guy was involved in drugs and selling women. Don't tell anyone I told you though. I'm glad they left."

My heart raced. He actually remembered Victoria and the others. "When did they leave?"

He paused for a moment. "Now that you mention it, that was just about thirty-five years ago."

"And you're sure?"

"Oh yeah, I remember," the elderly man said. "There were these ladies walking by. They were advocating for prostitutes, talking about feminism and all that. No offense. Anyway,

Anthony left. Said they were starting up a real business or something. I didn't believe him, but I was glad when they all left."

"Do you remember Blade? Anthony?"

"Oh, that piece of work? Is he who you're looking for?"

"No, I'm looking for Jade. She also went by the name Victoria. Did you know her?" I pulled out the photo and showed it to him.

He took it and squinted at the image. "To be honest, they all sort of looked similar. I wasn't friendly with them. And they always had these names you knew were fake. Like Blade, his real name was Anthony. Anthony Stanzel. His family, the Stanzels, are still around in San Francisco. By the look of him, you wouldn't guess, but his family had money. He was the black sheep. Lived like a junkie though, you know? I heard his father made him clean up his act, and that's when he moved out."

I mulled over the new information. He seemed to know a lot for not having fraternized with them. "Anthony Stanzel," I murmured. "That's something to look into. You've been very helpful, sir."

He tipped his hat slightly. "Hope you find who you're looking for. Though, I'd be surprised if those ladies are still around."

"Thanks again," I said.

I quickly pulled out my notebook, jotting down the name Anthony Stanzel. I glanced around the area, pondering why someone from a wealthy background would live in such an apartment. Of course, being the family's black sheep would explain some things. I needed to dive deeper into the Stanzel family. If they had done something to Victoria, their resources might have covered it up. Fingers crossed it wouldn't prevent me from finding her.

7

MARTINA

"You've GOT to be kidding me," I mumbled to myself. The resident of Victoria's old building wasn't kidding; the Stanzels were the elite of San Francisco. From my investigations, Mr. Maurice Stanzel, the patriarch of the family, owned hotels and a long list of real estate holdings. There were also donations to the opera and animal shelters. Could this man really be Victoria's old pimp's father?

If that wasn't strange enough, my research revealed that Maurice Stanzel and his wife had two children. There was Regina, their daughter, who was married to a surgeon and had three children in prep school. And then there was Anthony, presumably the infamous Blade. He was married with two kids and worked for his father's real estate firm.

Is it really possible that a pimp from thirty-five years ago had transformed into a real estate mogul? Something about this entire situation felt off-kilter. Could the old man have been mistaken? Perhaps Anthony, or Blade, as he was known back then, wasn't really a Stanzel.

There was one way to find out. I could show the photo to Nancy and see if the man in the image was one and the same.

Thirty-five years could change a person's appearance, but given she knew him for over five years, she should recognize him if it was Blade.

I glanced at the clock, realizing the evening was creeping in. I needed to order pizza soon, especially if Zoey would be getting home by seven as she'd said. But another thought crossed my mind. Was it too late to call Nancy on a Saturday evening? Did she have plans? I had promised her I'd start working the case as soon as I could. She had told me not to rush—after all, it had been thirty-five years—but if my findings were correct, this could be a significant breakthrough.

I looked down at Barney, my loyal companion, curled up in his bed next to the sofa. "What do you think, boy?" I asked.

Barney cocked his head, looking up at me. I took his reaction as an affirmative. Decision made, I pulled out my phone and dialed Nancy's number. After three rings, she answered, her voice tinged with uncertainty. "Hello?"

"Hi, Nancy, it's Martina Monroe. How are you doing?"

"I'm doing fine. Is everything okay?" she responded, a hint of concern in her voice.

"Yes, of course. Like I mentioned earlier, I actually got around to working on your case today, and I have some information about Anthony."

She hesitated for a moment. "Oh." The apprehension in her voice was clear. "Give me a second."

I imagined she was seeking a more private place. She probably didn't want her family or her kids to hear about her past, especially about her former pimp. Even if she had been transparent about her youth, it wasn't a topic to casually discuss.

When she returned to the line, her voice was steadier. "Okay, just wanted a bit of privacy. You found Anthony?"

"I might have." I began laying out my findings. "I went to San Francisco today and spoke to some residents around the building where Victoria was last known to live. There's an elderly man there. He claims he's been there for over forty years. He mentioned that Anthony's last name was Stanzel. Does that ring any bells?"

There was a brief silence before she answered, surprise evident in her voice. "You know, it does. It kind of does. If I saw a picture of him now, even after all these years, I'd probably recognize him. I did live with him for five years, after all."

"That's what I hoped to hear," I said. "Do you have a computer or a smartphone? There are photos online."

She responded promptly, "I have a computer in my office here."

The pieces were beginning to fall into place, and I felt the weight of the mystery start to lift.

"If you Google Maurice Stanzel or Anthony Stanzel, you should get some hits," I suggested.

"Was he in jail or arrested?" Nancy queried with hesitation.

"I'm afraid it's quite the opposite. He apparently comes from a very wealthy family, assuming it's the same Anthony."

There was silence from the other end, punctuated only by the soft clicking of keys.

Next, I heard a sharp gasp. "It's him... I can't believe it's him. I... I don't know what to say."

"I was as surprised as you are," I admitted. "From what I've found, it seems like Anthony is now working for his father's real estate firm, is married, and has kids. But you're certain it's him?"

"Absolutely," she replied, a hint of bitterness evident in her voice. "He's got those same beady eyes. I should tell them what he was like back then," she muttered, a spark of anger flaring.

I quickly interjected, "I'd advise you against that. Just because he appears squeaky clean now doesn't mean he is. Don't underestimate how far the rich will go to protect one of their own. If Anthony was involved in drugs and prostitution thirty-five years ago, his family wouldn't want anyone to know. Not to mention, who's to say they're not still involved in criminal activity? Having legal businesses doesn't necessarily make them clean." I paused, hoping my point hit home. "I've encountered more than one crooked family in my time as a private investigator. If you're concerned that he might have harmed Victoria all those years ago, remember that people don't just change overnight. Even thirty-five years can't erase that kind of darkness."

"Then what will you do?"

"I'll question him," I reassured her. "But I don't want to mention your name or involve you, especially if he's still involved in illicit activities. I'll dig deeper to see what I can find."

Nancy's voice trembled with gratitude. "Thank you, Martina. Gosh, you've already made so much progress."

I shrugged, even though she couldn't see it. "I had some extra time on my hands. I'll look more tomorrow." Just then, I heard the opening of a door in the background. Zoey must be home.

"Thank you again, Martina. I know I told you not to rush, but now I'm a bit anxious."

"Not to worry," I said, hoping the new development meant I would find Victoria sooner rather than later.

"Thank you again." Nancy's voice was soft. "Have a good night."

"You too," I replied, feeling the weight of our conversation press down on me.

I ended the call just as Zoey walked in. "Working?"

"Just got off a call with a client," I replied. "Found some interesting things today, but I'm off the clock now. What kind of pizza should we order?"

"Super veggie!" Zoey exclaimed with enthusiasm.

"And a salad," I added.

She held up a box of candy, grinning. "And Red Vines."

"Sounds like our night is set." I was eager to spend the evening with my daughter. However, at the back of my mind, my thoughts churned about the case. Something felt off about this whole situation. How could such a prominent family be involved with drugs and prostitution? And had they really stopped all criminal activity? If they had been criminals, my gut instinct said no.

8

VICTORIA

THIRTY-FIVE YEARS EARLIER

My eyelids flickered open, but I squeezed them shut to avoid the blinding brightness. Where was I? I attempted to shift my body, only to realize I was restrained. Panic surged through me. Was I drugged? I slowly opened my eyes, letting them adjust to the bright lights above. I looked down to see myself dressed in a hospital gown, secured to the bed. Why was I tied up? Had I been arrested?

A wave of memories came crashing back. The frantic run through the streets, the brutal thud of a head hitting the ground, the chilling sight of a man bleeding profusely, as if he'd been struck by a blade. That man... There was no way he survived. The sheer volume of blood reminded me of water gushing from a fire hydrant. Blade would surely be looking for me. I had seen too much. And if witnessing him attacking that man wasn't reason enough, I had also defied him a second time. The thought made my heart race. I was undoubtedly marked for death.

A beeping sound from a nearby machine drew my attention, and a nurse, clad entirely in white, hurried over. "Oh, you need to settle down, dear," she soothed.

Filled with panic, I said, "What happened? How did I get here?"

She attempted to reassure me. "Firstly, calm down. You're in San Francisco General Hospital. We're taking good care of you."

"How did I end up here?"

"You were found on the street, passed out, bruised, and bleeding. Someone called 911, and you were brought here. We've been taking care of you for the last three days."

"Three days?" I echoed, incredulous. "I think I'm fine now. I should go."

She shot me a sympathetic look. "Oh, no, dear. You've got broken ribs, a sprained wrist, and a nasty concussion. Looks like you received a hard hit to the head. The police will be here soon to take your statement."

My eyes widened in terror. "No, no police," I protested.

The nurse's brow furrowed in confusion. "Someone did this to you, and they need to be held accountable."

Before I could respond, a uniformed officer with a mustache and piercing green eyes approached. "She's awake," the nurse reported.

He eyed me carefully, then said, "Good to hear it. Victoria, are you ready to make a statement?"

"You know my name?" I stammered.

"Your ID was in your jeans pocket," he replied.

The realization hit me hard. With my name, they could find me. "Nothing happened," I lied. "I just fell."

The nurse raised an eyebrow skeptically. "If your boyfriend did this to you, it's not okay," she said, her tone a mixture of concern and sternness.

"No, really, I just... I fell, that's all. I promise," I insisted, my words tumbling out faster than I'd intended. I could feel the sweat forming on my brow. The absence of my regular fix was making itself known. The hospital's substitutes weren't strong enough.

"We noticed you might be experiencing withdrawal. We've been administering methadone to help you. We're working to get you on the right path," the young nurse interjected.

"Do you mind giving us a minute, nurse?" the officer asked, his tone courteous yet firm.

"Yes, officer. I'll be right at the nurse's station," she replied, then left the room.

As I took in the officer's features more closely, a flicker of recognition crossed my mind. I had a feeling he recognized me too.

"Victoria... so that's your real name?"

I looked away, avoiding his piercing gaze. "I don't have any statements to make."

He sighed, exasperated but patient. "Here's the thing, Victoria. You were beaten up badly. We've received reports that you fled an area where a homicide occurred. Now, if you don't want to rat out the person—Blade, I'm guessing—who did this to you, that's one thing. But a young man lost his life, and we believe you witnessed it."

"I didn't see anything. I really didn't," I protested, my voice shaking.

"Victoria," he began, his tone softening. "The person who found you said that you were semi-conscious and kept murmuring about 'blood' and 'so much blood' before passing out. We think you know who killed that man. Do you recall saying any of that?"

"I didn't see anything. I don't know anything," I repeated desperately.

He nodded, understanding the subtext of my words. "Here's the thing, Victoria. That young man's family deserves answers, and I'm trying to provide them. You can cooperate and tell us what you saw, or I could arrest you for obstruction of justice."

"You can't do that. I didn't do anything!" I snapped, defiance rising.

"I can," he said sternly. "Think of it this way: you're here in the hospital. They're helping you get clean. If you cooperate with us, we can help you turn your life around."

Could they really help me get clean? Help me find a job, a place to stay, and help me get Shannon back? If Blade came after me, I could always lie. Pretend I saw someone I didn't recognize. "How will you help me?" I questioned cautiously.

"We'll do everything we can to protect you."

Tears formed in my eyes. "Can I call my mom?"

"Of course," he replied gently. "When the nurse comes back, she'll help you get in touch with your family. It's probably been a long time, huh?" the officer said, a hint of compassion in his voice.

I nodded. I remembered him. He was the one who had always been a bit kinder, didn't treat us like garbage, unlike the other officers. It always baffled me. Why were they always coming down so hard on the girls? It wasn't us buying sex. If they got rid of the men wanting to buy women, there wouldn't be prostitution. If there were better educational and work opportunities for those without money, there wouldn't be a need for such desperate measures. If they cared just a teeny bit more, they wouldn't have to see us as stains on their pristine streets.

But I couldn't dwell on that now. My number one priority was getting Shannon back. If they promised to help, I'd make up a story, but I'd never tell who was behind it all. He'd kill both me and my baby. My mom too. He was that kind of evil.

9

MARTINA

I waved as I approached Hirsch at the small bistro table. He, like my Zoey, loved to be on time—usually early. They both seemed to think if they were on time, they were late. It wasn't my modus operandi.

Hirsch waved back, and I hurried over, placing my bag on the back of the chair. "How's it going?"

"Great. I must admit, I'm pretty pumped about this."

A waiter approached and set a menu in front of me. I set it down, ignored it, and said, "Me too. It's just the distraction I need, not to mention what I want."

Hirsch frowned, looking sincere. "How are you doing? I mean, about the whole Wilder situation?"

"Well, I'm sad. But given how it all went down, I realized maybe he wasn't who I thought he was. And maybe that's for the best. We had a long talk last night on the phone. There was some arguing, some crying, but ultimately, a breakup."

"You don't think maybe in the future, if he returned to the Bay Area, you would reconsider?"

I shook my head. "No, I think anybody who would take a job without even talking to me about it, but then asks me to move, one, doesn't know me at all, and two, isn't the right one for me. I don't follow people around unless I'm paid to."

He chuckled. "True. I thought he was a good guy, but maybe just not right for you."

"And I think that's true. I think Wilder's a wonderful person, just not my forever match. And that's okay. I only have six months before my daughter goes off to college. I've got my job that I love, and now I get to work with you again. I'm sad, but I know if I'm meant to be with someone, I'll know it. And Wilder and I are not meant to be."

The waiter returned. "Sorry, I haven't got a chance to look at the menu yet. Can you give us five more minutes?"

"Of course."

I shrugged and glanced down at the menu. I could order the obvious choice—what I always ordered—but I was more in the mood for some comfort. Decision made. Salmon with mashed potatoes and a side of broccoli. Nutrition with a side of comforting mashed potatoes drenched in buttery goodness.

"Well, I'm glad you're willing to work with us again."

"Does Sheriff Baldwin know?"

"No," he replied. "But if he did, he'd say we are more than lucky to have you, even if for only a few hours a week. And I'm inclined to agree."

"Who else do you have slated for the squad? How many people can you get?"

"Two full-time resources are budgeted. I'll use half my time, and I plan to approach Jayda and Ross, see if they're willing to give us half their time. Plus, your consulting hours to fill in the other half. If we come across something really big, I might be able to wiggle another half or full resource."

I wondered if he was referring to Vincent. "Well, if those are the only resources you have, that's about the best team you could possibly get. Jayda, Ross, you, me... It'll be good to get the gang back together again."

"Absolutely." The waiter took our orders, and we got down to business. "So, when will you approach Jayda and Ross?"

"Today. I wanted to get your input first, in case you thought maybe there's somebody better for the team, but..."

"But you know I think Jayda and Ross are the best?"

He nodded.

"I looked over my schedule and talked to Stavros. I can probably give about fifteen to twenty hours a week maximum. Maybe I can do some work from home, you know? Maybe only go into the sheriff's department a few days a week, if that'll work?"

"That's totally fine. We could even meet for just a couple of hours. Most of our work is usually outside the walls of the sheriff's department."

"True." I smiled and didn't even realize it until he smiled back. As much as I enjoyed Wilder's company, I didn't remember ever sitting there and thinking, "Wow, this feels so right." Something in my gut was telling me it was never right with Wilder. It was fun, and I was grateful for the time we had, but that didn't mean I had to drag out the breakup and attempt a long-distance relationship that was destined to fail.

"How's Kim?"

His once bright smile faded. "She's getting antsy. And 'antsy' is probably not the right word. She's sad."

"No luck?"

He shook his head. "Her doctor thinks it's secondary infertility. We might not be able to have a second child. We're currently deciding whether or not to go the fertility clinic route. Her doctor gave us the name of a good endocrinologist, but we're trying to decide if that's right for us."

"That's tough. I can't imagine what she's going through."

"She's grateful we have Audrey, but we always wanted a slightly bigger family. Sometimes I feel guilty for being upset we can't have another child."

"You could borrow Zoey if you want. But she's a teenager," I teased.

Hirsch tried not to laugh. "You know, she's at our house often enough, she's like a second child."

Zoey was one of Audrey's favorite babysitters, and Audrey adored her and Zoey adored Audrey. "I guess it's the end of our double dates."

"For now."

Such an optimist.

The waiter presented our meals. Before taking a bite of my salmon, I said, "Any idea which case you want to take on first?"

"Well, my first thought is to get a couple we can knock out of the park right away. Something that just needs DNA testing or advanced forensics that will help us close them out quick."

With a half-grin, I said, "Prove the squad's worth it. And then angle for a bigger squad and a bigger budget?"

"You know I can't keep secrets from you."

I laughed, stabbing the salmon with my fork. "You can be pretty sneaky. But when it comes to work, I've got you figured out."

Midway through the meal, he leaned forward, curiosity evident in his eyes. "How is your new case? The one about the thirty-five-year-old missing person?"

I took a deep breath. "It's interesting, to say the least. My client is looking for an old friend she hasn't seen in thirty-five years. Both were sex workers. My client managed to escape that life, start fresh, and now she's clean and has a family. She wants to find her old friend. I don't have a last name, but I think I found her old pimp."

He raised his eyebrows in surprise. "Wow, already?"

"This weekend, I had a few extra hours on my hands. So, I went into San Francisco and started asking questions around where she used to live. Turns out the pimp is from a rich family in San Francisco. When you worked at SFPD, did you ever hear about the Stanzel family?"

Hirsch dropped his fork, disbelief evident. "You're saying the Stanzel family is connected to prostitution?"

I nodded. "So, you've heard of them?"

He wiped his mouth with his napkin, his face growing somber. "Yes. Are you sure about this?"

"From what I've found, Anthony Stanzel was a pimp thirty-five years ago. His father wanted him to clean up his act, and so he did. Now, he works for his father's real estate firm and has a wife, kids, with no hint of criminal activity. When you worked with SFPD, did anyone suspect something rotten about the Stanzel family?"

Hirsch leaned in, voice low. "No, and they practically own half of San Francisco. And by that, I mean they have a strong grip on the SFPD. They're 1099 members and make huge donations. They're good friends with the police commissioner. They're protected."

I pursed my lips, weighing my options. "So, if I want to question Anthony Stanzel, I need to tread carefully."

"Very carefully," he affirmed. "What proof do you have that it's him?"

"I questioned some residents of his old building, looked up his name online, got a picture, showed it to my client who also worked for him back then, and she confirmed it was him."

Hirsch looked around the restaurant, ensuring privacy. "Keep that to yourself until you can prove it, undoubtedly. Thirty-five years is a long time. And like I said, they're not just elite, they're powerful. Make sure you cross your Ts and dot your Is."

"They've never been suspected of any criminal activity?"

"Not that I know of. And if anyone did suspect something, it was buried. And I mean, buried deep."

The weight of the information hung heavy, but it only made me want to learn more. I'd tread carefully, but I certainly wouldn't back off.

After lunch, Hirsch and I said our goodbyes, planning to meet later in the week with Jayda and Ross. The assumption was they'd accept the part-time positions, splitting their time between homicide and cold cases.

I settled into my car, taking a moment before turning on the engine. I pulled out my phone, dialing the offices of Anthony Stanzel.

"Stanzel Real Estate. How can I assist you?"

"I'm hoping to make an appointment with Anthony Stanzel," I replied smoothly.

"May I ask who's calling?"

"My name is Martina. Does he have time to meet today?"

The voice on the other end paused for a moment. "Give me one second. What's this concerning?"

"It's about a real estate project."

"All right. He has an opening tomorrow at 2 p.m. Would that work for you?"

"Yes, thank you." I provided a few more details, sealing the appointment before ending the call.

As I gripped the steering wheel, I thought, *Anthony Stanzel, I'm coming for you. I hope you're ready.*

10

PRISCILLA

THIRTY-FIVE YEARS EARLIER

AFTER ALL THIS TIME, he still thought he was better than me. Just because you're born into something doesn't make you worthy. I had fought tooth and nail, refusing to sell my body to get by. I had overcome drug addiction and capture. I'd run from violent johns and clawed my way out of danger countless times. And now this little pipsqueak—not so little, actually. Had he ever heard of a gym or a pair of jogging shoes? He was disgusting. Standing next to his father in a shiny suit, I could barely see the resemblance.

"What's the situation, Priscilla?"

"I spoke to our contacts within the police department. They found your girl. She's not talking to them."

"I can take care of her," the idiot son said.

His father glared at him and said, "Not so hasty, Anthony."

Anthony pressed. "Where is she at?"

"Let's just calm down. We'll figure out a solution. Have you come up with an alibi yet?"

"I'm working on it."

"Well, I think your best bet is an alibi as a way of keeping her quiet. But I don't think another dead body is going to help the situation any. Even a whiff of connection to this family, and you're done for—both of you."

Maurice slammed his fist down on the desk. "This family will not have a single scuff. But the police say she won't talk, and from what you've said, it sounds like maybe she knows better."

"So, we just let her go?" Anthony asked incredulously.

"Yes, let her go. If she wanted to run away, let her run. She's a junkie, anyway. She'll probably end up dead of her own accord."

"I'll let our contacts know," I offered.

"Now that the girl is taken care of, what do you want me to do?"

Maurice eyed his son with disgust. "Priscilla, tell him what he needs to do. Anthony, listen to Priscilla." And he left the room, leaving me to deal with the idiot.

"You know I don't take orders from you, right?"

"You heard your father. You absolutely do. I have one main concern: to keep this family's name pristine. And your father has trusted me to do just that. You will obey me and your father, or there will be consequences. Members of this family can have 'accidents.'"

"Who do you think you are? You can't threaten me."

He puffed out his chest, and his hands were balled into fists. I'd like to see him try to take me down. I wasn't some drugged-out prostitute anymore. I was clean, healthy, stayed fit, and knew how to protect myself. He'd be lucky to make it out with his balls intact.

"Look, all we need to do is work together, and everyone succeeds. Now, I'll give you your instructions. Do you think you can follow them?"

"Let me have it."

He said it, but his eyes told a different story. They declared that he was going to do whatever he damn well felt like. He was a loose cannon. No matter how much his father protected him, one had to wonder: how far was he really willing to go to preserve his family name? If you asked me, I'd say the old man should cut his losses. I didn't think Anthony was worth another moment of our time.

But just in case there was any doubt about the girl's cooperation, I decided to have a little chat with her myself. If she was cooperative, great. If not, well, I was going to have to teach her a lesson myself. I wasn't going to let some junkie ruin the future I'd built. I had poured out too much blood, sweat, and tears to end up here. Nothing would stand in my way—not this piece of garbage named Anthony, and certainly not one of his unfortunate girlfriends. I just hoped the girl knew what was best for her. That would be to keep her mouth shut and to run far, far away.

11

MARTINA

WEARING MY BEST BLACK SLACKS, paired with a turtleneck and a blazer over it, I steeled myself to meet Anthony Stanzel. Inside his office, our hands met in a firm shake. He looked like he did in his pictures online. Tall, with dark hair and beady eyes. He looked more corporate than street hustler. "Thank you for coming in today," Anthony began, a hint of intrigue in his eyes. "I admit I'm a little curious. It just said in the notes that you have some real estate you'd like to discuss."

"Yes, that's correct."

"Please have a seat."

As I settled into the chair opposite him, I remembered the script I had rehearsed. I intended to approach the topic delicately, not wanting to start off aggressively. I didn't plan to confront him directly with statements like, "Is this your former sex worker? Were you a pimp?" Subtlety was the name of the game. However, one look at him and I realized he didn't fit the typical image of a pimp. But they weren't always the oily-haired, bare-chested slimeballs that movies portrayed.

"Thank you," I began, choosing my words cautiously. "I was

actually looking at an apartment building not far from here, in the Tenderloin, and your name came up."

His expression changed momentarily, indicating that my statement had surprised him. "I don't believe we have any property holdings in that area," he said, his voice even. "I'm curious as to how my name came up."

"Sure," I responded. "I was talking to some of the residents, and they said you used to live there. I assumed you had owned the building."

He furrowed his brow. "How long ago was this?"

"Thirty-five years ago."

"What was the address?"

"On the corner of Golden Gate and Jones."

He nodded slowly and his face softened. "Golden Gate and Jones... My goodness, it's been years since I even thought about that old place. I was just a kid back then, during my college days. You see, I attended San Francisco State, and I rented an old apartment at the time, trying to prove I was my own man." He chuckled, but it lacked authenticity.

"So, you don't own the building?"

"Oh, no," he replied, sitting up a bit straighter. "I was just a kid back then. Worked odd jobs until I realized that my father's money was far better than a minimum wage job and a dingy apartment."

"Oh, okay. I guess the person I talked to was mistaken then. They assumed you owned the building, but maybe it's that you just lived there during college," I said, acting as if I accepted the reasoning.

"What's your interest with that building anyhow? Are you looking to purchase it?"

"Oh, no, I'm actually looking for a friend of mine. She used to live there."

He studied my face. "So, you're not really here to talk about real estate?"

"Yes and no. You see, I have a friend, a friend of my mother's, who I've been looking for." Slowly, I fished the photograph out of my purse. It showed Victoria and Nancy as young women with hope in their eyes. I could tell by his demeanor that Anthony had secrets, but prying them out wasn't going to be easy. I certainly wasn't going to let him know that Nancy was looking for Victoria. I slid the photo across the desk, pointing at one of the faces. "The girl on the left, her name is Victoria. I'm looking for her."

His eyes darted to the photograph, and for a split second, his body twitched, but he recovered quickly. He slid the photograph back to me. "Don't know her."

"Are you sure?"

"Positive. Never seen her before in my life."

I challenged him, "Interesting. My mother said she was sure you knew her, that you'd dated."

Fidgeting in his seat, he said, "To be honest, I dated a lot of girls back then. Maybe I did know her, maybe I didn't. I just... I don't remember her."

"So, you haven't seen her in thirty-five years?"

"Ma'am, I'm not sure I've ever seen her. You came in here under false pretenses, which I don't appreciate. I'm very busy, and I'm going to have to ask you to leave."

Clearly, the photo struck a nerve. "I apologize. I didn't mean to upset you, Mr. Stanzel. I actually looked you up, and it seems like you're one of the pillars of the community. You've done so much good for San Francisco. I thought you'd be open to answering questions about my mother's friend."

"Who is your mother?" he asked, skeptically.

"You probably wouldn't know her. Her name is Hetty. She

used to work in San Francisco, at a coffee shop. I guess Victoria used to go there a lot, and they became friends."

He shrugged, but I could tell he was trying to place the name Hetty and the coffee shop. He wouldn't because I'd made up the story. He leaned forward, "Doesn't ring a bell. Like I've told you, I don't know that girl, never did. Now, please, if you don't have any questions about the actual real estate dealings of my company, I need you to leave. And if you don't, I'll have security escort you out."

He was awfully defensive for a man with nothing to hide.

Out of my chair, I took a step away from the desk. "That's fine. I'm leaving. Thank you for all of your help, Mr. Stanzel." I smiled, an expression that hinted I knew more than I let on. With confidence, I strutted out of his office.

His defensiveness and obvious recognition of the photo strengthened my belief Anthony Stanzel and Blade, the pimp, were one and the same. A man who abused and sold young women not just for profit but, I suspected, for pleasure. Yet, if he did know Victoria's whereabouts, he certainly wouldn't tell me. But I had to wonder, had he turned over a new leaf since his college days?

Regardless, it was clear I had to look elsewhere to uncover Victoria's fate. The process would be involved, considering the length of time, but one way or another, I was determined to find her, to unveil the truth. And if Anthony Stanzel had any more secrets, I planned to find them.

12

VICTORIA

THIRTY-FIVE YEARS EARLIER

I NEVER TRUSTED THE COPS. The idea that they wanted to help me get sober and put my life back together seemed farfetched. As much as I wanted to believe him, I couldn't. I told him I was interested in their help, hoping they would leave me be. My plan was to make an escape in a few days, once I'd healed up.

When the pain medication wore off, my body ached everywhere. They had been giving me methadone to help with my addiction. Without it, I wasn't sure if I would make it through the day.

As I lay in pain, the friendly nurse returned to my bedside. I attempted a smile. She had been kind to me and genuinely seemed to want to see me get better. It was rare to find someone willing to help someone like me.

"How are you feeling?"

"Sore, but better."

"Ribs can take a while to heal. How are your headaches?"

"Getting better. How long do you think it'll be before I can be discharged?"

"Give it a couple of days," she answered gently. "The social workers will come by to talk to you. I know the police said they'd help, but I think it's best if you talk to someone not connected with crime, you know?"

I stared at her name tag, which read "Nurse Gray." It didn't fit her at all. In my eyes, she was more like sunshine.

"I appreciate how kind you've been to me. Thank you."

"You're very welcome," she replied, a soft smile on her face. "It seems like no one's helped you in a long time."

Nodding, I said, "I've been trying so hard. I have a daughter, you know? My mother has temporary custody of her now. I'm trying to earn some money, get an apartment, and get her back."

"I believe the social worker can guide you. There are programs to help you get clean."

"I want to be clean. My baby deserves better."

Nurse Gray patted my arm. "You deserve better too," she assured.

As she left quietly, a small glimmer of hope kindled in me for the first time in what felt like forever. I hoped for a different life. I hadn't visited my daughter, Shannon, in over a month, and I worried she'd forget me. Mom put her on the phone once, but she hardly spoke. I tried not to take it personally. Phones can be intimidating for little ones, like how a voice emanates from an object on the wall. I didn't blame Shannon. She was just a toddler. Oh, how I missed her.

Together, we'd have a good life. I'd get an apartment where Shannon would have her own room. I imagined getting her one of those little beds with pink frills and a canopy. I'd give her everything I'd wanted as a girl. I never wanted her to worry about money or face any bad men lurking in the shadows.

The first time I met a bad man, I didn't know he was bad. He was a neighbor who offered to help my mom with the yard. Grateful, she'd invited him in for lemonade. He seemed real nice. The next time he visited, I was about six years old, and I thought he was one of the nicest men I had ever met and wished he would be my dad. I didn't really know my dad—didn't remember him anyway—he had left when I was Shannon's age.

One day, as Mom was rushing to work without having a babysitter for me, he offered to watch over me. Mama said he was a godsend.

That was when the games started.

They didn't seem too weird at first, but the next time he stayed with me while Mom was at work, it felt wrong. He made me promise never to tell. I didn't want to get him or Mom in trouble, or for her to have to worry about who would watch me while she worked.

Shaking away the haunting memories, I vowed to never let that happen to my Shannon. Never.

A woman in a crisp suit, with glossy hair and bright lipstick, approached. She looked like a social worker but more polished.

"Are you Victoria?"

I nodded. "Hi."

"I'm here to talk about your future."

"Are you the social worker?"

She shook her head, "No. I'm here to ask you about what you saw on the street."

Who was she? Unclear, but I was sure she couldn't be trusted. Though the woman was beautiful, her eyes were devoid of warmth. "I didn't see anything."

"That's good to hear. Now, I'm here to make sure that doesn't change. Do you understand?"

"Yes. I didn't see anything, and I won't remember anything. I swear. I just want to get clean and never turn back. I have a daughter. I have to think of her. I'll do anything to keep her safe."

She gave me a smile—one of satisfaction. She stepped closer, making my heart race. This woman could hurt me; her demeanor screamed it. Instead, she handed me an envelope, "This is for your future, Victoria. Use it wisely. Leave the city. Don't come back. If you do, things are going to be very unpleasant. Understand?"

My eyes widened in fear, but I quickly nodded. "As soon as they discharge me, I'll go. I promise I'll never look back. I won't ever come back to the city."

"Good. I spoke with the nurse. You'll be out in a couple of days. I'll ensure you leave safely. I will arrange a car for you. We can take you home or to the BART station."

"The BART station will be fine." I didn't want them to know where I was going. It was better to run and make sure nobody followed.

"Very well." Without another word, she left my room.

Though she was terrifying, a part of me felt she might've just given me a gift. I opened the envelope, revealing $5000—enough for an apartment. Enough to get Shannon back. A mix of fear and hope swirled inside me. Everything was going to be okay.

13

MARTINA

PACKING up to go and meet Hirsch, I was surprised by a knock on my office door. Glancing up, I said, "Hey, Vincent, how's it going?"

"Good. I got some info for you."

I had enlisted Vincent's help with some of the research into Victoria. We were checking all possible leads. We knew Victoria had a daughter named Shannon, born approximately thirty-seven years ago. We also knew that Victoria had lived in San Francisco and was somehow connected to Anthony Stanzel. But with Anthony not talking, our best lead was to pursue the daughter. If we found the daughter, hopefully we'd find Victoria.

"What did you find?"

"Well, 'Shannon' was the 21st most common girl's name that year. So, I did a search of birth records for the year and found eighteen Shannons born in CoCo County. This is assuming, of course, that Victoria had her baby in the county where she lived."

He stood up and wiggled his eyebrows. I could've been

annoyed that he was drawing this out, but I wasn't. His behavior meant that he had found something significant.

"And?" I prodded.

"Eighteen Shannons were born in CoCo County that year," he repeated.

"But how many were born to a mother named Victoria?"

He raised his pointer finger and declared, "Aha, that's the right question! Exactly three."

It was looking like the case would be simpler than I had anticipated. "What do you know about the Victorias?"

"One is Victoria Stone, married to Victor Stone. They currently have three children and still live in Concord. The second Victoria lists the father's name as Davy Green. I checked the records: they were married but are now divorced. This Victoria Green, now Victoria Sable, lives in Walnut Creek. And the third..."

"And the third?"

"The third is Victoria Hightower, mother of Shannon Hightower. No father listed. I did a search for Victoria Hightower in CoCo County and found nothing."

Of the three Victorias, I would guess that Victoria Hightower was our Victoria. If she had been married when Shannon was born, she probably would've shared that fact. Based on Victoria's past, it was possible she didn't know who the father was.

"Did you do a wider search to see where she might be?"

"As you can imagine, there are more than a few Victoria Hightowers, not just in CoCo County but all around California," he replied.

"What about Shannon Hightower?"

"That I can help you with," Vincent smiled. "Shannon Hightower, daughter of Victoria Hightower, currently lives in Pleasanton with her husband. There are a few other Shannon

Hightowers in the area, but only one born thirty-seven years ago."

"Sounds like you may have found Victoria's daughter. Do you have any photos of Shannon? DMV records, perhaps?"

"Even better." Vincent stepped inside and set his laptop down on my desk. With a few taps, he pulled up a DMV photo of Shannon Hightower, now known as Shannon Bernstein. I quickly grabbed a photograph of Victoria, placing it next to Shannon's for comparison.

Vincent pointed at Shannon's hairline. "They both have a widow's peak. And that nose—they have the same nose. Plus, the blonde hair..."

Turning to Vincent, a chill went down my body. "You found Victoria's daughter."

"That's my guess. I also got an address and a phone number."

I glanced at my shiny watch and said, "I'm meeting Hirsch to discuss some new cold cases."

"Yeah? You excited to be back with the squad?" Vincent's tone was encouraging, but there was a slight falter, a hint that maybe he felt left out.

"It's not the whole squad. I'm just part-time, maybe 10-15 hours a week. Jayda and Ross are just part-time too. Hirsch wants to start with some easy closures, hoping it'll justify more funding," I replied, trying to ease his concerns. I didn't want him to feel like the odd one out.

"I understand. I'm happy for you, and for Hirsch."

"Thanks. I should get going."

"Okay," he said quietly. Something was off. Vincent would normally be doing some sort of dance or a silly jig.

"Everything okay, Vincent?"

"Yeah, I'm just tired, that's all."

I wondered if that was the only reason. Was he upset about

not being invited to the new cold case squad? Or was it something else? I remembered his upcoming wedding. Maybe the stress was getting to him. "How's Amanda?"

His eyes lit up at the mention of her name. "She's doing well. The wedding's only a few months away, and she's got some family stuff going on. It's been a little rough."

I nodded, trying to convey understanding. "You'll get through this. Let me know if you need any help or just to talk."

"Thanks, Martina." He left without saying much more. I felt for the guy. Family situations could be tricky.

Speaking of family, my mother had been nagging me recently about not talking to my brothers. Not that she spoke to them often herself. But she did keep in touch, ensuring they were okay.

In a family full of addicts, my mother and I were recovering alcoholics. From what I understood, my brothers still struggled with various substances. We were never close. For my daughter's sake, I preferred not having that kind of influence around her. Sometimes, it was easier to pretend they didn't exist. It might sound cold, but they'd had run-ins with the law and associated with some really dangerous people. It was best to maintain distance.

As I walked out, I called Hirsch. "Hey, Martina, are you on your way?" he said.

"Would you mind if we pushed the meeting an hour? I got a lead on my missing person. We think we found her daughter."

"Go. Our cases won't get any colder."

"Okay, thanks, Hirsch."

Parked in front of the Bernstein residence in Pleasanton, I had made the decision to just show up. I wanted an authentic response and since, according to employment history, Shannon worked from home, she should be there. And my vibe from the Stanzels made me wary of letting information flow too freely.

Taking a deep breath, I hurried up to the front door and knocked.

The door opened a moment later. The woman from the DMV photo stood in front of me. Sandy blonde hair, brown eyes, and that telling widow's peak just like Victoria. "Hi, I'm Martina Monroe, a private investigator. Are you Shannon?"

She looked puzzled. "Yes. I'm Shannon."

My mind raced, wondering if the Stanzels had gotten to her already. "I was hired to find a woman. And I have reason to believe you're the woman's daughter. Her name is Victoria."

Unflinching she said, "That sounds right," still staring at me with a hint of suspicion.

"Are you in contact with your mother?"

"No. I haven't seen her since I was two years old. I was raised by my grandmother."

Victoria is missing. "Do you know the circumstances around her disappearance?"

"Grandma said she was an addict and had been in the hospital when they last spoke. She feared my mother had crossed paths with the wrong person—someone responsible for her hospitalization."

I pulled out the photograph of Victoria and Nancy. "Is this her?"

She accepted the picture. Recognition flashed in Shannon's eyes. "Yes, that's her. My mother."

We found Victoria's daughter.

She cocked her head, questioning, "Who's looking for her?"

"A friend from your mother's past. She had the same troubled life as Victoria but managed to turn things around. Now that's she's older and has a family of her own, she's trying to find Victoria. She didn't know much about her, except that she had a daughter from Concord, but that was all she knew."

Shannon shook her head, eyes filling with concern. "Have you found her?"

"No. Until today, I didn't even have her last name. But I'm committed to finding her."

"I fear she might be dead."

I hesitated before asking, "Have you ever tried to find her?"

"My grandma filed a missing persons report, but the police didn't find anything—or do anything to find her, according to Grandma. A few years ago, I hired a private investigator before my wedding, but he found nothing. Initially, I thought you were working with him. That someone else is looking for her is surprising."

A cell phone rang, and she said, "Oh, that's my work phone. Give me one sec."

Standing in the doorway, I waited and hoped she had more information about her mother that could help us find Victoria. Shannon returned. "Sorry about that. It's a busy Monday."

"I'm sorry to have intruded. I was excited to meet you. Maybe we can set up a time to discuss your mother's case."

"I'll have to check my schedule. I'm a marketing consultant and up to my eyeballs in work. I have your card. I'll call. I will. I really would like to know the truth."

Me too. "That would be great. In the meantime, if you could share the PI's contact, and your grandmother's, it might help our search."

"I'll get you the PI's info but let me talk to my grandma first. She's not in good health."

"Understood."

She retreated into the house, and I waited for all of thirty seconds before she handed me the PI's card. I thanked her, and she promised to be in touch. This was certainly a turn of events —hopefully one that would lead us to Victoria.

14

___

MARTINA

AFTER CHECKING in with the reception desk at the CoCo County Sheriff's Department, I waited for Hirsch to come and get me. It wasn't like I could waltz in and act like I owned the place—anymore. But perhaps that would change once they officially brought me on as part-time help. The timing of Victoria's case and working with Hirsch again was truly serendipitous. Victoria's missing persons report had been filed in CoCo County because her permanent address was at her mother's, and I needed to review it. It was unfortunate I didn't get to talk much with Shannon, but surely, we would get another chance soon enough.

A few moments later, Hirsch, Jayda, and Ross approached with wide smiles. "You must be the welcoming committee," I remarked.

Ross offered a playful curtsy. "Welcome back, Martina, our favorite private investigator."

"Don't let Vincent hear you say that," I retorted with a grin.

"He's our second favorite," Jayda quipped.

After a round of heartfelt embraces, I faced Hirsch. "All right, boss, lead the way."

He simply smirked as we headed toward the new mini Cold Case Squad headquarters. The air was filled with an electrifying mixture of excitement and nostalgia. Being reunited with the three of them brought back a flood of memories. Our regular meetings with Dr. Scribner, Kiki from forensics, and the rest of the squad.

Sheriff Baldwin had hinted, after our last case had overlapped, that he envisioned a collaborative future between Drakos Monroe Security & Investigations and the CoCo County Sheriff's Department. It had taken eight months for that to happen, but I thought maybe, after this part-time stint with Hirsch and the team, there'd be more opportunities in the future.

Inside the modest conference room—a stark contrast to our previous Cold Case Squad room adorned with whiteboards and expansive tables—I was almost too restless to sit. Yet, we all found ourselves seated around a circular table, each of us seemingly content.

"So, Hirsch," I started. "What have you got in store for us?"

"Well, first of all, thank you, all three of you, for agreeing to work with me on cold cases again. As you all know, funding was always a challenge. But I see this as a victory for us and hope for a future expansion."

Jayda chimed in. "So, we tackle the easy cases first? The ones that might just need some DNA analysis or benefit from recent technological advancements in forensics?"

"That's precisely what I had in mind," Hirsch affirmed. "I'm aware that you, Martina, are working on another case for your firm. Jayda and Ross have active cases too. We need to establish some ground rules—how much time we can all commit, how frequently we should meet. Essentially, it's up to us four to chart the way forward."

I said, "Sounds good. And, yes, I do have another case, but it's connected to CoCo County. A cold case."

Hirsch turned his attention toward me, as if surprised. "Yep, I've just confirmed the full name of my missing person." Ross and Jayda shot me some puzzled expressions. They obviously had no clue what I was referring to, so I explained the case and the connection to CoCo County.

"So, either way you were coming back here?" Ross asked, half teasing.

"That's right. Because I want to see that missing persons report. The daughter insinuated the police didn't put much effort into the search. To this team, it wouldn't shock any of us to hear if zero resources were spent looking for a missing sex worker. But any details I can find about Victoria will help me retrace her final steps and find her. We already have her connected to a very prominent family."

Hirsch leaned in. "Did you speak to them?"

"I did."

Ross interjected, "Who's the family?"

With their questions, I realized how much I missed having a whole team to discuss the details of a case. "The Stanzel family. They're the elite of San Francisco. My client insists that Anthony Stanzel, the son of the patriarch, was their pimp thirty-five years ago. He beat them and supplied them with drugs to keep them compliant—the whole nine yards."

"Seriously?" Jayda exclaimed, clearly exasperated.

Nodding, I said, "I met with Anthony. He wasn't thrilled about my questions regarding his past. He lied, claiming he never saw the girls in the photo—my client and her friend, Victoria Hightower, the person I'm searching for."

Ross nodded thoughtfully, leaning back. "You think her disappearance might be linked to this 'Richie Rich' from San Francisco, who was once her pimp?"

"Exactly. I need to see the missing persons report, which could provide details about Victoria from that time. I also intend to question her mother, though her daughter wants to speak to her first. She mentioned her mother isn't in good health."

Jayda cocked her head, studying me. "Martina, you've got yourself another big old crazy case. Sounds like it will keep you pretty busy. Can you really take on more right now? I mean, I heard about..."

I felt Jayda's hand on my arm. She was the one who had set me up with Wilder, her old college friend. From the look she gave me, she knew Wilder and I were history. "Time will tell. But as of right now, it's keeping me occupied, which is good. But I've worked with prominent families before. They dislike their skeletons being dragged out into the open. If Victoria knows something damaging about them, they'll do almost anything to keep it hidden. I've been discreet. I didn't tell Anthony Stanzel who hired me. I don't want him targeting my client."

"Do you believe the Stanzels would retaliate against your client?" Hirsch asked, concern evident in his voice.

"I wouldn't put it past them. Remember the first case we worked together, Hirsch?"

He nodded in acknowledgment.

"My next step is to pull up the missing persons report and go from there. I only spoke with the daughter briefly, but she said Victoria was hospitalized before she disappeared. I need to find which hospital and then pray someone there will remember her from thirty-five years ago."

Ross chuckled lightly. "Sounds like a quintessential Martina case."

Hirsch agreed with a head bob. "All right, Martina, you'll look for the missing persons report for Victoria Hightower. It can be one of our first official cases. The rest of us will look for some easier cases to close."

"Sounds like a great plan, boss."

A thought struck me. If I was already being hired through my firm to work the Victoria Hightower case, it was a bonus for the CoCo County Sheriff's Department. If I didn't bill Victoria's case to CoCo County, that meant there was potentially another part-time person who could join the Cold Case Squad. "You know, I'm not working Victoria's case alone. One of my investigators helped me find her daughter. He's pretty good."

Hirsch smiled.

Did he understand what I was implying? "That's right. Vincent did the research, tracking down all the girls named Shannon born thirty-seven years ago, matching them up with a mother named Victoria. He found all the matches and gave me an address for the daughter. That's how I knew who she was. I'm already working on the case for Drakos Monroe, which means I don't need to bill CoCo County, which means..."

Hirsch said, "We have an opening for a part-time consultant."

"I have one I could recommend."

Hirsch nodded. "I must admit I miss his sunny disposition."

With that, everyone knew who we were referring to. Vincent was a constant source of humor and levity during our investigations. He was diligent and intelligent but carried a playful spirit that brightened every case. "I'll talk to him about it."

"Let's find that missing persons case. And a few others to close out."

We didn't need further instruction and strutted toward the file room. Inside, it felt like déjà vu from when I first started working with the Cold Case Squad. Towers of banker's boxes loomed, filled with unsolved mysteries. Now, I was on a mission to locate one from thirty-five years ago—Victoria Hightower.

All four of us scoured the room, sifting through files,

choosing the initial batch for the new cold case team. After ninety minutes of relentless searching, I exclaimed, "Ha! I found it!" I began to read aloud, "Victoria Hightower missing..." I paused, finishing the text silently before announcing, "I know where I'm going next."

"Where?" Hirsch asked.

"The missing persons report says she was hospitalized at San Francisco General. She called her mother from the hospital the day before she was reported missing. She told her mom she would be home that day but never arrived. When her mother called the hospital, they said she'd been discharged and didn't know where she was."

The team nodded, like they understood it was a solid lead. I continued, "The report mentions she had spoken to the police while there. So, I'll need to liaise with SFPD to see if there are any police reports from the time Victoria went missing and was hospitalized. That could help locate her, or at least shed light on why someone might've wanted her gone."

Hirsch responded, "So, you have your hands full."

"Definitely. It would surely help if someone from law enforcement accompanied me to the SFPD to gather info," I hinted, casting a suggestive glance at Hirsch, a former SFPD homicide detective.

Hirsch's blue eyes twinkled. "My afternoon's pretty open."

It was exactly the response I hoped for. As a PI, I could go undercover for information, but a badge often yielded better results, especially in hospitals and with police departments. More so when the person flashing the badge used to be one of their own. We devised a strategy and exited the CoCo County Sheriff's Department. Hirsch and I were partnering on a case once again. In that moment, all of my being knew we *would* learn what had happened to Victoria Hightower.

15

MARTINA

WITH MY PARTNER by my side for the first time in almost a year, I felt reassured we would get the information we needed with minimal pushback. Procedures from thirty-five years ago might have been laxer than they were now, but obtaining medical records without a warrant was impossible. Luckily, I had Hirsch and crew who could secure one if necessary. However, our real interest wasn't in the medical records. We hoped to find someone who'd been on staff at the time—perhaps an old nurse or a doctor who was still employed. It was a stretch, but we had to try.

The interior of San Francisco County General Hospital greeted us with an overly chilly embrace. Air conditioning set too low had visitors bundling up, their sniffles and coughs echoing in the sterile space. I'd always hated hospitals.

Hirsch stepped forward to the receptionist, flashing his badge with a warm smile. "Hi, my name is Sergeant Hirsch, and this is my partner, Martina Monroe. We're hoping to speak with someone about a patient from thirty-five years ago."

A woman, likely a volunteer, with gray hair, neatly pinned in a bun, peered at us over her wireframe glasses. "That's quite a request, Sergeant. Fortunately, I've been here forty years, if you can believe it. Maybe I can help. Do you have more details? That will likely help me direct you to the right department."

Smiling at the woman, Hirsch said, "We're investigating a missing person case. She was last seen here, at this hospital. We're hoping to find any information we can. Her family, especially her daughter who was just two at the time, misses her dearly. We believe she had been attacked and was admitted to the emergency room. It was a situation involving a boyfriend."

She nodded knowingly. "Ah, domestic. I know just the person to help. There's a nurse in the ER; she's been here for forty years. Forty years! She's planning on retiring soon, but I'm sure she'll be eager to assist, especially in a case like this."

"That would be wonderful. Do you know if she's around today?"

"I think I spotted her earlier. She's always been the kind to go above and beyond. I'm sure she'll be eager to help if she knew a family was in distress. Just give me a moment."

As she reached for the phone, Hirsch leaned closer. "You might be a lucky charm, Martina."

I smirked. "It's about time we had some luck. And if we can get someone who remembers Victoria from thirty-five years ago and the SFPD cooperates and provides us useful information, we'll be golden."

"It's a big department. I doubt they'll have any digitized records from that era. But we can always request the physical files."

"I'll take whatever we can get."

Concluding her call, the woman smiled. "She'll be out in ten minutes. Is that all right?"

"Absolutely. Thank you."

"You're welcome. I hope you find what you're looking for."

With another thank you, we took a step back to distance ourselves from the screeching of coughs and sniffles.

Ten minutes later, a slight woman in her sixties, about five feet in height, approached us in the reception area, wearing pink scrubs. She said, "Sergeant Hirsch, Ms. Monroe?"

We walked over to her. "Yes, hi, my name is Martina Monroe, and this is Sergeant Hirsch from the CoCo County Sheriff's Department."

"Hi, I'm Lottie Gray. An ER nurse. I heard you're needing information about a patient from thirty-five years ago."

I nodded. "We're looking for a missing person by the name of Victoria Hightower. We believe she was last seen at San Francisco General before she disappeared. We were hoping you might remember her."

She squinted slightly, pondering the information. "I was definitely here back then. Can you give me more details about her?"

"Of course," I replied before taking out the photo from my backpack and handing it to her. "The woman on the left is Victoria."

While she studied the picture, I said, "She was brought in, we believe, due to injuries, possibly inflicted by a boyfriend. She called her mother and told her people were helping her and that she was trying to get clean. Victoria has a daughter who was two years old at the time, and she likely talked about becoming sober to regain custody of her."

Nurse Gray's face took on a look of recognition. "Yes, I think I do remember her. Between the face and the story, it does sound familiar. The police came here to speak with her, which was out of the ordinary."

Yes. She does remember!

"That's right. We believe she spoke to the police while she was here. Can you tell us why that was out of the ordinary?"

"Well," she began, her gaze distant. "Victoria had apparently been on the run from someone. She was badly beaten, but someone found her passed out on the street and brought her to the hospital. It took her a couple of days to even realize where she was. Yes, she had an addiction, and we started giving her methadone a few days before her discharge."

Hirsch inquired, "Do you remember why the police were here?"

"The staff called them in because of the severity of her injuries. She had significant head trauma, broken ribs. Whoever hurt her was trying to kill her, I think. She mentioned not wanting to file a police report. She was scared to say anything."

"But the police still came?"

"They did. I got the impression she might have witnessed something. They asked her repeatedly about what she might have seen, but she insisted she didn't know or see anything."

"Did you believe her?"

Nurse Gray sighed. "I had the feeling she was protecting someone."

I knew exactly who Victoria was trying to protect.

Hirsch continued, "But she never mentioned who?"

The nurse shook her head. "No. But she did have a visitor."

My ears perked up. "Really? Who?"

"I thought she was family," she said. "It was a woman, and she was there when Victoria was discharged. I had assumed she was taking her home. Now, in light of what you're saying, it seems strange."

"Do you remember what this woman looked like?" I asked, hoping she had the key to unlock our case.

"She was stunning," Nurse Gray began, her eyes distant with the recollection. "She told me she was Victoria's cousin. She had dark hair, fair skin, and bright blue eyes. Truly a stunner. And well-polished, in a suit. I remember being a bit surprised, not just by how attractive she was, but by the evident disparity between her wealth and Victoria's situation. It gave me hope for Victoria, who despite everything had a sweet soul. You could tell she genuinely wanted to get better for her daughter."

Was this supposed cousin a member of the Stanzel family ensuring Victoria never mentioned Anthony to the police? This could be a valuable piece of information.

"And the visitor didn't mention her name?"

"No, not that I can recall. It was a long time ago, but her case touched me. Those times were hard for women, and many were taken advantage of."

She glanced at Hirsch, momentarily sizing him up but not necessarily in distrust.

Hirsch chimed in. "Do you remember the police officer who came to talk to her?"

She chuckled. "He had a mustache. Though, to be fair, a lot of men sported big bushy mustaches back then. I'm rather glad that trend died out."

I couldn't help but agree. "Was he from the San Francisco Police Department?"

"Yes, absolutely," she confirmed.

"Older, younger?"

"Younger. Maybe in his late twenties or early thirties."

I smiled, appreciating her help. "Thank you so much, Nurse Gray."

"I hope you find her. For her family's sake. I genuinely wished she was one of those who made it through."

"I understand," I said, touched by her concern.

There was something about Nurse Gray that made an impression. She was one of those souls who believed in redemption for all. It didn't matter one's background or profession, she genuinely cared. I silently wished there were more people like her in the world.

Emerging from the hospital into the chilly air, I looked over at Hirsch. "Ready to head over to SFPD?"

I knew he'd left SFPD due to a disagreement with his former supervisor on how to handle cases. Hirsch thought you should have evidence to close cases, not just because you needed better closure stats. He nodded with determination. "Let's find out what happened to Victoria Hightower."

"That's the spirit."

16

VICTORIA

THIRTY-FIVE YEARS EARLIER

Seated in a wheelchair, with a plastic bag full of my belongings, I waited. The nurse verified that I was free to go. Both she and the social worker had been so kind to me, but I knew I had to turn my back on the opportunities. That woman told me I had to leave the city and never come back. The social worker offered a rehab center and women's shelter in San Francisco. I couldn't risk it. There were other rehab centers and other shelters, I was sure. Anxious, I wanted to call my mom to ask how Shannon was doing. I couldn't wait to see them both. I was determined to be better for them. And as that kind nurse had said, I was going to be better for me, too.

It was strange to think there were such nice people out there, like Nurse Gray. But there were also awful people like Blade. Nurse Gray appeared from around the counter. "Okay, so you have a visitor. Your cousin, Priscilla, said she's going to take you home."

That woman, apparently Priscilla, was pretending to be my cousin. She claimed she would take care of me. And to an extent, she had. She'd given me money and promised to take me out of the city. I was eager to leave it all behind. "There she is now," Nurse Gray remarked. She looked down and said, "Take care of yourself, Victoria. I'm rooting for you. I think you're going to do great things."

"Thank you for everything. I think you're just about the kindest person I've ever met."

She patted my shoulder lightly and returned to her nurse's station.

"How are you feeling?" Priscilla asked, feigning concern.

I could tell she wasn't sincere, but part of me believed she might care, even if just a little. Otherwise, why not just kill me? I had assumed she was connected to Blade. After all, who else would care what I saw? But if she was working on behalf of Blade, why was she trying to help me? "Doing a lot better, thanks."

She grasped the handles of my wheelchair and steered me toward the elevator. As the doors closed, she said, "I have a car waiting downstairs, but there's something else."

I glanced up at her. "What is it?"

"I've spoken with my associates, and they're concerned you might not really disappear, that you'll cooperate with the police."

I shook my head vigorously. "No, absolutely not. I'm putting this all behind me. I'm never looking back. I want to see my daughter and my mom. I want to be clean. I don't ever want to talk about any of this. I don't remember anything. I swear."

"That may be, but I'm afraid your word isn't enough." The elevator doors dinged and opened. She pushed me out into the lobby.

Once outside, she commanded, "Okay, you can get up now."

I stood up and froze.

She nodded toward the black sedan. "Get in the back seat."

Where was this heading? Was she going to kill me? Was I

walking into my own death? What did she mean my word wasn't good enough? I was too afraid to move.

"Get in the car. I'll explain everything once we're inside."

I complied even though I didn't know if she was going to kill me. But if she was going to do it, it might as well be in the back of the car. Trying to run in my state wouldn't get me far.

Once we were seated inside, she handed me another envelope, a larger one with a little hook that kept it securely closed. She shut my door and then climbed into the front seat.

"Drive north," she told the driver.

I said, "My mother's house is in Concord."

From the front seat, she turned around and said, "I know exactly where your mother and your daughter live, and so does the family. That's not where I'm taking you. Look inside the envelope. You'll find a new identity and some extra money. I'm sorry, but it's the only way. You'll have to start over. You can never see your mother or daughter ever again."

I gasped.

"If you don't follow my instructions, they will kill them and you. Do you understand what I'm doing for you right now? They wanted to kill you. I had to fight for this."

None of it made sense. "Why would you fight for me? You don't know me."

She looked directly into my eyes and said, "I've been where you are. I was you once. I fought to not be that person anymore. I believe you have the possibility to change too. Don't prove me wrong. We're going to take you somewhere safe. You're going to go to rehab, stay in a shelter. Everything is outlined in the envelope. I've given you a new birth certificate. From there, you can establish a new life. Make it count, Victoria. This is your only chance. I'm sorry it's come to this."

Did she mean she was once like me? Had she worked for Blade too? "Where are we going?"

"North."

Was that just a vague answer to keep me calm? Were they just saying that so I wouldn't be freaking out, trying to run away, fearing they were going to kill me? I opened the envelope and pulled out the documents: a birth certificate with a new name, addresses of shelters, phone numbers, contacts. Why did she care so much? She said she had been in my position, but this still seemed like a lot.

"Is this all from you?"

She turned around again. "It's from my associates."

"Blade?"

She shook her head. "His family. They're very sorry for how he's treated you, and they want to make it right. But between us, Blade is a disgrace to his entire family. He's repulsive, an imbecile. He doesn't deserve to breathe, but he's family. I'm sorry for what he's done to you and the others. We're going to make sure it never happens again."

"So, he's not going to be a pimp anymore?"

"He won't be. Hopefully, we can keep him away from innocent people. His tactics are not in alignment with his father's ideals."

What did that mean?

"So, they run legal businesses?"

"It's best you don't know any details."

"Okay."

Something still wasn't sitting right with me. "Are you sure this isn't some sort of trick?"

She sighed. "I'll say this one last time, Victoria. Learn your new name and background story. Start a new life. This is literally your only chance for survival. If you don't follow through completely, you, your mother, and your daughter will pay for it. Start over and don't look back."

If what she was saying was true, it was the only choice I had.

17

MARTINA

INSIDE THE SAN FRANCISCO police station, Hirsch pulled out his phone and said, "I'll call to see if an old friend can help us. One I'm sure isn't on the Stanzels' payroll."

I gave him a thumbs up.

Hirsch had worked in the SFPD homicide department for ten years before he'd moved to the CoCo County Sheriff's Department. He knew who was good police and who would help us. It was always good to have friends in high places.

Hirsch said into the phone, "Lieutenant Tippin, it's Hirsch."

Hirsch cracked a smile, and I could tell they were on friendly terms, if that wasn't already obvious. "I'm here in the lobby. Can you meet with me and my partner?"

After a brief pause, Hirsch said, "All right, we'll see you then."

He put the phone in his pocket and said, "That's Lieutenant Tippin. He's a good guy. I believe if we explain to him what we're looking for, he can put in the request. Like I said, and as you can probably tell by the number of phones ringing and people bustling around, they're busy here. So, don't get your hopes up that you can get the records overnight."

"I can be patient," I responded.

Hirsch raised his brows at me. "You can?"

"Yes, if I try really hard," I said with a coy smile.

"Okay, I'll believe it when I see it."

Just then, a man with a shiny bald head and a wide grin approached. "Hirsch!"

They shook hands. "Tippin, I want you to meet my friend and partner, Martina Monroe. She's a PI and consultant for CoCo County."

"Is that Monroe of Drakos Monroe Security & Investigations?"

"Guilty as charged. Nice to meet you, sir."

He shook my hand and said, "It's nice to meet you too. It's a pleasure. And I'm more than happy to help in any way I can."

Hirsch interjected, "Is there somewhere more private we can speak?"

Tippin gave him a quizzical look but didn't question it. "Of course."

Considering the sensitive nature of the investigation, it was best we went somewhere private. If the Stanzels were big donors to the SFPD, we didn't need anybody overhearing what we were up to.

Seated inside a small conference room, I explained the case and everything we'd learned so far about Victoria and her past. "So, as you can see, we need to keep the investigation quiet. I've heard the Stanzels are important around here, and if they're tied to my missing person, I'm afraid they might try to bury it."

He scratched the top of his head and said, "I haven't heard any rumblings they're shady, and they're friends of the department. You really think they're somehow connected to a former prostitute and junkie?"

"I've all but confirmed it, sir. What I need is the police report from when Victoria Hightower was in the hospital, beaten badly, presumably by Anthony Stanzel. I doubt she actually mentioned him in the report, but I'd like to understand what happened."

"Did her family hire you to find her?"

"No, actually, a friend of hers from back then did. I don't want to disclose who it was, considering she worked for Stanzel too."

"Boy, if what you say is true, that's big," Tippin began. "And keeping it quiet, that's smart. Because if it's true, the Stanzels won't be happy about it."

"What I need in addition to her report taken at the hospital are any records relating to her statement. I've got estimated dates for when she was in the hospital."

He nodded. "I'll check the records. See if we have anything related to Victoria Hightower around that timeframe."

"Thank you," I said, relieved.

"You can go ahead and have it sent over to Drakos Monroe. Martina will handle it along with some of her staff," Hirsch added.

I explained, "I'm just part-time at CoCo County."

Tippin nodded. "Understood. Your reputation precedes the both of you. I remember a few years back, you were working cold cases, solving the unsolvable."

"That was us, sir." Hirsch beamed.

"I'm glad you're still out there fighting the good fight."

The look on Hirsch's face told me he was remembering a time in that department when nobody appreciated him fighting the good fight, so to speak.

"I'll see if I can get this to you relatively quickly, Ms. Monroe," Tippin assured.

"Call me Martina."

"Martina, I'll make sure they're sent over to your office as soon as we have them."

"I appreciate it."

"Delighted to meet you. And Hirsch, let's keep in touch."

"Of course."

As Hirsch and I exited the station, I said, "Not bad for a Monday."

"True. But now our biggest obstacle—fight the traffic over the bridge to get home."

"Our toughest mission yet."

He chuckled. "How about we stop and get a coffee and a bite before we head out?"

My stomach rumbled, and I realized lunch had been forgotten. "Sounds great." I was feeling good about the case. A lot of things were getting connected, but the picture wasn't clear quite yet. My gut told me Stanzel was at the heart of all this. But what did it mean? Had they killed Victoria to keep her quiet? They didn't want people to know that Anthony Stanzel was a pimp who physically assaulted his workers? I'd seen rich folks do far worse for less.

18

PRISCILLA

PRESENT DAY

STARING into Maurice's dark beady eyes, I said, "We have a problem."

"What do you mean 'we have a problem'?"

"I just got a call from one of our contacts at the San Francisco Police Department. Someone is looking for all records relating to Victoria Hightower from thirty-five years ago."

It took him a moment to recognize the name. "Why is someone looking into records for Victoria Hightower?"

I was as surprised as he was. "I don't know. All I know is the guy in the records department said somebody made a request for anything relating to Victoria Hightower around the time she had been hospitalized."

"Maybe her family's looking for her again. There might be nothing to worry about."

"I'm not so sure."

"If you really think it's a problem, reach out. You know her new name. Make sure everything stays quiet."

I felt conflicted. I had done so many bad things, all for the sake of self-preservation. If anything got out, it would ruin the family, ruin me, and devastate many. "All right, I'll get our guy on it, try to find out where she is now."

"You've been keeping tabs?"

I shook my head, somewhat defiantly. "It's been thirty-five years. We haven't heard a peep from her. For all I know, she's dead. She's kept her end of the bargain."

If she was out there and told the police what she knew, it would ruin the family. And me. Would they retaliate against me, since I had said it was handled? "We should find out who is looking for her."

A knock interrupted our conversation. "That's Anthony."

Opening the door, Anthony walked in, clad in an expensive suit and a silk tie, his hair freshly cut. Time may have refined his appearance, but he was still the scum he was all those years ago, but now with a trainer and a new wardrobe. "Priscilla says we have a problem."

"I told you. That PI came in asking about Victoria. She even had a photo of her."

"What was the PI's name?"

"She didn't give her full name, just a first name: Martina."

"Well, that's not a common name. We'll look for all PIs named Martina. Have a chat with her, ask why she's digging."

I preferred that approach rather than trying to find Victoria living under an assumed identity. For all I knew, she was married and her name was no longer the one we had given her. She'd upheld her end of the bargain; it was only fair that we upheld ours. I would much rather stop the investigation than disrupt her life.

These men had taken so much from her and many others. It wasn't fair, and I knew I was complicit, but I'd done it for self-preservation. No one looked out for me. I had to fend for myself. Times had changed. I no longer needed the Stanzels. I had money, independence. However, our ties bound us together indefinitely. And our current dealings meant a revelation like Victoria Hightower's past could detonate everything we had built.

She had information that could shatter the glass house we'd been living in.

From the outside, our world was shiny and clean, but the inside was dark and dirty—stained with the souls of the innocent. In my mind, I wasn't part of it, but I was just as guilty. Maybe I deserved to be punished. But I wasn't planning on trading in my Gucci suits for an orange jumpsuit, and neither were the Stanzels or their associates. It was selfish. But there was only one person who looked out for my best interests—me. My priority? Find this PI, Martina, and quickly.

19

MARTINA

STANDING IN THE LOBBY, I spoke softly to Mrs. Pearson. "Shannon and her grandmother are coming in today to talk about Victoria."

"I can't believe you found them," she replied. "Have you told Nancy yet?"

"Not yet, but the case is definitely heating up. I think we might actually find her or at least find out what happened to her."

Mrs. Pearson nodded. "Well, Martina, I knew if anybody could, it would be you. How's it looking though? Do you think you'll find her alive?"

"Honestly, I don't know. There are plenty of reasons to believe she may not be alive. But stranger things have happened. I've seen it, you've seen it, everyone in this building has seen it. I'm not giving up hope."

"Nancy will appreciate that."

"After I speak with Victoria's mother and daughter, I'm going to give Nancy a call and update her."

"I know Nancy's so grateful that you've taken her case. And for her years of friendship with Victoria. I think if you can't find

Victoria alive, she would most definitely like to meet her family."

"So, how do you know Nancy?"

"Church."

"Really? How long have you known her?"

"A few years now, probably... oh, actually, my goodness, probably a decade."

"And she's shared her history with you?"

"She has. If she hadn't told me, I wouldn't have known. She turned her life around so much, it's really incredible. She's a wonderful person, mother, and grandmother. I really hope you find Victoria."

So did I. On the off chance Victoria was still alive, chances were she could turn her life around too. Drug addicts don't typically have a long lifespan, especially ones caught up in sex work. I tapped the desk and said, "That's them. They're here."

"Good luck, Martina."

"Thanks, Mrs. Pearson." I stepped toward Shannon and, presumably, her grandmother. "Hi, good to see you, Shannon."

She turned to the other woman. "Grandma, this is Martina Monroe."

"It's nice to meet you. You can call me Martina."

"You too. Please call me Peggy."

"Peggy, I understand it's hard for you to get around now, but I can lead you back to the conference room, and we can talk more about Victoria. Can I get you anything? Do you need something?"

"Some water. I'm a little parched," Peggy replied.

"I'll have some tea if you have it," Shannon said.

"I'll get it, dear," Mrs. Pearson sang out as she hurried back to the break room.

"That's Mrs. Pearson. She is the linchpin of the entire organization. She knows everyone and everything. Want to go ahead and follow me back?"

I walked slowly to ensure that Peggy would be able to keep up. I opened the door and led them into the conference room. It was one of the smaller rooms with a window and colorful art on the walls. It was where we brought clients who needed a ray of sunshine, and I thought Victoria's family most certainly could use as much light as possible.

As they seated themselves, Mrs. Pearson hurried in with tea and water. Both women thanked her, and I said, "Thank you."

"I'm not done yet. I'll have your latte in a moment," Mrs. Pearson noted with a wink, revealing just how well she knew me.

We sat quietly. Shannon sipped her tea, and Peggy held her bottled water with a shaky hand before taking a drink. Mrs. Pearson returned, and I thanked her. She shut the door behind her, and I took a sip of my drink. Mrs. Pearson made the best lattes.

"Thank you both for coming down. I have a few questions about Victoria," I began.

Shannon interrupted, "Before we get started, I'd like to say something."

"Of course, anything."

"I spoke with the PI I hired before and told him that you were looking for Victoria, my mother. He said that your firm is the best there is and wished me luck. But I also asked him to forward any kind of records he found."

"I really appreciate that." I had purposefully held off on speaking with the private investigator who had, or had not, found Victoria, not wanting his information to bias the investigation, especially since we were uncovering so many clues. I glanced down at the folder she had. The printed emails from the PI revealed that he had found very little. He hadn't located any of her medical records or police reports detailing her last known movements. He did track down where she had lived in San Francisco, but there was no mention of the Stanzels anywhere. Had he not found them or just didn't mention it? Considering how influential the Stanzel family was, the PI could have been compromised, so it was best he didn't know any more than necessary.

"Looks like he was unable to find much other than where she lived before she disappeared," I commented.

Shannon nodded. "He said she appeared to have vanished, which most likely means she is no longer with us."

"I understand how one might come to that conclusion. However, since I've restarted the investigation, I've learned a lot more details about her last few days before she went missing."

"You have?"

"Yes, I have. But before we delve into that, I want to know more about Victoria. Especially from you, Peggy. You're her mother. What can you tell me about her?"

"Like, what kind of girl she was?" Peggy asked.

I nodded. "In missing persons cases, it's crucial to understand who the person is; their likes, personality, things they enjoyed doing."

Peggy seemed to understand. "Even when Vicky was little, she liked to be in the garden, be in nature. She was such a free spirit. But then, something changed. She became... cold, angry. Mad at the world."

"How old was she when she changed?"

"Probably around six or seven years old. She used to be this ray of sunshine, and then she transformed into a sort of gloomy, introverted girl who just wanted to read books and keep to herself."

"Did she have a lot of friends growing up?"

Peggy shook her head. "No, she kept to herself. I never really understood it."

From my experience, something must have happened in young Victoria's life at age six or seven if she went from being a happy-go-lucky girl to an introverted, withdrawn child. That was often indicative of trauma. "Do you recall anything significant happening when she was six or seven years old? Maybe a divorce or loss of a pet?"

I didn't think it was either of those things, but it was worth asking.

"No." She hesitated. "But you know, I was working a lot back then. I was a single mom, and sometimes a neighbor had to watch her. He was a godsend; he watched her all the time. I didn't have to worry about childcare. Maybe that's why she became so different; I was gone so much."

I felt a twinge of suspicion. Were the neighbor's intentions pure? A friendly male neighbor spending a lot of time with a young girl followed by a stark personality change? It didn't bode well.

"The neighbor who helped watch her—did he have a family? Children of his own?"

She shook her head. "Nope, just a bachelor living on his own. He wasn't my type; otherwise, perhaps I would've remarried," she said with a sad smile.

My alarm bells rang louder. "And how did her middle school and high school years go?"

"Oh, she just went wild. Lots of boyfriends... she—" She hesitated, glancing at Shannon. "Maybe you shouldn't listen to this."

"I knew she was a prostitute, Grandma. There's nothing you can tell me that could make me love my mom any less," Shannon interjected gently.

I admired Shannon's resilience. "Well, by 'wild,' I mean lots and lots of boyfriends. There were rumors that she was using drugs, and I found evidence a few times. She was eighteen when she had Shannon."

It was consistent with child sexual abuse. Some children tried to normalize the abuse by engaging early in sexual behavior. "And is Shannon's father in the picture?"

Peggy shook her head. "Victoria didn't know who the father was, or so she said."

That explained the blank space on Shannon's birth certificate where the father's name typically would be.

"Even in her older years, when she was acting out quite a bit, did she have any hobbies? Did she still like to read or maybe write?"

"Oh, yes, when she was reading or writing in her journal, she seemed... quieter, calmer, you know."

"And when did she move to San Francisco?"

"She was about nineteen. Shannon was just a baby. She said she could make a lot of money in the city turning tricks. 'Why not get paid for doing something I like to do anyhow?' she'd reasoned. I worried for her, especially when I could tell she was using more and more drugs. I think she soon realized things weren't going as she had hoped. When she met that Blade character, she was no longer independent. She wasn't making the money she had hoped to make. She told us she was trying to get away from him. The last time we spoke to her, she was in the hospital about to be discharged. She told us she'd be back home that day, but we never heard from her again."

"That matches our findings. Was Victoria close with any family members? Maybe an aunt or cousin."

"No. I'm an only child and we weren't in contact with Vicky's father's family."

The so-called cousin, who was not her cousin, had picked her up, and then she was never heard from again. If I were a betting woman, I'd bet just about anything the Stanzels were behind Victoria's disappearance. "Can you think of anyone she may have been in contact with?"

"No. But you said she had a friend who was looking for her. Must've been a close friend."

"Yes, it was. She said she was also in 'that life' but managed to escape. She deeply regretted not being able to save Victoria too."

"Sounds like a wonderful girl. What's she doing now?"

"She's grown, has her first grandchild, and is clean. We met because she attends the same church as our receptionist."

"Oh my!"

"What I've learned so far about those last days is quite concerning. I'd like to share some information with you, but due to its sensitivity, I must ask you to not share it with anyone else—not the PI you've worked with previously and not the police. Even though I am working close with the CoCo County Sheriff's Department regarding the missing persons case you filed thirty-five years ago."

"I wish we'd found you years ago. We might've learned the truth by now."

"Sometimes, things happen for a reason. Nancy came to us, eager to find her friend, to convey how much she meant to her. We've identified 'Blade' and questioned him. We believe there was a police report filed based on her injuries. We've requested those records, which might offer more insight into what happened to Victoria after she left the hospital." I paused, then continued, "We suspect that her pimp, Blade, is a member of a highly influential, wealthy family. So, until we can prove what transpired, we need to keep this between us. Of course, I'll share this information with Nancy too."

Shannon nodded. "I understand the need for discretion."

Shannon placed her hand on her grandmother's arm, who seemed to be in shock.

Peggy squinted behind her thick glasses. "Wait. Now, I know why you look familiar. You were on the news years ago. You solved all those tough cases with the police. The sheriff's department."

"That's right. And I've been in contact with Sergeant Hirsch, and we're working the case together."

Tears formed in Peggy's eyes. "You're going to find her. I can feel it. And I think—I *know* she's alive. A mother knows."

That sent a chill down my body. Mother's intuition was real. If her mother believed she was alive after all these years, she may well be. I looked them squarely in the eyes, asserting, "I will find out what happened to Victoria. You have my word."

Armed with more knowledge about Victoria, supposing she was alive, I knew where to start looking for her. Many individuals, when given a second chance, revert to their intrinsic inclinations. For Victoria, it was nature, reading, and writing. If she was clean and alive, she'd likely be in a rural area, not the city. If she was hiding, she'd probably be keeping a very low profile, perhaps cocooning herself like she had all those years ago.

20

MARTINA

Vincent looked around at the familiar faces and grinned. "I guess this'll do."

Hirsch shook his head. "Glad to have you back, Vincent."

It hadn't taken much to convince Hirsch to ask Vincent to join the new Cold Case Squad, and Vincent accepted almost immediately. Vincent was one of the best Drakos Monroe had to offer, and Hirsch knew that. Vincent had an uncanny knack for exploring perspectives others hadn't considered. In those over-looked ideas, he often discovered pivotal clues.

"It's good to have some fresh faces around here," Ross remarked.

Jayda added, "Looks like we lucked out—two for the price of one."

"Just on this case," I clarified. "Because the case was ours first. But of course, any other missing person cases we get from CoCo County, we can collaborate with the sheriff's department to find the missing and bring them home."

"I appreciate that," Hirsch said.

Vincent sat down. "So, what's the game plan for the Victoria Hightower missing person case?"

I took a deep breath. "Well, from what we've learned, in the last days of Victoria Hightower's life, she was beaten and on the run. She ended up in a hospital where a police report was taken. Then, a so-called cousin left the hospital with her. Victoria's family never saw or heard from her again, even though she had told them she'd see them later that day."

Ross nodded. "So, we find that so-called cousin."

"Exactly," I said. "My hunch is that her disappearance is somehow connected to the Stanzel family."

"Do you think the cousin is part of the family?" Jayda asked.

"Maybe. We need to delve deeper into the Stanzels. Understand their associations, especially all known female connections. Starting with family members. It had to be someone who was around thirty-five years ago."

Vincent, leaning back, interjected, "The wealthy are never easy to approach. But if you're fortunate enough to have connections in high places, they can be invaluable." He said it with an air of mystery, suggesting he had some hidden knowledge. It would explain his extra cool-guy attitude. He definitely had something up his sleeve, and I was interested in what it was.

I gazed into his eager eyes. "I agree. That's why I think it's a good idea to put someone undercover, to get closer to their organization. Someone young, who could blend in easily." Everyone in the room knew about Vincent's affluent background. With his blond hair and fresh-faced appearance, he had the unmistakable look and, at times, the attitude of the wealthy. While I wasn't suggesting he came from a lavish background, I had heard tidbits about Amanda's family being quite well-off. It would make sense to pick Vincent for the undercover role.

"Me? Undercover?" Vincent faked surprise.

What info did he have? I was dying to know. If he was dragging it out this much, it had to be good.

He continued, "When I found out the Stanzels were

involved in prostitution and drugs back in the day, I was floored. Even I'm acquainted with some of their family—some cousins. So, out of curiosity, I dug a bit. Turns out, there are some rumblings they might not be as shiny as they claim."

"Rumblings from whom?" I asked, taken aback.

Vincent looked around the room, clearly weighing his words. "Seeing as you all seem to be on the right track, I made a few calls ahead of our meeting. Remember my friend Jess, the FBI profiler?"

"The one you went to college with?" I recalled. Vincent had been Jess's dorm room RA, and they had maintained a pretty tight friendship that we had benefited from on previous cases.

"Exactly. She's well-connected, especially within the FBI's San Francisco organized crime task force."

My eyebrows shot up. "You think the Stanzels are tied to organized crime? And you're only sharing this now?"

"Don't shoot the messenger," Vincent replied with a shrug.

That sneaky little guy. I knew he had something good. "What intel did Jess and the task force provide?"

He hesitated. "Officially, they don't have any concrete evidence. But, off the record, one of their operations picked up mentions of the Stanzels. Not necessarily as the heads, but they're mingling with those who are."

I glanced at Hirsch. "Sounds like we might need to loop in the FBI. Hopefully, they'll be open to collaborating with us on the Stanzels."

Vincent nodded. "Organized crime has a way of hiding in plain sight, often even unbeknownst to their own family members. But if you think about it, if Anthony was into pimping back then, maybe there's a connection to today's sex trade."

I pondered for a moment. "Can you get Jess and the FBI on a call to discuss the possibility the Stanzels are connected to organized crime and Victoria's disappearance?"

He smirked and glanced at his watch. "Actually, I've set up a meeting with the task force in about thirty minutes. Anyone up for a call with the FBI?" He scanned the small conference room playfully, as if challenging us.

Oh, Vincent. You have to love the guy.

"And if we had other plans?"

His smirk grew into a cocky grin. "I knew you'd be available. I've got to say, it feels good to be back." He waved jazz hands in the air with flamboyance.

I couldn't help but chuckle, glancing over at Hirsch. The look in his eyes mirrored mine: a mix of amusement and relief at having Vincent back on the team, especially when trying to solve a tough thirty-five-year-old case. It seemed, much like with the old cold case squad, we might've just stumbled upon something far bigger than a single missing persons case.

"Great work, Vincent," I acknowledged.

He shrugged. "Just a hunch that paid off."

That's precisely why multiple heads—whether two or five—were always better than one when trying to solve a case.

21

VICTORIA

THIRTY-FIVE YEARS EARLIER

THE DRIVE WAS LONG. We started passing through a national forest, and every inch of the journey heightened my nerves. With every turn, I grew convinced this new identity and money were a ruse. They were taking me to a secluded, wooded area to silence me—to bury me and the memories of what I had seen forever.

The woman in the front seat was a mystery. Priscilla told me she was working on behalf of Blade's family. But in what capacity? Who was she really? And why did she want to help me? She had hinted at a shared past, but how did she fit into the puzzle? Was she family? Friend? Foe? It was unclear. What was clear was if what she said was true, I'd survive, but I'd be without my daughter, without my mother. They would probably assume I was dead and perhaps hate me if they ever discovered I wasn't.

To my surprise, when the car stopped, it was at a bus station in Portland, Oregon. Not the middle of the woods as I had feared. Priscilla pulled out a duffel bag from the trunk and opened my back door, beckoning. "Come on."

"Okay," I said, clambering out. She handed me the duffel. It wasn't too heavy and probably contained clothes.

As I stood on the curb next to her, she clarified, "This has some clothes, some toiletries. There's some additional money in there too. Be careful. Start over. Start fresh. I don't want to see you again. Do you understand? Because if I do, it'll be the end for you."

I had to know. "Why are you doing this? Are you related to Blade?"

She looked at me, her gaze firm. "Like I told you, the less you know, the better. Just know that my help is help from Anthony's family. Be grateful and go before they change their mind."

I didn't hesitate and turned toward the bus station, my heart racing. She had warned that once she left me there, my past had to remain just that—the past. The daunting reality of never contacting anyone from my previous life weighed heavily on me. I briefly considered whether this isolation was worse than death. To my daughter, Shannon, whether I was gone from her life or dead would make no difference. She'd grow up mother-less. With a heavy heart I had to hope she turned out okay.

Staring up at the board, I needed to choose my next destination. Where could I start a new life? I once dreamt of having an apartment with a back yard. Maybe a ground floor unit with a patio where Shannon could play. A sandbox, or even a small swing. It seemed like a distant dream. The pressing matter was my sobriety and shelter.

Across the station, a pair of women dressed like nuns caught my attention. They were calling to me like a pair of friendly penguins. My instincts told me that maybe, just maybe, my first step wasn't to leave town but rather to find refuge and sobriety and then think of what to do next. If I relapsed, I was as good as dead. The effects of the methadone were already wearing off. I needed more and to get clean for good.

Swallowing my pride and mustering all the strength I had left, I approached the two women. "Hi, are you nuns?"

With a kind smile and a hint of curiosity, the older one said, "Yes, dear. Is there something we can help you with?"

I nodded, finding the words difficult to come by. "I hope so. You see, I'm from out of town, and I... I have a problem. I need to find help. The hospital gave me methadone, but I need... I want to get clean, stay clean."

The woman's gaze softened. "What's your name, dear?"

I hesitated, to make sure I got it right. "I'm Maisie."

"Maisie," she repeated. "We can absolutely help you. Are you all on your own? No family?"

It hurt to say it. My paperwork said I was Maisie—a childless woman with no family, but saying it out loud might break me. But I had to. I had to protect my mother and daughter. "I don't have any family. I just got out of a really bad situation. I need to get clean and start over."

"We'll take good care of you," she assured.

As I looked into their compassionate eyes, I felt a surge of hope. I believed them when they said they would take care of me. Although I had never had much faith in God or any higher power, there was something about the way they looked at me— as if I were truly human, someone worth saving. It made me entertain the idea that perhaps, just maybe, there was a force greater than all of us, watching over the downtrodden, the desperate, and those in need of a helping hand.

I felt an overwhelming sense of gratitude toward the women. For the first time since I was a little girl, amidst the chaos of my life, I whispered a quiet prayer, placing my trust in the unknown.

22

MARTINA

With the recent revelation, my mind spun, swirling in countless directions. The questions were endless, but my primary hope was that the FBI would provide a lead that would guide us somewhere significant.

"I'm going to grab a coffee before the meeting. Need anything?" I asked.

"I'll join you," Vincent replied.

Ross smirked, looking Vincent up and down. "Are you sure you need more caffeine, young man?"

Vincent shot back with a grin, "Don't worry, old man. I can handle it."

Like Vincent said, it was good to be back. Not that we didn't have a soft spot for our Drakos Monroe team, but the camaraderie here was unparalleled. We had been through thick and thin together, having each other's backs, whether we worked side by side or apart.

As we approached the familiar coffee maker, Vincent said, "How's it going, Martina?"

Exhaling deeply, I responded, "I'm relieved to be working on a case and potentially following some promising leads."

"It's a welcome distraction, isn't it?"

His cheerful tone made me wonder if it was a mask for his family woes. "How are things with the wedding planning?"

He sighed, the weight of the world seeming to press on his shoulders. "It's Amanda's family. They come across as loving, but ever since we got engaged, her family's expectations have mounted. The wedding planning is an endless list of tasks for Amanda. She's so upset she's saying she wants to elope. But the wedding is just a few months away."

"I may not have much experience with demanding families," I admitted, "but you should prioritize your happiness and Amanda's. If a private ceremony is what you both want, then those who genuinely care will understand."

He shrugged, as if unsure. "Amanda's father is almost treating it like a business function. He's inviting every associate, friend of a friend, and contact. It's becoming a massive spectacle. I fear he'll hold it against Amanda if we don't cave to his demands."

"It sounds like she's under an immense amount of pressure."

"We didn't realize the pressure until we got engaged," Vincent said, his eyes clouded with worry. "It makes me so mad that her father is putting such a burden on Amanda when all she wanted was to marry me. Sometimes, I think maybe I shouldn't have proposed."

"Nonsense." I grabbed a mug from the shelf, placing it under the spout and pressing the button. "Have either of you tried having a heart-to-heart with her parents?"

"Amanda has tried, but it wasn't a productive conversation."

"Family can be tricky."

Vincent sighed. "I see that now. She wants to elope, but I'd feel bad about canceling all the plans. Amanda already has her dress, the favors and the cake have been ordered, and the catering is set."

As my coffee finished pouring, I set down a mug for Vincent. I gave him a nod, and he indicated he wanted the same. "You know," I started, thinking aloud, "what if you and Amanda eloped before the big day that's currently planned? That way, you have a day just for the two of you, then you can celebrate with everyone later. It'll be something special, just for the two of you."

"That's very sneaky, Martina," Vincent said with a half-smile. "I think I like it."

Being sneaky seemed to be a trait that bonded all of us in the Cold Case Squad. Holding my coffee, I could see that Vincent's spirits were slightly lifted.

While he was undoubtedly happy to be back at the CoCo County Sheriff's Department, I could sense the heavy weight of Amanda's family issues surrounding their wedding. Sometimes it was more challenging to watch someone you care about struggle than to face hardships yourself.

Back in the room, as we sat and chatted, I noticed Vincent's familiar charm. While he had opened up to me, he seemed more guarded around the others. Even though Ross could be a little brash, he was really a big lovable lug. Jayda had a sense of humor off the clock, but she wasn't one to worry about feelings on the job. She was all business. Hirsch was warmer but usually pretty focused on the job too. Despite all of that, I believed they would be just as sympathetic and warm as I was toward Vincent if he chose to share.

Vincent flipped open the lid of his laptop, adjusting the Polycom closer to him. He began dialing. "Jess said she can't make the call, but a couple of members from the Organized Crime Task Force in San Francisco will join us."

"Great."

After inputting the passcode, some chatter came over the line. "Hi, this is Vincent from Drakos Monroe Security Investigations and CoCo County Sheriff's Department," he said, a hint of amusement evident.

"Excellent. This is Special Agent Vine and Special Agent Honeycutt from the San Francisco Organized Crime Task Force. Who else is on the line?"

I spoke up. "Martina Monroe from Drakos Monroe, now also working on a case with the CoCo County Sheriff's Department."

Hirsch chimed in. "From CoCo County's Cold Case Squad, I'm Sergeant Hirsch. We also have detectives Jayda and Ross on the line."

A voice from the other end responded, "Nice to meet y'all. Vincent, can you get us started? Agent Holley said you might have a missing persons case that is connected to someone we think might be linked to organized crime in San Francisco. Can you brief us?"

"I'll defer to Martina. She's leading this case. But to clarify, it's also a missing persons case from CoCo County."

"Understood."

I took a deep breath. "The case started with a client wanting to find an old friend..." I explained everything we knew and had learned since the case was opened.

Whispers passed on the other line before someone asked, "So, you're saying a sex worker lived with Anthony Stanzel?"

"Not just lived," I clarified. "He was her pimp. And not just her pimp, but also my client's. Both worked for Anthony, known by his street name 'Blade' back then."

"And you're certain it's Anthony Stanzel?"

"My client identified him from a photograph. She's adamant it's him."

Hirsch jumped in. "We heard you suspect the Stanzels might have ties to organized crime."

Special Agent Vine said, "We don't have solid evidence, but we suspect they do. In our ongoing operations within San Francisco, the Stanzels have been heard and seen during our surveillance. They are definitely known associates of the DeMarco crime family, but we haven't been able to link them to criminal activity."

"What are the DeMarcos into?"

"Historically, drugs. But the product du jour is sex trafficking. Male, female, and young. We think they're shipping some overseas, but others are being positioned all over the Bay Area in massage parlors and nail salons."

"So, that ties in with Anthony once being a pimp, right?" Vincent suggested.

"Y'all might be onto something. If the Stanzels were involved in the sex trade back then, perhaps they never left. This information could be very useful. We'll definitely dig deeper into the Stanzels—maybe they're just really good at covering their tracks. We'll look harder."

That was exactly what I thought. "That's my concern regarding Victoria Hightower. Victoria was brought into the hospital after a pretty bad beating. A nurse told us the police came to take a report. We're waiting on the records from SFPD. My suspicion is that, given Anthony was her pimp, he likely was the one who had assaulted her, landing her in the hospital. Perhaps they made her disappear so she couldn't testify or bring charges against him."

"That makes sense," Special Agent Honeycutt said. "Considering their influence, they'd do anything to protect their name."

"I've already questioned Anthony Stanzel," I continued. "And while he denied knowing Victoria or our client, his defensiveness was obvious. But I'm hoping your team can provide insight into the woman who took Victoria from the hospital. Do the Stanzels have any women in their operation who might have done their dirty work?"

"From thirty-five years ago?"

I exchanged glances with my colleagues and responded, "Yes, ideally from that time frame. Perhaps someone closely affiliated with or a part of the family? Based on the nurse's description, the woman is likely in her mid to late fifties now. She had dark hair and blue eyes. Attractive."

Special Agent Vine said, "We know of several women in their family circle. But there's only one associate who is often at their business lunches with the DeMarcos."

Special Agent Honeycutt added, "Sounds like Priscilla Keene."

"That's what I was thinking," Special Agent Vine confirmed.

Yes. A name. "What do you know about Priscilla Keene?"

"Business associate—from what we know—for decades."

"Did you do a background check on her? Where is she from? Is she related to them?"

"No blood relation that we know of. To be honest, we haven't looked at her too close."

"She could be the last person to have seen Victoria."

And with a name, we could find her and question her about Victoria. The FBI hadn't dug into Priscilla Keene, but I certainly would.

"Well, it sounds like we have some homework to do," Special Agent Vine added.

"Us too. We'll start digging into Priscilla Keene as soon as we're off the call. I'd like to question her about Victoria's whereabouts."

"Fine by us. Let's meet up again in a few days and share notes. If the Stanzels and Keene are connected to your missing person, and you can prove it, it could break our case against them wide open."

Glad to be of service, but that wasn't my immediate concern. My concern was Victoria Hightower, and my gut said if I found Priscilla Keene, we just might find Victoria.

23

MARTINA

IT WASN'T difficult to find Priscilla Keene. As the FBI had informed me, she was frequently at business meetings and a significant figure in the Stanzel Empire. However, her background check unveiled a curious anomaly. For the last thirty-five years, Priscilla Keene had faithfully worked for the Stanzels. The strange part? No records of her employment, property, or even birth existed from before that time. It was as if Priscilla Keene hadn't existed before her association with the Stanzels. That begged the question: who was she before she became Priscilla Keene? And what was her relationship with the Stanzel family? How had a woman with seemingly no past so deeply entrench herself within such a powerful family?

These questions regarding Ms. Keene's earlier years weren't my primary concern. My immediate mission was locating Victoria Hightower, and I believed that a visit to Priscilla could shed some light on the matter. Venturing into the city alone, I determined it was time for a candid conversation with Ms. Keene, woman to woman.

Given her presumed closeness to the Stanzels, I didn't expect Priscilla to openly discuss Victoria with me. Yet, I hoped to gauge her reactions and discern any signs of deceit. Every individual has a tell, and it was my job to uncover Priscilla's.

I found myself again in downtown San Francisco, preparing to enter the same building where Anthony Stanzel had his office.

With the chilly January weather on my side, I used a hat and scarf as a disguise, trying not to attract any undue attention. Though I doubted anyone was on the lookout for me, it was better to not risk recognition.

Under the pseudonym Veronica Martin, I hoped to extract information regarding Victoria Hightower's whereabouts. With a purposeful stride, I crossed the grand lobby and took the elevator to the 22nd floor. As the doors dinged, I was thankful Priscilla and Anthony's offices were on different floors. I wanted to avoid any chance run-ins with him. The last thing I needed was to set off alarms. After all, if Priscilla had any knowledge of Victoria's involvement with Anthony, a sudden appearance on my part could jeopardize everything.

However, there was also the possibility we were entirely off the mark. If Priscilla had no connection to Victoria, then she wouldn't have alerted her associates about my presence.

At the reception desk, a polite voice pulled me from my thoughts. The receptionist, with an inquiring gaze, asked, "Your name?"

"Veronica Martin," I replied.

"And you're with?"

"Martin and Associates."

She nodded, making a few clicks on her computer before dialing a number on her phone. After a brief conversation, she looked up with a smile. "She'll be right out."

"Thank you." My eyes were drawn to the large floor-to-ceiling windows with views of the San Francisco Bay. The sky was a sheet of gray and the waters choppy. Sunshine was noticeably absent both from the building and the city itself. Was Priscilla a contributor to this gloom? I was hoping to find out.

The door creaked open, revealing a woman in a sleek black suit, elevated by three-inch heels. Her shoulder-length hair was impeccably styled, and her piercing blue eyes bore into me. She fit the description to a tee. At sixty years old, she radiated a beauty that made me question her true age. Or if she'd had some cosmetic surgery. To a casual observer, she might seem to be in her mid-forties or, at most, early fifties.

"You must be Ms. Martin," she greeted with a practiced smile.

"Yes."

"Call me Priscilla," she said warmly, leading the way. "Come in, let's talk."

As I followed her into her lavishly decorated office, I took a seat across from her large desk. She opened the conversation. "I haven't heard of Martin and Associates. What can you tell me about your firm and what brings you here today?"

I hesitated briefly before admitting, "Well, now that I'm here, I'll come clean."

"Oh?" Her impeccably sculpted brows lifted in a mix of curiosity and amusement.

Drawing in a deep breath, I laid out my cards. "My real name is Martina Monroe. I'm a private investigator. I'm searching for a woman named Victoria Hightower. She vanished thirty-five years ago from San Francisco General Hospital. I have reason to believe you're acquainted with her and that you might have information on her whereabouts."

For a split second, Priscilla seemed like a statue, her face devoid of emotion. She didn't even blink. But in that lack of expression, I knew. She knew exactly who Victoria Hightower was. Did she also know where she was?

"Do you recognize the name, Victoria Hightower?" I pressed further.

Shaken from her brief stupor, she shook her head and attempted a casual demeanor. "I don't think so. Is she in real estate?"

It was a clever deflection, but I wasn't fooled. "Victoria was someone you encountered thirty-five years ago." I retrieved a photograph from my purse, placing it before her. "She's the one on the left—blonde hair, blue eyes. I suspect you were the last to see her before her disappearance."

She glanced at the photo fleetingly before sliding it back to me. This tiny gesture cemented my beliefs. She was familiar with Victoria, whether she admitted it or not. A seeming calm enveloped her as she responded, "I'm sorry, but I don't know anyone named Victoria Hightower. Perhaps you have mistaken me for someone else?"

"No, I think you were there when she was discharged from the hospital thirty-five years ago. I believe you identified yourself as her cousin. You know of her whereabouts or, at the very least, what transpired that day."

Her tone took on an edge of finality. "I have no idea what you're talking about. Unless this pertains to business, I'm very busy, and I'll kindly ask you to leave."

"Ms. Keene, I've been in this line of work for quite some time. Your defensiveness speaks volumes, and I have a hard time believing your claim about not knowing Victoria. Since you're unfamiliar with my methods, let me clarify: once I begin an investigation, I don't stop until I find the truth. We can handle this the easy way or the hard way. I just want to find Victoria. Her family and friends miss her and are desperate to learn what happened to her. And let's not forget that she's registered as a missing person with CoCo County. The county may have their own motivations in solving the case, but my sole focus is to locate Victoria and provide answers to my clients. The deeper aspects of the case, the motivations and actions of those involved, particularly any malevolent acts, are secondary. So, I must ask: did you have a hand in what happened to her, or was it Anthony Stanzel?"

Priscilla, visibly flustered, stood up abruptly. "I deeply regret that you've mistaken me for someone else, someone tied to this missing person you're searching for. But I'm not that person. If you won't leave willingly, I'll have to call security. Do we understand one another?"

I held her gaze, my resolve unyielding. "Oh, I understand you perfectly clear. But rest assured, this won't be our last encounter. Ms. Keene, or whoever you *really* are. That's a promise."

Without waiting for a response, I pivoted and made my exit.

While I had not expected Priscilla to spill any details about Victoria's disappearance, her evasive behavior was proof enough of her involvement or at least her knowledge. My next step was to update the FBI and share my findings.

Priscilla Keene, a woman whose records only went back thirty-five years, remained a conundrum. If she truly was sixty, as her current documents indicated, then what was her life story for the twenty-five years prior to her connection to the Stanzels? Priscilla Keene was a mystery as was her allegiance to the Stanzel family and her determination to protect them. Thankfully, I wasn't one who backed down from a challenge. I would learn the truth about Priscilla and what she had done to Victoria.

24

PRISCILLA

PRESENT DAY

My THOUGHTS RAN in overdrive as I paced outside Maurice's office. As if the visit from Martina Monroe wasn't bad enough, what I'd learned was far more distressing. I had a gnawing feeling that I would have to take drastic measures to keep our secrets buried.

Despite some of the things I'd done, I never wanted an innocent woman to suffer. But it was a dog-eat-dog world, and, unfortunately, it might just come down to her or me. I hadn't gotten this far in life by choosing other people over my own interests.

But a nagging question lingered in my mind. Why was it always a woman who had to be sacrificed? All to cover up a man's indiscretions! Of course, the women were left to clean up the mess.

What I had considered proposing to Maurice made me feel uneasy. It wasn't a decision I had come to lightly. But, judging by everything I knew, there seemed to be only one way to silence her permanently.

The door opened, and Maurice's expression immediately told me he knew I brought bad news. Peeking over his shoulder,

I caught sight of Anthony, whose mere presence made me recoil.

"Come in, Priscilla," Maurice said. "Take a seat." He gestured toward the small table and chairs in the corner of his massive office. I chose a chair as far from Anthony as possible. I didn't want any part of his presence tainting me—least of all, ruining my Prada.

"Thank you both for coming," Maurice began. "Priscilla, do you have an update about the PI named Martina? And any news on the whereabouts of Victoria?"

"Our PI is still searching for Victoria. She's either dead or changed her name. If anyone can find her, he will."

"And the PI named Martina?"

I took a deep breath, bracing myself for the difficult conversation ahead. Contrary to popular belief, I wasn't made of ice. There was still a small, empathetic part of me that cared. "Yes, her name is Martina Monroe. She's with Drakos Monroe Security & Investigations. And she paid me a visit. Came into my office and asked about Victoria. I denied all knowledge of Victoria, but I don't think she bought it."

Maurice leaned in. "And do you think she'll be a problem? Can we just pay her off like the last PI who came looking for Victoria?"

This was the difficult part, the moment I'd been dreading. "I doubt it."

"Why?" Maurice questioned.

"Well, for starters," I began, "Martina has a decorated history as a cold case investigator. She's partnered with the CoCo County Sheriff's Department and has been involved in some pretty high-profile cases. Cases they solved that seemed impossible."

"So she's good," Anthony surmised with a scowl. "And there's no way you can flip her?"

"Doubtful," I said. "I had our guy dig into her history. Martina is a single mother, an Army veteran, and a partner at Drakos Monroe. She firmly stands on the side of justice and is rumored to work in the gray area when it favors the innocent. She has no pity for the guilty. According to our guy, she's the best there is." I glanced over at Anthony, who appeared unbothered. He wasn't absorbing the weight of my words.

This Martina Monroe could very well take him, his entire family, and even me down for good. That realization gnawed at me. She had uncovered that I wasn't born as Priscilla Keene. I had changed my identity, and even the Stanzels were unaware of my true identity. They didn't need to know, and for my own survival, I couldn't let Martina Monroe unravel everything I'd built over the last thirty-five years.

Maurice leaned forward, considering the situation. "Okay, so she's a goody two shoes. Being a single mother, is there a way we could sway her through her child?"

"We could threaten her," I replied cautiously. "But based on the reports from our PI, she would come back at us with a vengeance and wouldn't stop until she gets what she wants."

Anthony smirked. "Sounds like she should be on our team."

There was no way Martina Monroe would ever work with us. Taking a deep breath, dreading the next words out of my mouth, I said, "The only way to protect the family name and the organization is to eliminate Martina Monroe."

Maurice raised his hands defensively. "Whoa, whoa, whoa! That's drastic, Priscilla, even for you."

"She'll never stop." I believed that was true.

Anthony interjected, "I'm not as convinced as you are that she won't quit. She surely hasn't solved every case. I mean, come on, everyone has a price."

I shook my head firmly. "Not this time." I proceeded to share all the intelligence I had gathered on Martina Monroe, emphasizing why I believed she would continue to be a problem. "That's not all. Martina Monroe has a bigger stake in finding the truth than we originally thought. Our connection at the San Francisco Police Department informed me there was a records request made for anything related to Victoria. It was for the police report taken while she was in the hospital before she disappeared."

Maurice's eyes darted to Anthony, his face hardening. "This is your mess," he growled, his voice low and menacing. "Why did you act like such an animal?"

"It was a long time ago, Dad," Anthony defended, clearly attempting sincerity. "I've changed. I've seen the error of my ways. I don't behave that way anymore."

Publicly, perhaps. But I'd seen the concealed bruises on his wife's face. We could do everyone a favor if we selected a different target to eliminate. Anthony Stanzel was a liability. We could pin everything on him. He would make the perfect scapegoat for our other businesses. Plus he would turn on his family in a heartbeat if it came down to them or him. He had no sense of loyalty. Anthony only followed the money.

Maurice interjected, "So, what does the police report say?"

"It names the person who assaulted her and sent her to the hospital. Street name: Blade."

"But it doesn't mention Anthony's real name?"

"No, but there's more." I leaned over, retrieving two documents from my briefcase. I spread them out, pointing to the highlighted sections of the summary prepared by our PI. Maurice's eyes scanned the notes, and I watched as his expression shifted from indifference to shock, eventually landing on a grim realization. The only way to halt Martina Monroe would be if she was no longer a threat.

"You're sure about this?" Maurice asked.

I nodded, maintaining my resolve. "Yes. From everything

I've heard, once she gets this information, she and the CoCo County Sheriff's Department will throw everything they have at us."

Maurice sighed deeply. "Okay. I concur with your assessment. She won't relent, especially not with this evidence. Does she already have a copy?"

"It should be in her hands any moment."

"Any way to stop it?"

"No, it's already been sent."

Maurice shook his head in frustration. "Of all the PIs in California," he lamented, "she's the one with the capability and motive to want to bring us down."

"Let's have *the two of us* discuss details tomorrow with our guy."

Maurice agreed. "Set up a time with my admin."

Without further discussion, I collected the documents, ensuring Anthony couldn't see them. He was too reckless to be entrusted with such information. There's no telling what he might do. Personally, I favored a plan to eliminate Anthony and let him get the punishment he deserved. But Maurice would never sanction it. Regrettably, another innocent woman would bear the consequences of his mistakes.

25

MARTINA

Vincent knocked on my door. I glanced up from my monitor to find him holding a large envelope under his arm.

"Mrs. Pearson asked me to bring this to you. A messenger sent it over from the SFPD," he explained.

"It's probably all the police reports relating to Victoria Hightower."

"That's what I thought, so I brought it over right away."

I glanced up at the corner of my monitor to check the time. "I don't have any meetings for the next few hours. Do you have time to hang out with me in a conference room and sift through all of them? It looks like there's quite a few."

"Sure," he replied.

As we headed toward a conference room, we made a pit stop at the coffee maker. I placed my mug under the dispenser and pressed start. "How are you doing, Vincent?"

"Good. Amanda and I had a talk, and she had a discussion with her parents."

"Oh?"

He lowered his voice. "It's kind of a secret, but we're planning to elope before the big shindig her parents have planned.

But we're still going to do the whole ceremony and everything they want."

"Are you happy about that?"

"I am happy because Amanda is happy. If this eases her stress and makes it so our wedding is about us, and then we celebrate with cake and booze, I'm in." He grinned.

"Glad to hear it."

"Thanks for the suggestion. I told Amanda, and she was like, 'Yes, let's do it!' So, that's the plan."

"Do your parents know?"

"No, actually, just you. We told her parents we'd go forward as planned—no more fights. Amanda's so chill about the whole thing now. She's like, 'I don't care what they want me to do because the two of us will have our own time together to celebrate, just us.' We found a place down in Big Sur that does elopement packages. We'll get married on a bluff overlooking the Pacific Ocean."

"It sounds incredible."

He looked genuinely happy. "Thanks again for the suggestion. Honestly, I am so thrilled and can't wait to marry Amanda."

I retrieved my mug, trying not to feel a pang of sadness. I didn't know if I would have married Wilder had we stayed together longer. But deep down, I knew that's what I wanted one day. It just wouldn't be with Wilder.

"I'm sorry. It looks like I upset you," Vincent observed.

"No, I'm very happy for the two of you. My day will come," I reassured him.

"Yes, it will. Hey, there might be a few single guys at the wedding reception." He nudged me playfully.

"I think I'm taking a bit of a break. Plus, now that I have more free time, I was looking into being a sponsor at a rehab clinic not far from the office. I could give back to addicts in need who are under outpatient and inpatient care. I'm trying to expand my volunteering efforts."

Becoming a sponsor was wonderful for my soul, and I looked forward to working at the clinic and all the new experiences it would bring.

"That's awesome, Martina."

"Thanks. Are you ready?"

He lifted his mug and replied, "Yep."

Feeling good about Amanda and Vincent's upcoming nuptials and potential new volunteer opportunities at the rehabilitation clinic, I was ready to dive into the police reports relating to Victoria Hightower. We were nearly certain—99% sure—that Priscilla had taken her out of the hospital. But if we could figure out why they wanted her to disappear, it could really help the investigation.

I ripped open the envelope. "You take a stack, I'll take a stack."

"Sounds good to me."

The first page I looked at was a solicitation charge. Victoria had been arrested for prostitution, but the charges were later dropped. A note said she was in the custody of her boyfriend, Blade.

I shook my head. Why was it always the women—sex workers —getting busted and not the johns? If sex workers had other opportunities to make money, opportunities for education and a better life, would they still choose to engage in prostitution? I highly doubted it. Yet society looked down on them as if they weren't worth the time. It wasn't right; everybody deserved to be treated like a human being, not like trash discarded on the roadside.

I flipped to the next page, studying the report. It read a lot like the one before. It was from a year before her disappearance, suggesting she continually got into trouble. The report listed half a dozen incidents, but none of this was offering any new insight. I hadn't yet found a police report in which she had been violently assaulted, one that could explain her hospital admission.

Then Vincent spoke up. "I found it."

He handed the paper over to me. It was dated just five days before she went missing. Victoria had been admitted to the hospital with multiple bruises and contusions, broken ribs, and a concussion, likely from a significant blow to her head. The doctor stated she might have been hit with an object or thrown against a wall or the ground. There was external bleeding but, fortunately, no signs of internal bleeding. The report also high-lighted older, unhealed injuries, implying Victoria had been hurt before.

My suspicions pointed toward Anthony Stanzel, but his name wasn't anywhere in the report. According to the police officer's notes, Victoria claimed she didn't know her attacker, saying it was a stranger. The police were skeptical. They believed she was too scared of her assailant and assumed it was her pimp, Blade.

Having worked numerous domestic and intimate partner violence cases, I knew many victims were hesitant to identify their abusers, fearing even worse retaliation. It wasn't fair but unfortunately a valid concern.

I noticed a small asterisk at the bottom of the page and pointed it out to Vincent. "You see this? There's a note here suggesting she might have witnessed a crime. Someone found her unconscious just two blocks from a homicide scene."

"No. Did you find a homicide report in your stack?"

"No, it must be in yours."

Vincent quickly shuffled through the remaining papers in his stack. One page caught his attention. "This is odd. It's just a summary, but..." His voice trailed off, and he shot me a look of disbelief. "This can't be right."

"What? What is it?" I asked, my voice edged with impatience.

"Look at the victim's name."

I took the report from him, and my breath caught in my throat. For a moment, disbelief clouded my judgment. Surely, this was some mistake. My hands trembled as I scanned the homicide report, and when I flipped it over, I found a sticky note from Lieutenant Tippin. It simply read, "Call me."

"We don't breathe a word about this until I've spoken with Lieutenant Tippin," I instructed.

"My lips are sealed."

Clutching the report, I left Vincent in the conference room and hurried to my office. My heart raced, each beat echoing the weight of the information in my hand. Once inside, I closed the door and reached for the telephone.

26

MARTINA

STARING at Lieutenant Tippin's sticky note, I dialed his direct line. After a few rings, the line picked up.

"Lieutenant Tippin," came the voice on the other end.

"Hi, it's Martina Monroe. We met a few days ago. I'm working with Detective Hirsch on the missing persons case—Victoria Hightower," I said, trying to sound composed.

"Yes," he replied gravely.

"I just got the package. Did you look at it? And the associated homicide report?"

"I did. I've been expecting your call. Have you talked to Hirsch?"

"No, not yet. I need to confirm... is this right?"

"It is. I didn't have them send over the entire investigation. I thought we could talk about how to handle it," he responded with caution.

With a heavy heart, I said, "I have to tell him."

"Understood, but you understand he can't work the case, right?"

"I know. But now that it's connected to my missing persons

case, and since it was contracted through my firm, I will investigate. And I *will* solve it and bring them to justice."

"I would think no differently," he affirmed, a hint of respect in his voice.

I took a deep breath. "Just so you know, this is serious. I've almost confirmed the Stanzels' involvement in Victoria's disappearance. I think I know who whisked her out of the hospital—Priscilla Keene, one of Maurice Stanzel's top executives at the real estate firm."

"Oh, boy," he murmured.

"We have to find the truth," I said determinedly.

"Without a doubt. But this is not only a super high-profile case, but it's also very sensitive. You really have to work quietly on this. I'm guessing you know how to work discreetly?"

"Of course," I confirmed. "Do you have someone I can work with from SFPD? Someone you trust."

There was a momentary pause before he said, "Well, I trust myself."

"Do you typically work cases?" I inquired, surprised by his offer.

"Not typically, but I still remember how," he replied with a hint of amusement.

"Like riding a bike?" I quipped.

He chuckled. "I'm looking forward to working with you, Martina. When can you meet?"

"My time is yours. This is my top priority. Aside from my daughter, there's absolutely nothing more important than this case. I'm sure you understand that."

"Absolutely. You're close on their trail, and if they're involved, I have no doubt we'll prove it."

Motivated, I said, "I like your spirit. I can meet you today. It'll probably take me about an hour to get to SFPD headquarters. Or should we meet somewhere else?"

He didn't respond right away. "That's a good point. Maybe I should come to you."

"Okay, but you know I need to talk to Hirsch."

"Yes, but while we can keep him informed, we can't compromise the case. Make that clear to him."

I was sure Hirsch would understand. He was a professional and I knew he wouldn't want to jeopardize a prosecution. "Okay. What time can you get here? When I tell Hirsch, I want it to be face-to-face. He'll be upset if I don't tell him."

"How about this? It's ten' o'clock now; let's meet at one. Will you be able talk to Hirsch before then?"

"Yes."

"Good luck, and I'm looking forward to working with you."

At the end of the call, my whole body was tense. I got up, exited my office, and rushed over to the conference room where Vincent was gathering papers.

"Lieutenant Tippin from SFPD's coming here with the full case file. I need to talk to Hirsch and let him know what's going on. He's not allowed to work the case."

Vincent nodded. "Makes sense."

"Don't tell anyone until I've told Hirsch. He has to hear it first, from me."

"Understood. Let him know we won't stop until we close it out."

"Without a doubt. Lieutenant Tippin will be here at one o'clock to help us with the case. Are you available?"

"For this? Absolutely."

I nodded and rushed out of the office.

27

MARTINA

Butterflies swarmed in my belly as I approached Hirsch's office. I hadn't called ahead, not wanting to alarm him and make him think something was wrong. In some ways, this was just the opposite. But I didn't know how he'd react. I thought he might be glad, but at the same time, I sensed he'd be frustrated. He couldn't work the case himself and would have to deal with that, despite knowing it was in good hands.

I knocked on the door.

His eyes widened in surprise. "Martina. Did we have a meeting?"

"No," I replied, trying to sound calm. "Do you have a minute?"

His surprise turned to worry. "Sure, come on in."

I closed the door behind me and sat across from him. He looked at me intently. "What's going on, Martina? You're scaring me."

"I'm sorry. I don't mean to worry you. There's been a development in the Victoria Hightower case."

His eyebrows raised in curiosity. "Did you get the police records?"

"Yes, we did, and we're starting to form a theory about why we believe they wanted Victoria to disappear."

Hirsch leaned forward. "Well, what is it?"

I took a deep breath, choosing my words carefully. "According to the police records, when they questioned Victoria in the hospital about how she sustained her injuries, they also asked her about a crime that was committed less than two blocks from where a Good Samaritan found her and brought her to the hospital. They think she might have been a witness."

"A witness to what?" Hirsch asked, his voice filled with anticipation.

"To a homicide."

All the color drained from Hirsch's face.

I hesitated before delivering the final blow. "The victim is your brother, Nick."

His eyes wide, he said, "So, you're saying Victoria, the person we believe disappeared because of the Stanzels, was a witness to my brother's murder?" Hirsch's voice was laced with disbelief.

"Yes," I responded, my voice steady. "We think your brother's murder might be connected to Victoria's disappearance. If she witnessed Nick's murder, the killer might have been the one to make her disappear."

Hirsch struggled to speak, his words jumbled. "So, we don't have we..." He wasn't making sense, but I could understand why. The shock was palpable. I had known that Hirsch became a homicide detective due to his brother's murder, a cold case that had been unsolved for thirty-five years. His passion for working cold cases came from that personal tragedy. He knew the agony of being a family member left with unanswered questions about the death of a loved one.

I took a deep breath, steadying myself. "We're going to find out who killed Nick, if it's the last thing we do. I spoke with

Lieutenant Tippin of the SFPD. We're going to work together, quietly, on this case. But only with Lieutenant Tippin, given the Stanzels' power and connections to the police commissioner. We can't let word get out that we've discovered the connection. We're going to find out who killed Nick, but, Hirsch, you can't be directly involved."

He sat back, a look of bewilderment in his eyes. "Okay," he murmured.

"We're going to uncover the truth and those responsible will pay."

Hirsch turned away. I caught a glimpse of a tear being brushed from his cheek. After a moment, he managed to speak. "I know you will, Martina."

I couldn't leave without offering comfort. Despite being in a professional setting, I embraced my best friend. As I pulled away, I whispered, "I'm off to meet Lieutenant Tippin now."

He whispered, "Thank you."

I nodded at Hirsch, his eyes red-rimmed, as I hurried out, determined to solve both Nick's murder and Victoria's disappearance.

28

MARTINA

AFTER PULLING MYSELF TOGETHER, I stared into the mirror. My eyes were still a bit puffy. My heart hurt for Hirsch, and I could only imagine the turmoil he was going through. And I knew he needed time to process it all and tell his family we were reopening the investigation into his brother's murder. As upset as I was for Hirsch and his family, a part of me buzzed with anticipation. Deep down, I was certain we would discover who was responsible for Nick's death. That tragedy had marked the most defining moment in Hirsch's young life: the inexplicable loss of his sibling and the agonizing years of wondering why he had been killed. Had it been a random mugging gone fatally wrong? That was the explanation the police had given the family, but with what we had learned about Victoria and the Stanzels, I was seriously questioning that assumption. I swallowed the grief of reopening Hirsch's wounds and converted it into a driving force to unmask the killer once and for all. The Hirsch family deserved answers.

After everything Hirsch had contributed to in his career, after all the families he had aided, it was now his turn to receive some justice. This wasn't a time for sorrow. It was a time for action. Splashing a little more water on my face, I dabbed my eyes dry with a paper towel. Staring back at my reflection, I mustered as much confidence as I could and whispered, "You've got this, Martina. Let's go find out who killed Nick."

Back in my office, the phone rang. "Hello?"

"Lieutenant Tippin is here to see you, Martina."

"Thanks, Mrs. Pearson."

Eagerly, I made my way to the lobby, where Tippin awaited, standing next to a hefty banker's box. As our hands met in a firm shake, I greeted him. "Thanks for coming over."

"No problem," he replied with a nod.

"Shall we find a conference room? You can set your things down, and maybe we can get some refreshments?"

"Sounds great."

We settled into the first conference room on the right, with him placing the banker's box on the table. I was silently relieved. This wasn't just some flimsy file. I was hopeful that inside that box might lie the physical evidence that could link the murder back to the killer, or perhaps even to Victoria and the Stanzels.

"Before we start, do you need some coffee or tea?"

He smirked slightly. "You know, honestly, maybe in about an hour. But right now, my adrenaline is high and I'd love to get started."

"Understood." My tone shifted from somber to energetic.

With deliberate motion, Tippin lifted the box's lid and began laying out binder after binder. There were five in total.

"Have you gone through these files?" I asked.

He shook his head. "No, but the moment I saw the connection to your missing person case and Hirsch, I felt the need to bring them in."

"Any concerns about leaks from your department?"

His brow furrowed. "Are you asking if I think the Stanzels might have friends in our department? I wouldn't be surprised.

But I'm not certain who would leak information to them, which is why I wanted to meet you here instead of at the station. Assuming they're involved, which they might not be."

It was possible. It could be a coincidence and Victoria and the Stanzels had no connection to Nick's murder. "So, if the Stanzels are involved, there's a chance they already know we're onto them."

"It's possible."

If they had looked into my background, Priscilla or Anthony Stanzel would have surely found my connection to Hirsch. But if they were innocent, why would they want to know about me? Why would they pry into my life? Was I being paranoid?

"So, I guess we read," he said, glancing around at the walls, finally settling his gaze on a lone whiteboard. "As we go through the details, we can jot down key points of the investigation on the board."

I nodded but then hesitated for a moment. "You know, three minds are better than two."

His eyebrow quirked up. "You have someone you can trust?"

"One of my investigators, Vincent Teller. He's been with us for almost six years. Previously, he was a researcher for the CoCo County Sheriff's Department."

"That should be fine. You say he's good?"

"He's excellent."

"All right. You're right—three minds are better than two."

I gave a brief nod. "I'll be right back."

I made my way over to Vincent's cubicle. "Hey, Vincent."

"How'd it go with Hirsch?"

"Well, he was surprised. Took it hard. He's going to contact his family and Kim. He gets that he can't be part of the investigation."

Vincent nodded his understanding.

"But that doesn't mean you can't. Tippin is here with the case file on Nick's murder. Do you have time to help us read through the files?"

"Of course, anything for Hirsch."

He quickly shut down his computer, and I led him back to the conference room where Tippin sat, engrossed in a binder. "Lieutenant Tippin, this is Vincent Teller. Vincent, meet Lieutenant Tippin of the SFPD." The two men shook hands.

"Nice to meet you, sir."

I gestured to the desk covered with binders. "We have five binders full of files, one murder investigation, and a whiteboard."

Vincent smirked, a playful glint in his eyes. "I see why you brought me in. Not just for my young eyes but for my cunning skills and the ability to piece it all together on a beautiful murder board."

I couldn't help but laugh, shaking my head. *Our Vincent.*

Tippin gave Vincent a little side eye. I said, "Trust me, he's one of the best."

"All right, let's dive in."

Vincent moved to the whiteboard and began sketching out a framework for our murder board—areas for suspects, locations, evidence, known associates. He was precisely the strategic mind we needed.

We each grabbed a binder and read quietly. After I studied the witness statements, I noted a recurring theme. Despite there being at least seven witnesses, not a single one had identified the murderer. The only distinguishing characteristic listed was the man had dark hair, no race listed. That anomaly struck me as odd. As I made my way through the remaining files, I began to get a feel for the progression of the original investigation. But it wasn't until several hours—and a pizza delivery—later that the incident began playing out like a vivid movie in my mind. With the team ready to discuss, I said, "Okay, based on the witness statements and the autopsy report, this seems like it should've been solved years ago."

"But they didn't have DNA analysis back then. And as we all know, eyewitness testimony isn't very reliable," Tippin pointed out.

"True. But let's break down what happened. Correct me if I'm wrong, but from what I've gleaned from the last"—I glanced at the clock on the wall—"six hours, Nick Hirsch had been in a convenience store in downtown San Francisco. As he was leaving, he witnessed a man assaulting a woman. He tried to intervene, but the assailant attacked Nick instead, beating him before pulling a knife and severing his carotid artery. By the time witnesses reacted, the attacker had fled and the woman Nick had tried to help had vanished."

"That's precisely how I interpreted it," Vincent confirmed.

"And from our discussions about Victoria Hightower, she could very well have been the woman in distress," Tippin added. "Nick, playing the Good Samaritan, lost his life for trying to assist."

"Exactly," I replied. "What about the car? Any mention of that in the statements?"

"The only thing I could find mentioned was that his car was missing from the scene," Vincent noted, flipping through a binder.

"The assailant, or an accomplice, must've returned to move and dispose of the car, ensuring it was never found again," Tippin surmised.

Vincent moved to the whiteboard. "Witnesses couldn't give a detailed description of the attacker. Just a mention of dark hair. Probably because everything happened so quickly, and they didn't recognize him. But if someone knew him, they could've easily identified him."

"Right," Tippin agreed.

"And if you were the victim previously being attacked by this person, you'd undoubtedly be able to ID him, correct?" Vincent questioned.

"Yes," I replied. "Victoria Hightower was the eyewitness to Nick Hirsch's murder."

"And that's why the Stanzels had her silenced," Vincent concluded.

"Exactly," Tippin echoed with a sigh. "But how do we prove it?"

Vincent and I exchanged a glance before turning to Tippin. "First off, do we have any forensic evidence?" I inquired.

Tippin pointed to the board. "Right here. The autopsy report shows they took samples from Nick's clothing. There's a chance the killer might've left some of his blood on Nick, especially if he'd cut himself during the attack. They didn't run DNA analysis back then because, well, the technology wasn't as advanced."

"We can send it to an independent lab for testing."

Tippin hesitated. "That might be tricky with our budget constraints."

"This is a Drakos Monroe investigation. It's taken care of," I reassured.

"You sure about that?" Tippin questioned skeptically.

"Even if I wasn't part owner, Hirsch is my best friend. There's no cost too high to find out the truth about his brother."

"Okay, so we send out all the evidence for DNA analysis—touch DNA, anything we can get off the evidence collected at the scene."

I nodded. "And we leave no stone unturned until we find Victoria Hightower. She's likely the only one, other than the killer, who can ID Nick's killer."

Vincent chimed in. "You know what else we could do?"

I raised an eyebrow. "You have another idea?"

Vincent continued, "The FBI is already looking into the Stanzels due to their connection with the DeMarco family. Maybe they can check their records. It was a long time ago, but if they can find any financial records, anything suggesting a payoff from thirty-five years ago, and figure out who this Priscilla Keene really is, we might be able to show probable cause linking them to Victoria's disappearance. And if we can uncover the motive, it could lead us back to Hirsch's killer."

I grinned at Tippin. "How's that for your first case in a while?"

Tippin smirked back. "I'll have to dust off my boots. But I'm ready."

"All right. Let's get the FBI on the line and tell them what we have."

"I'm on it," Vincent affirmed.

Tippin turned to me, an amused expression on his face. "You two seem to be old hats at this."

Before I could respond, Vincent interjected with a chuckle, "The toughest cases either find Martina, or she finds them. We're still deciding which."

"And I don't like unsolved cases."

"Your closure rate?"

"One hundred percent," I boasted.

Tippin whistled, clearly impressed. "I have a feeling I'm in for a wild ride."

Vincent did a playful two-step and with a mischievous glint in his eyes, said, "Welcome to the team. Buckle up."

29

PRISCILLA

PRESENT DAY

I PACED MY OFFICE, the weight of anticipation heavy in my steps. What was taking him so long to get back to me? We needed to trace every movement Martina Monroe made, and we needed to stop the investigation before she exposed all of us.

When the phone finally rang, I snapped, "It's about time."

"Got good news and bad news," the voice on the other end replied.

"Just give it to me."

"We know exactly where she is. She wasn't hard to find," he said, a hint of admiration in his voice.

"And the bad news?"

"We also spotted Lieutenant Tippin entering Drakos Monroe offices. They must've made the connection to Sergeant Hirsch from CoCo County. My guess, based on Martina Monroe's reputation, is they're investigating the murder of Nicholas Hirsch."

I sighed, a feeling of dread settling in. "Is there any way they will find out what happened?"

"With any other investigator, I'd tell you there's no way. It's buried deep. But this is Martina Monroe. She's made headlines for solving unsolvable cases. Twenty-year-old cold cases. She's even taken down sitting sheriffs and homicide detectives. A mayor. She's relentless."

This was not the news I wanted to hear. "That's exactly why we need to stop her. What's the plan?"

"Look, I'm not saying we can't take her out. Nobody's beyond the reach of my rifle. But if we go that route, you'll have the entire CoCo County Sheriff's Department on your tail. And then there's Drakos Monroe. They've got a reputation for working in the shadows, doing whatever it takes. Rumors say they've even taken out targets themselves."

The gravity of his words hung in the air between us.

Rex continued, "You really don't want to mess with them, Priscilla."

"So, what am I supposed to do?"

"It's risky, but there are other ways to make her back off."

"Like?"

"Well, she has a daughter. And there's only one person in this world she probably cares about more than Hirsch: her daughter."

The implication was clear, but it made my stomach churn.

I stopped pacing and stared out at the Bay Bridge, taking in its beauty amidst my turmoil. How had it come to this? Sure, I had done questionable things to get ahead, but threatening the innocent? One could argue it wasn't the first or thirtieth time. All for the Stanzels? I was beginning to question why I had been protecting them all this time. When I started out with Maurice, they weren't into half the horrific things they were into now.

The voice on the other end pulled me back. "What do you want me to do?"

"Can you find out what she knows? Maybe tap into the servers at Drakos Monroe Security & Investigations?"

Rex laughed, a sound I found grating in the moment. "It'd be easier to get into the White House."

Shaking my head, I felt backed into a corner. "Do whatever it takes to stop this investigation. And for Pete's sake find Victoria!"

"You got it," he said confidently.

I ended the call, my mind racing. What would Martina Monroe uncover? I knew Maurice said to do everything possible to preserve the family's name and keep them out of prison. Not that I was considered family, but if they uncovered the truth, I would most certainly go to prison. I'd disappeared once, I supposed I could do it again.

30

MARTINA

We waited in silence for the response from the FBI team. We had just provided our latest theory regarding the disappearance of Victoria Hightower and its connection to Nicholas Hirsch's murder. We were hopeful the FBI would shed some light on events from thirty-five years ago, potentially revealing the origins of the criminal activities of the DeMarcos and the Stanzels. Above all, our aim was to find Victoria and establish if she had been simply in the area, or if she was the eyewitness in Nicholas Hirsch's murder. If our theory that Anthony Stanzel was our murderer was wrong, we still had to ascertain who was responsible for making Victoria vanish—and to find her. One thing was clear in my mind: if Victoria had indeed witnessed a murder, it was the most plausible reason for her disappearance.

"Admittedly, it's an interesting theory, and it makes sense," came the reply from Special Agent Vine. "But as of now, all you have is a theory. There's no evidence connecting Victoria High-tower to the Hirsch murder, and there's no link between the Stanzels and either Victoria or the murder."

We were prepared for skepticism. "We have a photo ID that indicates Anthony Stanzel was pimping, not just Victoria Hightower but several other young women. As for the Hirsch murder..." My voice faltered. I disliked referring to it as "the Hirsch murder." To me, Hirsch was August Hirsch, and even the idea my Hirsch had been killed was too much to think about. "We've sent the physical evidence from Nicholas Hirsch's crime scene to a private lab. We're hoping they can uncover any evidence that points toward the assailant. If there is any, I'm confident we'll get to the truth."

The anticipation in the room was palpable. "Our teams— the undercover team—have been briefed on your case. We'll brief them on this new development as well. The connections you found are compelling, and the team is probing into the Stanzels' activities further. Have you discovered anything new about Priscilla Keene?"

"Only that she seemingly didn't exist more than thirty-five years ago. But I've met her, and she's undoubtedly in her mid-fifties or early sixties."

"That aligns with our findings too. However, the challenging aspect is sifting through data from thirty-five years ago or even more. We're mainly looking for paper records, if they exist. I'm honestly surprised you've managed to gather as much evidence as you have on the Nicholas Hirsch murder."

"It's not been easy," I agreed. "But there has to be a way forward. Has your team found any leads on the DeMarco and Stanzel associates, anyone who might have been involved both then and now who operates in the shadows—does their dirty work for them?"

If the Stanzels were smart, they would keep their hands clean and hire out the dirty bits.

Special Agent Vine said, "We have a list of individuals believed to be part of the DeMarco crime family. However, as of now, there's still no evidence the Stanzels are criminals. So far, it just looks like social and real estate ties. The Stanzels might be entirely aboveboard. It's not illegal to sell real estate. They aren't obligated to verify the cleanliness of their clients' funds."

In my gut, I knew the Stanzels and Priscilla Keene were far from innocent, and I was determined to prove it.

"Do you have any confidential informants who could be useful?" I asked. "Someone we could push a little harder, maybe incentivize more? Given the stakes here at Drakos Monroe, there's nothing we wouldn't do to bring justice for Hirsch and his family."

"Understood. I'll inform our CIs of the new development. If they catch wind of anything related to your case, I'll let you know."

"Great, thank you."

"When do you expect the results back from the private lab?" Special Agent Vine asked.

"In a few days at most. We requested a rush on it."

"And how's Hirsch coping with all of this?"

"As well as can be expected," I admitted. "At first, he was in utter disbelief. It felt like he was grieving all over again. But he's expressed gratitude for reopening the case, and he's quite optimistic that we'll uncover the truth about his brother's death."

"You've made significant headway so far. It's incredible."

Tippin chimed in. "Have you identified anybody within the SFPD who might be on the Stanzels' or DeMarcos' payroll?"

"We have a few leads, but I can't disclose specifics at this time."

Tippin pressed. "So, you're not willing to share that information with us?"

"Not at this time. Doing so could jeopardize our ongoing investigations."

Vincent, looking concerned, asked, "How dangerous are the DeMarcos and the Stanzels?"

Special Agent Vine responded with a heavy tone, "The

DeMarcos have been known to take drastic measures to protect their business. As expected, they deal in drugs, a typical commodity for traffickers. But their involvement in the trafficking of young individuals, buying and selling them, is horrific but lucrative. They won't hesitate to kill to safeguard their operation."

A thought suddenly struck me. "Have you managed to rescue any survivors from their sex trafficking ring?"

"A few have been recovered."

"And their whereabouts?"

"Most were deported."

I pondered for a moment. "Is there a possibility of reaching out to some victims and gathering intel on what they know?"

"We questioned them when we brought them in. They were all promised a better life—for a price. They didn't know the price was their bodies and their children's until their debt was paid off. A debt they'd never pay off, by design. Anyway, the victims we talked to know some get shipped out. They don't know where to. They only have vague descriptions of the operators. But as far as trying to get info for your case, the victims are quite young. I'm not sure it would shed light on past events."

"What about those managing the massage parlors and nail salons? Are they younger members or potentially individuals higher up in the organization?"

"That's a valid point," the agent conceded. "However, getting them to cooperate without alerting the DeMarcos would be challenging."

"It seems our immediate steps are to await the lab results from the Nicholas Hirsch crime scene, ascertain Victoria's whereabouts, and determine Priscilla Keene's true identity. If we can find answers to those questions, we'll be closer to solving the Nicholas Hirsch case."

Special Agent Vine said, "While I agree with your strategy, Martina, it's not going to be easy. It's a tall order."

Vincent added, "Yeah, well, with the undercover agents and CIs, hopefully we'll find out if the Stanzels are criminals. If they've slipped up, there might be a weak link."

"True. We'll be in touch and let you know what we find on the Stanzels and Priscilla Keene. We'll dig deeper into her background, try to figure out what was happening back then."

"Thank you very much, Special Agent Vine."

I ended the call and leaned back in my chair, trying to process all the information.

"So far, they haven't been very helpful, have they?" Vincent remarked.

"Not yet," I replied. "But once their people get more information about the sex trafficking ring in San Francisco, it could help. Like you said, there's always a weak link. Someone among the missing who's willing to talk, to tell us the truth."

"But who?"

Before I could reply, my phone buzzed. A call from Zoey. I excused myself and walked into the hall. "Hey, Zoey, what's up?"

"Mom, something's off."

"What do you mean?"

"Well, I'm calling you from the grocery store. I didn't want to go home. I think somebody's been following me."

My pulse raced. "Why do you think that?"

"After I left school and was heading to Kaylie's, I noticed a dark sedan with tinted windows behind me. When I realized the car was still tailing me near Kaylie's, I took a different route. But the car followed every turn I made. So, I drove to the grocery store. What should I do, Mom?"

"Are you parked outside?"

"Yes, right in front of the entrance."

"Here's what I want you to do: Keep me on the phone, get out of your car, and run inside the store. Stay there until I get to you. Don't leave with anybody, not even a police officer, understood?"

"Yes." I heard the sounds of Zoey's car door opening and then her rapid footsteps as she ran toward the grocery store's entrance. "I'm inside now."

"Okay, I'll be there in ten minutes. Stay near the entrance. If a store worker asks what you're doing, just say you're waiting for me because your car broke down. I'm on my way."

"Are you worried?"

"I always worry about you. Stay calm. I'll be there soon."

I rushed back into the conference room. "I have to go. Zoey thinks she's being followed. I'll catch up with you later."

Without waiting for goodbyes, I bolted out, my heart racing. As I headed to my car, an unsettling thought crept into my mind. Would they really target my daughter? Just how far would the Stanzels go to keep their secrets hidden?

31

VICTORIA

THIRTY-FIVE YEARS EARLIER

Wandering through the garden, I was captivated by the aromatic sage and rosemary, the meticulously trimmed thyme plants, and the lush green of the manicured lawn. Quaint picnic tables beckoned for quiet reflection, and a distance away, the intricately designed sculptures added a touch of artistry to the natural beauty around. Yet amidst this tranquility, a weight pressed on my heart. There wasn't a moment I didn't miss Shannon or my mother. I wished more than anything that I could bring them here. I wished they knew that, despite everything, I was okay.

Sister Kate, with a warm smile lighting up her face, strolled up to me. "Maisie, how are you doing?"

"I'm... I'm feeling well. It's hard to believe—sixty days without drugs." And that I had escaped Blade and that woman, Priscilla. I still hadn't figured out why they had let me live. Even I understood it wasn't often girls like me got a second chance. Not that I hadn't paid a price.

"You should be very proud of yourself. We all are, here at the convent."

A sigh escaped me.

"What's troubling you, dear?"

"I miss my daughter. I miss my mother. They don't know what's happened to me. What if they think I just abandoned them?"

Sister Kate's gaze held understanding. "You never shared the circumstances of your past, and we respect your privacy. But perhaps it's time to discuss it. Maybe you don't need to stay hidden."

Tears welled up in my eyes. "Oh, no, I have to. If they found me, they'd kill me—and worse, they'd harm my family. I have no choice but to stay away."

"That does sound dangerous," she murmured.

"I wish they knew I was okay. But maybe it's better they think I'm gone forever."

Sister Kate gently took my hand. "In their hearts, they'll know."

"But will they? Will they resent me for leaving? My daughter is without a mother, without a father. By saving myself I've orphaned her."

"You're being too hard on yourself. If what you say is true, by staying away, you're keeping them safe. Would you like to pray with me?"

Nodding, I followed her to a secluded part of the garden, brimming with fragrant blooms, aptly named the "prayer garden." Sister Kate turned to me. "You know, you don't have to leave."

"I'd like to stay, at least for a little while longer, if that's okay. I'd be happy to help clean, and I'm eager to learn to cook. I'll do anything to help."

"That's heartwarming to hear," she replied. "We would love to have you stay. It's been a joy watching you find your strength and blossom here."

As we knelt on the fresh earth, I looked up at Sister Kate,

thinking perhaps I might stay here forever. Maybe even become a nun or at least assist them in their cause. In this serene garden, a realization dawned. I didn't deserve a new family, a partner, or more children. This would be my penance. I would serve, and I would give all I could. This was where I belonged now.

32

MARTINA

AFTER BREAKING SEVERAL TRAFFIC LAWS, I eased into the parking lot of the local Safeway grocery store—the one my family shopped at regularly. More often than not, Zoey visited the Starbucks inside, primarily to indulge in her penchant for sugary beverages. My nerves were firing, and I was anxious to see my daughter alive and well.

I studied the parking lot, driving slowly down each lane until I caught sight of a black sedan, just like Zoey had described. There was a man sitting behind the wheel, wearing black gloves, which he rested on top of the steering wheel. As I drove past, our eyes met, but I kept going. Within moments, the car peeled out of the parking lot and sped away.

I quickly pulled out my phone, recording the license plate number, then parked my car and rushed into the grocery store. There, at the Starbucks counter, was Zoey. I raced toward her, wrapping my arms around my daughter. "Hi, honey. I'm glad you're safe."

After I'd squeezed her a little too long, she said, "Jeez, Mom. I'm okay."

Releasing her, I said, "Good."

"Is everything okay?" she inquired, her brow furrowing.

"Yes. I'm just happy to see you. But I do need to call the office real quick, okay? I'll be right over there."

Stepping ten feet away to a corner near a vending machine, I pulled out my phone to call Vincent. To my surprise, my hand was shaking. He answered on the first ring. "Hey, Martina, is everything okay? Did you find Zoey?"

"Yes, Zoey's safe and sound, sipping on some sugary concoction."

"That sounds like her. How can I help?"

"When I got to the parking lot, I spotted a black sedan, just like Zoey described. There was a man inside, wearing black gloves. He had dark hair, ruddy skin, and he might be in his fifties. We made eye contact, and he sped out of the parking lot. Luckily, not fast enough. I captured his license plate number."

"Give it to me."

After I read out the number, he replied, "Give me five minutes. I'll call you back."

I took a deep breath, trying to steady my nerves. Zoey didn't need to see me in this state. It would only worry her more. I forced a smile and walked back over to her. She was chatting with the barista, whom she apparently knew from school.

I gently pulled her aside, and she said, "So, what was that all about? Was I just imagining things?"

"No. I saw the car that matched the description you gave me. I got the plate number. Vincent's running it now."

"So, there was someone following me, and you saw him in the parking lot?" she asked, her eyes wide with the realization.

I pulled her closer to me and nodded. "Yes."

"Is this related to Uncle August's brother's case?"

"I don't know, Zoey. We're working on finding that out. But for now, you're not leaving my side."

"Mom, I have to go to school, and I have a leadership meeting," Zoey protested.

"Well, you don't have school right at this very minute, so you'll be with me."

She sighed but didn't argue. It was rare for Zoey, despite being a teenager, and me, her mother, to be at odds. However, this was one time I wasn't going to let her take matters into her own hands. She was my only daughter, my only child. If I had to be a little strict and she was upset with me, so be it.

My phone buzzed, and I quickly answered. "What did you find, Vincent?"

"The car's registered to a private investigator named Rex Kleinman."

"What did you learn about him?" Why was a PI following my daughter?

"He works for himself. He's not part of a firm—he's independent."

"Do you know who his clients are?"

"No."

"Well, get me his address and phone number. I'll go talk to him." It didn't matter that it was getting late. Nobody followed my daughter and got away with it. This Rex Kleinman had some explaining to do.

"What about Zoey?" Vincent asked.

It was a good point. "I'm going to bring Zoey to the office, and then I'll go see Kleinman."

"You know we can handle it, Martina, if you need us to."

"Someone hired him to track my daughter. I will talk to him. You can come with me, but Zoey needs protection."

"Maybe she could stay at Hirsch's?"

"That's a good idea. I'll talk to you later."

"Let me know if you want company when you talk to Kleinman."

"Thanks." Ending the call, I walked back over to my daughter. "I need to go question the person who was following you. How about you go to the Hirsches' for the night? Is that okay?"

"I guess," she said with exasperation.

"Good. I'll call Hirsch."

I got Hirsch on the line and explained the situation.

"I don't like the sound of that, Martina."

"Neither do I, but I have a lead on who was following her. I'm going to question him. Can Zoey stay with you and Kim?"

"Of course."

"Are you home?"

"Not yet. Kim's home, but I'll leave work now too."

Figured. "Thanks, Hirsch. I'll drive her over and wait until you get there."

"You don't have to thank me, Martina. Zoey is family. She can stay as long as she needs to. We can even get a patrol on the house if that helps."

I hadn't even thought that far ahead. "For now, I'm happy with her being at your house with you. We should be there in about fifteen minutes. How long will it take you to get there?"

"I'll leave now and should be there in about twenty minutes."

"See you then." I ended the call and explained the situation to Zoey. "What about Barney? He's home all by himself."

Shoot. "I'll call Grandma to see if she can go check on him."

My mind raced. The PI who agreed to follow my daughter and the person who hired him would greatly regret those decisions to do so.

33

MARTINA

With Zoey safely at Hirsch's house, I could focus on my task at hand. Vincent joined me, as I checked out the office of the PI, Rex Kleinman. It was small and located downtown in a strip mall. But there was no sign of him or his vehicle. Not one to back down from a challenge, I directed Vincent to drive to his home. Sure enough, there was his car, parked right out in the driveway. Mr. Kleinman was in for an experience he would never forget.

Nobody followed my daughter and got away with it.

I knocked on the door.

Vincent said, "Maybe he's asleep."

I retorted, "I don't care. This guy will talk to me, and he will talk to me now."

Vincent didn't protest. A few moments later, a man with dark hair, dark eyes, and a ruddy complexion answered the door. Our eyes met, and he seemed to recognize me. Did he know who I was? He was wearing sweatpants and a T-shirt with the 49ers logo etched across it. He clearly wasn't expecting us. That was his first mistake. Strike that. His first mistake was following my daughter around town. The second was not expecting me to show up at his front door.

"By the look on your face, Mr. Kleinman, I would guess you know who I am."

"No, I don't think we've ever met."

"Is that how you want to play it? Fine. I'm Martina Monroe, and this is my associate, Vincent Teller. We're with Drakos Monroe Security & Investigations. I'd like to have a talk with you, Mr. Kleinman."

"Call me Rex."

"Rex, I'd like to have a conversation with you."

"It's kind of late, Ms. Monroe."

"Yeah, well, the matter is quite pressing," I said, arms crossed over my chest. The crossing of my arms was deliberate. That way, I could reach my holster and pull my weapon if I needed to.

I stared him down until he finally agreed. "Come on in, and don't mind the mess."

We followed him inside, and I studied his messy home. Dirty dishes filled the sink, and dust layered his end table. My guess was he was a bachelor who lived alone and maybe wasn't home very much.

He led us into the dining room and gestured for us to sit.

Adrenaline and anger fueled me, and I wasn't sure if I could actually sit still. But mind over matter, I sat down calmly. Vincent did the same.

"What can I help you with, Ms. Monroe?" he said, his tone patronizing.

"Mr. Kleinman—I'm sorry, Rex—I believe I saw you earlier in the parking lot of the Safeway. Do you know how I knew you were in that parking lot?"

"No. I was there to buy groceries."

"Oh yeah? What did you buy?"

"Milk."

"Do you have a receipt?"

"I don't always keep those things," he replied with a smirk.

"Okay, that was a fun little exchange, but here's the real reason why I'm here. My daughter spotted you. That's right. Did you think my daughter doesn't know how to spot a tail or to be aware of her surroundings? You were following my daughter, Zoey, and I want to know why."

"I think you have me mistaken for somebody else." He leaned back, rather casually.

I sat straight up in my seat and looked him dead in the eyes. "You were following my daughter. I caught you in the parking lot. The car matches the description she provided to me. I *know* you were following my daughter. And frankly, if you don't play straight with me and tell me the truth, I'll consider *you* the problem. Read my lips, hear my words: nobody messes with my family. Do you understand, Rex?"

My body was shaking with anger.

Yet, he was unflappable. He didn't look worried, more like smug.

"Who hired you to follow my daughter?"

"I'm telling you, I think this is a case of mistaken identity."

"Well, here's what I think it's a case of. I think somebody hired you to follow my daughter to get to me. Am I right? Don't answer that. I know the answer. What I want to know is who hired you. And if you don't want to cooperate with me and my firm, like I said, I have to assume you're the problem. One way or another, we will find out who hired you to watch my daughter. You obviously know who I am, so maybe you know a little bit about me. Not only do I have my firm behind me, but I also have several police departments. Not only will I catch you and bring the truth to light, but you'll land in prison for every little thing you've ever done wrong. You can bet on that."

"Do you make a habit of going into people's homes late at night threatening them?"

My blood boiled. "Let me clarify. That's not a threat. It's a promise. You think you can follow my daughter and get away with it? Think again."

"I think maybe you should leave. I'm tiring of this."

Vincent interjected before I could answer, "Martina, maybe we're all wrong. Maybe nobody hired him at all. Maybe he's a predator who had been planning to kidnap Zoey?"

Smart move, Vincent. "You're right." I turned back to Rex. "Maybe you don't have a client who asked you to follow my daughter. Maybe you wanted her for yourself. Perhaps you're a sexual deviant. And that's what everyone is going to believe when you get arrested for following a teenage girl around. Maybe you were trying to kidnap her."

"Oh, the great Martina Monroe's not above planting evidence?" Rex said with a hint of sarcasm.

"From what I understand, I don't need to plant any evidence. You were following my teenage daughter around. And if nobody hired you, as you claim, that means you're a predator. You're stalking my daughter. All I need to bring you in is my daughter's testimony she saw your car following her, and then I saw you in the parking lot. That's enough to arrest you for child endangerment or attempted kidnapping or stalking. I guess we'll have to pick one. So, what's it going to be?"

That seemed to get to him as he shifted in his seat, not quite as confident as he was just moments before.

"So," I continued, "I'll take your silence as a sign that I should call my pals at CoCo County Sheriff's Department and let them know we have a predator here who went after one of their own." Eyeing Vincent, I said, "Why don't you call Ross to come pick him up. He likes to pick up perverts and teach them a lesson."

"Will do," Vincent said.

"You're really going to do this?" Rex asked.

"Oh, yeah, you were following my teenage daughter, and you think I'm just going to let it go? Seriously?" I sat back while Vincent got up from his seat and called Ross.

Standing behind me, Vincent said into the phone, "Hey, Ross, are you up? Yeah, we have a situation. Zoey, Martina's daughter, was being followed by some creepy old dude in a black sedan. We're sitting in his house right now. He's probably one of those pedophiles. You should check the registry."

Vincent paused, listening, then added, "The name is Rex Kleinman."

Rex now put his hands in the air in a defensive posture. "Okay, okay, okay, there's no need for that."

"Are you now willing to cooperate with me?"

"Sure, sure, of course."

I wasn't buying it, not for half a second. "Who hired you?"

He shrugged. "I don't remember."

I turned to Vincent. "Have them pick him up for child endangerment. Have them bring backup. He could be armed."

I knew I was.

Vincent nodded. "Will do."

As Vincent provided the address and the details we had on Rex Kleinman, I turned back to Rex.

"You wanted to do this the hard way. Well, then we'll do it the hard way. Soon, a couple of homicide detectives Vincent and I work with from CoCo County Sheriff's will be here. You see, Zoey and me, we're part of the CoCo County family. Vincent and I both work with them and for my firm, Drakos Monroe. It's not a good idea to be on the wrong side of us," I said, attempting to impress the gravity of the situation on him.

Rex sat stony-faced.

Vincent stepped forward. "Detective Ross and Jayda will be here shortly."

"Excellent news, Vincent. Thank you."

A tense silence settled over the room, only broken ten minutes later by a heavy knock on the door.

"I'll get it," Vincent announced.

As he moved to answer the door, I kept my gaze firmly on Rex, studying him like a predator sizing up its prey. I wondered what was going through his mind. Was he just now realizing he'd bitten off more than he could chew? Or were the people who had hired him far more intimidating than he thought I could be? Could he be the weak link we needed to break the Stanzels?

Ross ambled in, with Jayda in tow. I stood up to greet them. "This is Rex Kleinman. My daughter, Zoey, called me, saying she spotted a suspicious black sedan following her from school to a friend's house. Even when she diverted to the grocery store, he was still tailing her. I arrived in the parking lot of the grocery store and saw this man sitting in his car, as if waiting for her to come out. He claims nobody hired him, despite being a private investigator. Apparently, he just had an interest in my teenage daughter."

Ross nodded. "Understood." Turning to Kleinman, he commanded, "Mr. Kleinman, stand up and place your hands behind your back."

As Ross read him his rights and escorted him out, Kleinman cast one last glance in my direction. I responded with a smirk.

But he shook his head, and something deep inside me stirred, as if it was a warning. I didn't think Rex Kleinman was the real danger, but whoever had hired him certainly was. The next challenge was figuring out if Kleinman would talk, and if not, who had contracted him. Because trying to get to me through my daughter was beyond unacceptable.

34

MARTINA

AFTER I'D SPOKEN with Zoey to let her know the man who had been following her was in police custody, Hirsch came on the line. "Martina, what's going on?"

"I'm on my way down to the station now. Ross and Jayda arrested Rex Kleinman, the PI who was following Zoey."

"He was arrested on what charge?"

"Well, he told me nobody had hired him to follow her. So, from what I could tell, he was following her to kidnap her. They're booking him on child endangerment."

Hirsch chuckled. "Clever. You think he'll talk?"

"I don't think so, but that's what's got me worried."

"How so?"

"If he keeps quiet, that means whoever hired him is a lot scarier than going to prison."

"The Stanzels? The DeMarcos?"

"Maybe."

Hirsch and I usually discussed all of our cases—ones we worked together and ones we didn't. When it wasn't a social event with Zoey or Audrey, or a barbecue, we still met once a week just to talk shop. I didn't want to leave him out of this investigation even though he wasn't able to actually work on it.

"I think we struck a nerve."

"I know I can't help with the case, but if they know we're onto them, maybe a press release about your missing person? Maybe even say she's a key witness to a crime, something to that effect to get them really scared."

"It could also backfire, but if we can't find Victoria, neither can they. I'll talk it over with Vincent and see how Rex reacts when I bring it up in his interrogation."

"Wish I could be there with you, but I know I can't."

"How are you handling all of this—the reopening of your brother's case and not being involved?"

"Mom and Dad are grateful, and so is my other brother. But it stirs up feelings of anxiety and desperation, not knowing why he was killed."

I hadn't told him the full extent of the police report, feeling it better to keep most details inside the investigation, but maybe I was wrong. "We think we know why he was killed, Hirsch."

"You do?"

"It wasn't a mugging. We think he died trying to save Victoria."

Hirsch was silent for a heartbeat. "It sounds like Nick—he was always standing up for the little guy. He was the best big brother there ever was."

I didn't doubt that. "I wish I could've known him."

"Well, I'll let you go. I know you have to talk to this guy. Thank you again, Martina. I know you'll find out what happened to Nick, and you'll make them pay."

"That I will."

Arriving at the station, I got out of the car and followed Vincent and the team inside. One of the uniforms was leading Kleinman into a conference room when Ross said, "Let's get him settled in for a minute. We'll interrogate him for a bit, see what he knows, and then let you go in there. My guess is he'll want to lawyer up."

"Unfortunately, I think you're right."

"All right, once you take a crack at him, let us know how it goes."

Vincent and I took a seat in the lobby. "It's like we can't stay away," Vincent said.

"Not even if we tried."

"How are you holding up, Martina?"

I had been working with Vincent for so long, he knew my tells. He knew that, when I was quiet, it was a sign I was upset or angry about something. "I'm feeling a lot of emotions. I'm angry, I'm furious—though I guess that's the same thing. And I'm a little worried about my daughter. I mean, I've taught her so much, to take care of herself, to be on the lookout, self-defense, but..."

"Because of that, she called you, and we've got this guy in custody."

"What if she hadn't seen him? Or if she had spotted him but didn't call me?"

"But she did."

I shook my head, trying not to dwell on what could have happened. Instead, I focused on the fact that my daughter was safe at Hirsch's house and the man who'd been following her was locked up. But it wasn't this man who was the real threat—it was whoever hired him. Unless he also did dirty work for his employers. Maybe he was the dangerous one and had planned to hurt Zoey. "I'm looking forward to talking to him once he's been handcuffed and at least verbally roughed up by Ross and Jayda."

"They'll show no mercy."

"I hope not."

A few moments later, Ross and Jayda returned with disappointed expressions. Ross looked us in the eye and said, "He wants a lawyer."

"It was expected."

"Well, we can't question him, but you can. Be my guest."

Vincent and I exchanged glances and headed toward the conference room. Inside, Rex Kleinman sat, handcuffed, looking rather annoyed.

"How are they treating you in here?"

He rolled his eyes. "I'm not talking to you either."

"Well, I'm not actually the police, so I can keep talking, I can keep asking questions. It doesn't matter if you've been Mirandized or not. This is personal to me. For my daughter. What kind of monster goes after a teenager?"

"Look, lady, I can't talk to you. I'm not going to talk to you. You're wasting your time with me."

Vincent and I exchanged glances, and I said, "Okay, if you don't want to talk, I'll do the talking. Let's see how it resonates with you."

He nodded, seemingly interested in what I had to say. My gut was telling me I knew exactly who had hired this man to go after my daughter.

"Here's my theory. I think the missing person I've been hired to find, Victoria Hightower, disappeared thirty-five years ago, but not on her own. The last person to see her alive was Priscilla Keene, who checked her out of the hospital after she'd been badly beaten by an unknown—or rather, unnamed—individual. I believe that person is Anthony Stanzel, then known as 'Blade,' a notorious pimp and abuser of young women. I suspect Priscilla was cleaning up Anthony Stanzel's mess on the orders of his father, Maurice Stanzel." I paused to check his reaction. He had a glint of interest in his eyes despite trying to act like I was wasting his time. I continued, "I believe that while Anthony was attacking Victoria, a Good Samaritan stepped in, as the police report suggests. During the ensuing altercation, Anthony lethally wounded this person, cutting his carotid artery, leaving him to bleed out and die. During that chaos, Victoria ran. She later passed out due to her injuries. Another Good Samaritan took her to the hospital, but the Stanzels and Priscilla Keene located her and made her disappear to ensure she could never testify against Anthony Stanzel for the murder of the Good Samaritan as well as for his crimes against her and the other women he exploited."

I studied Rex's face. It was unflinching, which made me think I was spot on with my theory. "So, what I don't understand is why the Stanzels and Priscilla Keene, or whoever hired you, would target me. That's the puzzling part."

Rex remained stone-faced, but Vincent chimed in, "You know what I think, Martina?"

"No, Vincent. What do you think?" I asked in an almost playful tone.

"I believe the Stanzels and Priscilla Keene are worried you're getting too close to the truth. They're afraid you won't stop investigating until they're brought to justice, so they're trying to intimidate you."

I mulled that over and said, "But there's one flaw in that theory, right?"

Vincent nodded, as if we hadn't rehearsed the conversation. "Yes, because what they don't realize about you is that even if they took drastic action against you or your family, the entire team at Drakos Monroe would seek justice on your behalf. As would the entire CoCo County Sheriff's Department and the San Francisco Police Department. They'd never get away with it."

I nodded, playing as though I was just now considering Vincent's words. "That's an interesting theory, Vincent. I think you might be onto something. What do you think, Rex? Is he right?"

Rex exhaled deeply and looked away.

That's what I thought.

Vincent continued, "Remember that case we had a couple of years ago, Martina? Actually, Rex, you might find this one interesting. We mostly solved the case—thanks to Martina. It was the murder of a young soldier. We figured out who did it, and we found him. He died before he could be sent to prison, but his crimes were made public, and her family got answers. However, there were others who helped him cover up the crime. They thought they'd gotten away with it. It didn't sit right with us, did it?"

I nodded. "That's right, Vincent. And do you recall what happened when the details of their involvement were exposed? It wasn't just the soldier and killer's names leaked to the press. Someone gave away the entire story, naming names. As a result, everyone involved in that cover-up ended up behind bars."

Vincent raised an eyebrow. "Imagine if that happened in this situation. If someone, say, took our theory to the press, revealing the Stanzels' involvement in not only a murder and a missing persons case but also an attempted kidnapping of a teen girl. And let's not forget their ties to the DeMarco organized crime family. That would surely ruffle some feathers."

Rex finally looked back at us, shaking his head. "You sure seem to have a penchant for playing with fire."

I leaned forward. "Some fires need to be put out. And it seems like we're the ones who'll have to do the snuffing."

"Or you could perish in the process," Rex shot back.

Vincent added, "You're entitled to a phone call, you know. Who will it be? Your lawyer?"

"Of course," Rex replied.

"Good luck with that."

As we rose to leave, feeling that we wouldn't extract anything further from him, Rex said, "You could choose to let this go, but they won't. Think on that."

I paused and turned to face him. "I don't expect them to. But if they're all in jail, what can they do?"

Rex leaned closer, his voice low and menacing. "Their reach is far and wide. Be careful, Martina."

Could we flip him? Instead of turning around and leaving, I shut the door. Vincent gave me a puzzled look. I leaned against the wall, eyeing Rex intently.

"What do you think they'd do if they thought you were talking to us?" I probed.

Rex met my gaze defiantly. "They know I'd never talk."

I pressed on. "But what if the media happens to suggest you're our source?"

He looked away, and I said, "If you cooperate, we can protect you. It's not just me working on this. Our reach is far and wide too. Cooperate. Help us, and we'll ensure they don't hurt anyone ever again, and we'll make certain they don't touch you or anyone you care about."

Rex went silent, pondering my proposal. The room was tense, with only the sound of our breathing. I could tell he was mulling it over.

"We'll let you think on that while you're in lockup over the weekend," I said finally, breaking the silence.

He gave the slightest of nods.

It was barely perceptible, but I caught it and nodded back.

As Vincent and I walked toward Ross and Jayda, a thought struck me. If it wasn't for my daughter, we wouldn't have Rex in custody. This might be the break we needed for the case. Pride swelled within me. My Zoey never ceased to amaze me.

35

MARTINA

STANDING ALONE IN MY KITCHEN, the only discernible noise was from the coffee maker. Barney was staying with my mom and Ted. And since I was working round-the-clock, he was still at their house. Hirsch had decided to take a few days off to protect Zoey. He'd said it was the least he could do since I was trying to find his brother's killer. The entire team agreed we wouldn't stop until we found the truth.

My phone buzzed. Glancing down, I didn't recognize the number. "Hello?"

"Is this Ms. Monroe?"

"Yes, who is this?"

"Hi, this is Shannon. I'm here with my grandma. I'm Victoria Hightower's daughter."

With all the crazy activity in the past week, I realized I hadn't provided any of the family or Nancy with an update on what was going on with the case. There was only so much I could disclose. We were on the right track, but we still had no clue about Victoria's whereabouts, whether she was alive or buried somewhere never to be discovered.

"Yes, of course. How are you?"

"We're doing well. We're just calling to see if there's been any developments in my mom's case?"

"There have been developments but nothing I can share right now. But we're starting to put the pieces together."

"You can't share anything?"

"Unfortunately, no. Except for the fact that we believe her disappearance is connected with other crimes. This has become a much bigger case. We now have several different organizations working on it."

"Oh, my."

"Yes, so I would have to ask that you continue to keep this very quiet. You might hear from me in a few days. One outlet we're considering is going to the media, but not yet."

"Okay, but you're making progress?"

"Yes, we're making progress."

"Is it more than what the other PI found?"

"The other PI didn't find anything." Or if he had, he acted like he hadn't. And with how this investigation was going, I wouldn't put anything past the Stanzels and Priscilla Keene.

"Right, okay. Well, thank you for the update. So, I guess I'll hear from you in a few days?"

"Yes, I will give you a call in a few days."

"Thank you, Martina."

I hung up and shook my head. This case had turned everything upside down, including my entire life, my daughter's, and even my dog's. I supposed I should call Nancy.

My coffee finished brewing, and I sat down and prepared to call Nancy.

She answered after just one ring. "Hi, Martina."

"Hi, Nancy. I'm just calling with a brief update on the case."

"Did you find something?"

After a lengthy explanation, I added, "We think we're

getting close, but we have to keep this quiet for a little while longer."

"Oh, dear, what have I done?"

"You've done a great thing looking for Victoria."

"Are you sure?"

"Absolutely. And I know that right now there are several people who want to thank you, but we're holding off on that until we come to a conclusion."

"Any sign of Victoria?"

The unfortunate truth was no. There was no sign of Victoria. Priscilla wasn't talking. I had a feeling she was the only one who knew what happened to her. "Not yet, but if we keep working the associated cases, it'll lead us to Victoria." *I hope.*

"Okay." ·

"I'll give you a call in a few days. We think there are some actions we may need to take, and I'll need the cooperation of you and her family."

"How is Victoria's family doing?"

"I just spoke with them. They're doing okay, anxious, and grateful that we're looking for Victoria."

"That's good to hear. Okay, I don't want to take up any more of your time. Thank you, Martina."

"You're welcome."

That was two things crossed from my list of tasks for the day. Keeping the families updated was important. Given my family was now at risk, the task had unfortunately fallen to the bottom of my priorities. Looking up at the clock, I took a swig of my coffee and headed toward my front door.

The sudden noise of three loud pops jarred my senses. For a split second, they sounded like innocent firecrackers. But the chilling realization hit me, and I instinctively flung myself to the ground, heart racing wildly as the chilly floor met my body.

Almost immediately, three more pops echoed in the stillness. Panic consumed me, and every worst-case scenario flashed through my mind. Then, tearing through the silence, I heard the roar of an engine and the distinct sound of tires squealing against the asphalt. Someone, or something, was speeding away.

Lying there, my heartbeat thumped in my ears. I gasped for air, trying to calm the storm of emotions swirling inside me. I found myself whispering a silent prayer, thanking God for the safety of my loved ones. The thought of Zoey being in the cross-fire was too awful to fully grasp. My heart ached at the thought —what if she had been here? The horror of that potential reality gripped me.

Tears welled up in my eyes as shock took over, leaving me in a haze. Every muscle in my body felt tense and achy. With trembling hands, I cautiously felt over myself, needing the tactile confirmation that I was unharmed. To my relief, there was no blood, no wound.

As I shakily rose to my feet, my gaze was drawn to the front door. The wood was marred by a sinister mark. The telltale, smooth indentation of a bullet. My heart sank further as I looked around my once-safe sanctuary. Aside from that terrifying sign on the door, there was no apparent damage. But the invisible scars, the remnants of fear and trauma, were very much there.

A heavy realization weighed down on me, one that overshadowed any relief I might have felt—someone was out for blood. And that blood belonged to me and my family.

36

PRISCILLA

PRESENT DAY

STANDING TALL, I delivered the news. "Message sent."

Maurice nodded from behind his grand desk, resembling a king in his castle—which, honestly, he kind of was. I had sat near that throne, but with Maurice and his mediocre offspring, I'd never actually have the throne for myself. Not that I wanted to be his partner for life, anyway. I had wanted my own empire and always assumed I'd branch off one day, but the Stanzels had reeled me in—the money and the modicum of power that allowed me to make mostly my own decisions had kept me in their clutches. The only thing I couldn't stomach was continuing to cover for that idiot, Anthony.

"And our PI is still in jail?"

Nodding, I said, "I just spoke to his lawyer. He went in front of the judge, and they denied bail."

"You're kidding? That's outrageous. He has no priors."

"No, but they're pushing this angle of child endangerment, claiming he was trying to kidnap a teenage girl—a girl who happens to be closely connected to a friend of the court's—Martina Monroe. To keep a guy like Rex in jail, it's clear she has far more power than we initially realized. Drastic measures are likely the only things she'll respect."

Maurice shifted in his seat, looking uncomfortable. "Hopefully, she got the message and will back off."

"According to Rex's lawyer, he thinks Martina Monroe will never back down. And I mean never."

Maurice eased back in his chair, contemplating his next steps. "And what about Rex? Can we trust him? Really trust him?"

"Can we truly trust anybody? He hasn't said a word to the police. If he had, he'd be out of jail. They're holding him because he claimed nobody hired him. So, Martina, with her clever mind, told her pals at CoCo County Sheriff that he was a pedophile stalking, intending to kidnap and harm her daughter."

Maurice nodded. "It's unfortunate we don't have her on our side. She sounds formidable."

I suppressed the urge to roll my eyes. Sure, Martina seemed impressive, but what was with his admiration for her? It felt juvenile. He likely saw her as a woman to be conquered—it was the way he had operated.

Maybe I had reached my fill of the Stanzels. I could break away, but it would mean changing my name, my life—everything. It might not be so bad. If Martina didn't get the hint from our latest message, I'd have no choice.

If only Maurice would agree to take the most logical action and eliminate the actual threat to their family—Anthony. He would never agree, but DeMarco might. DeMarco harbored no affection for Anthony.

"I know you don't like discussing this, but there's another option to make all this go away."

"And what's that?" he said, straightening up in his seat.

"Anthony's the problem. He's who the police really want, the only one who's muddied his hands. We're ghosts."

Maurice's face turned a shade of red. "I'm not sacrificing my son."

"You're willing to let go of the entire organization, your legacy, everything for him?"

"You don't understand," he snapped. "You're not a mother."

I bit back a sharp retort. It wasn't true, but he didn't know that.

He didn't know about the brief period all those years ago when I had been a mother. Back when I was working the streets, doing anything I could to survive after the childhood I'd endured, and I found myself with a positive pregnancy test. They told me it was a congenital heart defect, that it wasn't my fault. But deep down, I believed it was God punishing me. That was why he only let me hold her for a few minutes before she faded away. It felt like a cruel joke, a fleeting glimpse into what could have been. But it was because of *her* that everything changed. My baby girl. I never could bear to give her a name—it didn't seem right. I didn't even know who her father was. Her face was a permanent fixture in my mind, pushing me forward. After my brief moments with her, I listened to the universe's warning.

When the opportunity arose, I seized it. I stopped selling my body, became sober, and started anew. It was all because of my baby girl that I reinvented myself. Unfortunately, I became someone who had done terrible things—all for what? Designer clothes? Money? If my baby girl had survived, would she be proud or ashamed?

Starting over would not be as easy as it was thirty-five years ago—with electronic records, microchips, and all the technological advancements. Forged documents were harder to come by, but I knew the ropes. The real challenge would be acquiring them without raising suspicions—especially not from the DeMarcos or the Stanzels. They'd grow wary, and they weren't the sort you wanted doubting your loyalty. I had to play the role, be the team player, all the way until I disappeared.

"You're right," I conceded. "I won't bring it up again. But just so you know, it is an option."

His voice was icy. "No, it's not. Bring it up again, and you're done."

My body shook. How dare he threaten to cast me aside after everything I'd done for him? The things I sacrificed, pieces of my soul I gave away. Yet, I forced a smile and assured him, "It'll never leave my lips again. Forget I brought it up."

"Give me an update in a few days. Make sure the message was received and that no one's looking into us."

"Will do, sir."

I waved and painted on a sickly sweet smile, playing the part of Team Stanzel. How naïve I'd been, thinking they'd ever truly protect me. Everything in my being was sending me signals that I needed to stop protecting people who would so easily toss me to the wolves in order to save themselves.

37

MARTINA

THE RESPONDING officer took down my information and my account of the drive-by shooting at my house. I had worked dangerous cases before, but this hit different. I was shook, but I would be okay. Keeping people safe was one of my specialties. Surely, I could keep myself safe. That meant I had to start treating myself like I'd treat one of my clients or loved ones.

Zoey and I would have to move in to a safe house until the case was over. She would have to leave school temporarily. I suspected she wouldn't be thrilled about the plan, but with our house being shot at and the fact my daughter was being followed, we couldn't afford to take risks. We would arrange for someone from the police department to pick up schoolwork for her. She was just going to have to be understanding. *Fingers crossed.*

Ross came running up. I realized this was the first time I'd ever seen him run. I'd had my doubts he could. He was a large guy but not particularly muscular.

"Martina, I heard there were shots fired at your house. What happened?" he panted.

I explained the situation, and he responded, "They've gone

too far, way too far. We need to put the screws to Rex Kleinman."

Feeling overwhelmed, I managed to explain the plan to move Zoey and me to a safe house. Hiding wasn't an option for me in the long run, but Zoey's safety was paramount. If I was buddied up, I'd be fine. All my buddies were armed and could be very dangerous.

"That's a good plan." He paused and studied my face. "How are you holding up?"

"I'm hanging in there. Neighbors have been asking if everything's okay. It's not often we get shots fired around here."

He glanced around my neighborhood. "I wouldn't think so."

Suddenly, Jayda rushed up the driveway, pulling me into a hug. "I'm so glad you're okay." She stepped back. "What can I do to help?"

Jayda, forever the one to jump straight to solutions. "Nothing right this second. I need to call Zoey and my mom," I said, fighting back tears.

"Of course. Just let me know if there is anything you need, Martina."

I took a deep breath and dialed Hirsch's number, knowing Zoey was at home with him. "Hey, Martina, how's it going?"

"Not great, Hirsch." I quickly filled him in on the situation.

He voiced the same concern. "We need to get you and Zoey to a safe house."

"I've already come to that conclusion," I replied. I'd said it before, and I'd say it again: no case was worth dying for, not even this one. But although they could make me work more discreetly, they couldn't stop me. The investigation would continue.

Hirsch interrupted my train of thought. "I'll let you talk to Zoey."

"Thanks." When she came on the line, I said, "Hey, Zoey," my voice thick with emotion.

"Hey, Mom. I was just about to head out for school. What's up?"

"Honey, you're not going to school today." I explained, glossing over some of the more frightening details, and told her about the move to the safe house.

"You're coming with me, right?"

"Yes, but while we're ironing out details, you'll stay with Uncle August."

"Okay, Mom. I love you."

"I love you too, Zoey." Tears welled up in my eyes. Hearing the worry in my daughter's voice, and realizing how quickly she complied, made the weight of the situation truly sink in.

Next, I called Stavros and told him I was coming into the office for us to discuss the recent events. He assured me he'd have everything prepared by the time I arrived.

I turned to Jayda and Ross. "I need to head over to the office to talk to Stavros about our accommodations," I explained.

"Need a lift?" Jayda asked.

"I'd appreciate that."

Ross clenched his fists. "Don't worry. Nobody goes after one of ours and gets away with it. We've got your back, Martina."

His confidence was a relief. I felt reassured that if anyone could get to the bottom of this, it was the investigators from CoCo County.

JAYDA and I soon entered the offices of Drakos Monroe. As usual, Mrs. Pearson was behind the front desk, her magenta lipstick brightening the otherwise muted ambiance. Spotting me, she hurried over, wrapping her arms around me in a tight embrace. "Oh, Martina, I just heard! I'm so glad you're safe."

"Thank you, Mrs. Pearson."

"I told Vincent about your situation since I know you're working closely with him. He mentioned he has some new information. He said it could wait, but he seemed to think you'd want to know."

"Thanks, I'll find him." Chances were it was related to the case. Vincent knew that if I was in the office, I'd want to be updated.

"Will you be okay from here? Do you want me to stay?" Jayda asked, concern evident in her eyes.

"I'm good. I have plenty of protection now."

She hugged me. "Take care," she whispered.

I walked farther into the office until I spotted Vincent. "Hey, buddy."

"Martina, good to see you. Are you okay?"

"I'm managing. We've got the best investigators from CoCo County on the shooting. Stavros is sorting out a safe house for Zoey and me. Hirsch is with her. But I hear you have new info on our case?"

He nodded with a sparkle in his eyes.

He had something good.

"I just got a call from the lab. They finished the testing. We should get Tippin on a call, if you're up for it?"

Absolutely.

"Let's find a conference room."

38

MARTINA

THE PHONE RANG, its shrill tone echoing my heightened sense of anticipation. It was almost surreal, how quickly I'd shifted focus from the terrifying incident at my home just an hour earlier.

"Lieutenant Tippin here," a voice announced on the other end.

"It's Martina Monroe and Vincent Teller. We have an update."

"What have you got?"

I glanced at Vincent, who chimed in. "Before we delve into the forensics for the Nicholas Hirsch case, Martina, I think you should brief Tippin on this morning's events."

Tippin's tone shifted. "What happened, Martina?"

"As you're aware, we apprehended a PI tailing my daughter. He's currently incarcerated without bail. But today, as I was leaving for work, someone fired six shots at my house."

There was a pause, then a somber, "Martina, I'm deeply sorry. Is everyone safe?"

"We're all okay. My daughter was already at Hirsch's for safekeeping, but we'll be relocating to a safe house soon."

Tippin sighed. "No wonder Nicholas Hirsch's case went unsolved. If they're going to these lengths thirty-five years later to cover it up, I bet they buried every detail back then."

Vincent smirked. "But nothing stays buried forever, right?"

"Let's certainly hope not," I responded. "All right, Vincent, let's hear it."

Vincent leaned in. "The lab analysis of Nicholas Hirsch's belongings revealed, in addition to his own DNA and hair samples, the presence of two other contributors. Both were run through CODIS, but neither returned a match."

I furrowed my brow. "Two unknown contributors?"

Vincent nodded. "Yes. The male contributor's DNA was from a blood sample. The third contributor, a female's DNA, was found in blood and a clump of hair that appeared to have been pulled out from the root."

My pulse quickened as I made the connection. "You're suggesting a possible scenario where someone assaulted a woman and then attacked Nicholas Hirsch, inadvertently transferring the woman's hair to him?"

"That's the working theory," Vincent confirmed.

Tippin remarked, "Excellent. If we had a cold case division, perhaps this case would've already been cracked."

Vincent countered, almost stating the obvious given the depth of their original investigation and the level of resistance they'd met. "Probably not. Not with the current lengths someone is going to to keep it quiet."

"You're probably right. It likely would take a team that couldn't be bought by the Stanzels—assuming they are behind all of this."

Vincent was right. The SFPD had likely been compromised all those years ago and likely even today.

"We need a sample from Victoria's family to see if the hair matches."

Vincent offered, "Martina, let me handle that. You have other matters to focus on, like staying safe."

I knew Vincent was right. He could obtain a DNA sample from Shannon or her mother to determine if Victoria was at the scene of Nicholas Hirsch's murder. "What's the theory on the other contributor?"

"The male contributor," Vincent replied. "It was mixed with the blood from Nicholas's wounds—likely mixed while the attack occurred. The perp probably cut himself on the knife or split his hands during the attack. It has to be from the killer."

"So, how do we obtain a DNA sample from Anthony Stanzel? I doubt we have grounds for a warrant."

Tippin suggested, "We could follow Stanzel. If he throws away a soda can or pizza box, we can swipe it and test it. Or we could camp outside his house on garbage day and see if we can get a sample from something discarded from his house."

Dumpster diving. I was familiar with the activity. It wasn't a pleasant job, but it could bear fruit.

"That could work. But I don't think I can volunteer for that one." Not because I didn't want to, but because I couldn't be out in the middle of the night when someone was taking shots at me. I silently reminded myself, *No case is worth dying for.*

"I could do it," Vincent offered.

"I'd prefer you don't go alone. Remember the golden rule."

Vincent nodded. "No case is worth dying for."

"Exactly. We can ask one of our team to join Vincent for an evening of dumpster diving."

"Good plan. I'm starting to see how you solved all those old cases," Tippin added.

"It's always a team effort, and I happened to work with only the best," I said with pride.

"I can see that. I admit, I'm a little jealous."

He should be. "Okay, we'll keep you posted."

"Excellent. Thank you both. And Martina, stay safe."

"Thank you. Talk soon," I said, ending the call. Turning to Vincent, I said, "This is big, Vincent."

"I thought you'd want to know," he said with a wry smile.

"Now let's pray one of the Stanzels throws out some DNA."

"I'm not sure I've ever prayed for DNA before," Vincent teased.

Well then, I'd have to pray for all of us. This case needed to end because one, the victims' families deserved answers, and two, mine deserved to be safe.

39

MARTINA

It was bad enough that Zoey and I had to stay in a safe house with limited communication with the outside world. We sent only essential messages to my mother, assuring her we were fine and asking her to keep Barney with her. It had only been a few days, but I already felt like a caged animal. And I wasn't the only one.

Zoey wasn't allowed to go on the internet, which meant doing all her schoolwork offline on a loaner laptop from the office—to be printed and handed in by one of our team. As for the investigation, I had to conduct all my communications with my burner cell phone which had to be changed each day—so comms were limited. Each time I needed to go somewhere, I was transported in the back of a van. It was all very covert. I had been undercover before, but this was different. This was my life and my daughter's.

"What do you want for breakfast, Mom?"

"I was thinking maybe scrambled eggs, toast, and fruit," I said, pretty sure that was about all we had left.

"Okay. You want me to scramble the eggs and you can do the toast?"

"Sure." I could have protested, pointing out that my daughter was subtly implying I was only capable of making toast. But I had to admit, Zoey was a far better cook than I ever would be—probably because she actually enjoyed it and had spent so much time with my mom learning how. Don't get me wrong, I could put together a salad with grilled chicken like nobody's business. But when it came to actual cooking, it just wasn't my thing.

Zoey pulled the carton of eggs from the refrigerator and then began searching for the frying pan. "It's in the dishwasher," I explained, having had to use it for dinner the previous night.

"You can't put frying pans in the dishwasher, Mom."

"Why?"

"It messes with the coating. That's what Grandma said, anyhow."

You learn something new every day. I pulled bread from the bag and set four pieces into the toaster oven. "So, what are your plans for today, Zoey?"

"Well, considering my options are to read, watch television, or go to the gym downstairs in disguise, I think I'll read. Maybe bake something."

"I'm sorry you're having to go through all this, honey."

"Well, it's better than being dead, right?"

She had a point. "True. Everyone's working to get this resolved as quickly as possible."

"I know you are, and as much as I don't like being in captivity, I'm trying to be patient. Because, well, our lives are more important. I do miss little Barney, though, and of course, not being able to see my friends or go anywhere."

"I hear you."

Zoey set down the carton of eggs. "But at the end of all this, we'll be safe, and we'll know who killed Uncle August's brother. It'll be worth it, right?"

Sometimes it took my teenager to remind me of what was really important. "That's true."

"What time are they picking you up today?"

I glanced at the digital clock on the microwave. "In about twenty minutes."

"You're so lucky to get to leave this place, freed from our gilded cage," she said rather dramatically. Every once in a while, behind her teenage exterior, she reminded me of when she was a little girl—when her middle name should have been *Drama*.

"Any leads on the case?" she asked, stirring the eggs.

"Well, Vincent went dumpster diving in the middle of the night. We're hoping to get some DNA off of some trash and maybe catch the guy who killed Nick."

"Seems like a long shot."

Sometimes any shot—even a long shot—was enough to break a case open. Could this all be over in a mere forty-eight hours, once the DNA was run on a piece of trash from the Stanzel residence?

AFTER BREAKFAST, my security team picked me up and brought me into the office through the semi-covert entrance. A new team picked me up each day, on a rotation, to make sure no one was following us or had picked up on the fact I was being transported in and out of the office.

I spotted Vincent first. "Hey, Vincent, how was your night?"

"It's still continuing. We've got bags of trash that we're still sifting through. So far, we haven't come up with much."

"Really? That's surprising, especially since he has two kids."

"Well, so far we've only found food scraps. They don't seem to eat out much. I haven't found any to-go containers or aluminum cans."

"Sounds like a bust."

"Yeah, and I talked to Hirsch and Lieutenant Tippin this morning." He must've seen the displeasure on my face, perhaps because I wasn't the first to know. "Sorry, but anyhow, I talked to them, and while the garbage thing is a good idea, it won't be definitive for prosecution. Even if we match up the male DNA to a Stanzel, a good defense attorney could argue that it could be either the male or female contributors who killed Nick."

Processing this information, it kind of made sense. If we argued that the hair and blood from a female contributor were transferred by the male contributor who assaulted Victoria and then killed Nick, the defense could argue the other way around. They could say she had beaten up Anthony Stanzel and then killed Nick, or that she had been beaten up by Anthony and she transferred his blood to Nick.

"But the witnesses said it was a man who fought with Nick."

"Eyewitness testimony is highly unreliable, especially thirty-five years after the fact," Vincent pointed out.

True. "Any updates from the lab?"

"Not yet. Want to sift through the rest of the garbage with me?"

I smirked. "I thought you'd never ask."

"I do know the key to your heart," he teased.

I headed back to the room where he was sifting through the Stanzel garbage and asked Vincent about his wedding plans.

"Oh, yeah, they're definitely in full swing. We're waiting for this case to be over to decide when to elope, but we're looking into venues and have tentatively set a date about a month before the reception."

"That's great."

"We think so. The more details we work out and seeing how happy it makes Amanda... I can't wait. I'm really excited for it."

"That's wonderful. Now let's solve this case so you can run off and get married."

"You got it, boss."

With gloves on, I cut open one of the trash bags and wished I'd worn a mask. The stench turned my stomach. There were wrappers from Goldfish crackers and cardboard that they'd swiped out of the recycling. Nothing to get a DNA sample from, but maybe fingerprints. However, that wouldn't help us. "I think we should put a team on Anthony Stanzel. Try to see where he goes and catch him throwing out a cigarette or a soda can."

"That's a good idea."

Tired of sifting through garbage, I took off my gloves and said, "I'll go talk to Stavros to see who we have available to put a tail on Stanzel and keep an eye on him at all times. It'll be useful to know where he is, so when we have enough evidence, the SFPD can arrest him."

It was at that moment I realized Anthony could be on the run. Not only could they be trying to eliminate me, but they could also be hiding him. I threw my gloves in the trash and headed toward Stavros's office. I knocked on the door, and he waved me in.

"How are you? How's Zoey? How's the accommodation?"

"It's fine, but the coffee is terrible. As for Zoey, well, she's a trooper."

"I can't believe it's come down to this. How's the case coming along?"

"We've been sifting through garbage, and I'm not sure we'll get anything useful this time around. I'd like to put a tail on Stanzel in case he tries to run."

"That's smart. We should have a couple of people who are available." He trailed off as he returned his focus to the computer. He tapped the keys, studied the screen, and said, "We're a little tight since we've been transporting you to and from your safe house, but it looks like we might be able to arrange a few different teams to keep eyes on him. San Francisco is a difficult place to tail people. Maybe you should ask SFPD to track him. We can coordinate efforts."

"Good idea. I'll talk to Tippin."

After a quick thank you, I turned to head back to the garbage-sorting room when Vincent appeared. "I just got a call from the lab. They've processed the sample from Victoria's family."

"And?"

He looked around and said, "In your office."

I walked a few steps to the right into my office and shut the door once Vincent was inside. "Well?"

"The female contributor is a match for the mother of Shannon Hightower."

"So, it was Victoria who was at the Nicholas Hirsch crime scene."

"Yes."

"The only way to prove our theory is if we can prove Anthony Stanzel was there too."

"Yeah. I mean, the witnesses said it was a male, so we could probably argue it was him. But it's Victoria's testimony that we really need—proof that he's the killer, assuming our theory is right."

"Now we have to figure out how to find Victoria. All the usual channels have come up as dead ends. Wherever she disappeared to, she disappeared well."

We needed to find Victoria more than ever—and that was exactly what we would do.

40

MARTINA

Lieutenant Tippin didn't have much encouraging news for us. "Our guys haven't seen anything unusual with Stanzel since I started tailing him last night. But at least we have eyes on him. I wish I could provide more than a few trusted patrols to watch Anthony, but I'm afraid anything more might set off alarm bells. Especially after the FBI was cagey about who from my department may be on the Stanzels' payroll."

"Understood. The FBI called and said they had something to talk to us about, so maybe they have something we can use."

"Let's hope so," Tippin agreed.

My gut told me we needed to push harder on Priscilla Keene. I was convinced she was the last person to have seen Victoria before she vanished from her family's life. "We should press Priscilla Keene again."

"If she was the last person to see Victoria, and we can find something criminal on her, we could bring her in. Maybe we should put a tail on her too. But I'm not sure SFPD can spare it."

"Drakos Monroe can help out. After we talk to the FBI, let's talk strategy for putting a team on Priscilla."

"Boy, this investigation must be getting pretty expensive for your firm. Are you doing this all pro bono?"

"We'd do anything for Hirsch."

Tippin nodded, as if he understood.

Vincent checked his watch and said, "Okay, it's about time." And he dialed into the meeting.

We were greeted with, "Special Agents Honeycutt and Vine here."

"Martina, Vincent, and Tippin here."

"I know the clock's ticking. So, let's just jump in. Any new developments on your end?" Special Agent Vine asked.

We filled them in on our dumpster diving as well as the DNA match for the blood found on Nicholas Hirsch.

"It sounds like your theory is starting to pan out."

Vincent said, "It is. We just need to confirm Stanzel's DNA."

"Well, if he goes to any restaurants where he tosses anything in the trash, it's all yours," Special Agent Vine offered.

"That's what we're hoping for. Our dumpster diving expedition didn't yield much."

"We're thinking of putting a tail on Priscilla Keene too. We think she was the last person to see Victoria, and we need to find Victoria."

"Yeah, that one's going to be tricky."

I glanced at Lieutenant Tippin and said, "Why is that?"

"Our team informed us this morning that something has the DeMarcos and Stanzels spooked, and they're not meeting with anybody right now. Secondly, no one's heard from or seen Priscilla Keene in the last three days."

"She's missing?"

"She hasn't shown up for work in days and isn't answering her phone."

That was puzzling. "Has anybody checked her residence to see if she's home?"

"We haven't gone in. Maybe somebody from the SFPD can do a welfare check on Ms. Keene? My guess is she's not there—or if she is, she's no longer there, if you know what I mean," Agent Honeycutt cryptically added.

"You think the Stanzels would kill Priscilla Keene to keep her quiet?"

The room fell silent as we all considered the chilling implications.

"Your guess is as good as mine. If they went after you and your daughter, there's no telling how far they'll go to keep their secrets hidden."

Tippin said, "I'll have one of my patrols go and check out her apartment. We can say it was an anonymous tip as a pretext for the welfare check."

"Thanks, Tippin. Let us know what you find."

"Will do," Tippin affirmed.

We didn't have a DNA sample from Anthony Stanzel or any of the Stanzels. The last person we believed to have seen Victoria alive was Priscilla Keene, and she was now seemingly missing too. Did they kill Priscilla? She had been their long-time advisor, according to the FBI. "Could Priscilla be on the run?"

"Well, I asked my guys that very question. They said she's always been a loyal Stanzel employee. But maybe they'd flip her before they'd flip one of their own—if so, she'd know it. Thirty-five years or not, blood is thicker than water."

That's what I was afraid of. We needed Priscilla Keene, but even more so, we needed to find Victoria. "Okay, we've got the PI who was following my daughter in custody. He's still not talking to us. Despite several nudgings, he's keeping his mouth shut. The Stanzels seem to have him more scared than we do.

But one of the things we threatened him with was going to the press."

"You're going to do a press conference?" Special Agent Vine asked.

"We think it might be the only way. The key to this entire investigation is Victoria Hightower. What if we had her daughter and her mother pleading for her return or information about her? We could talk to a local station about a human-interest piece—you know, long-time missing person and the family that never gave up—an inspirational kinda story."

Vincent nodded. "I could see it. I know people. We can put this together pretty fast. Of course, we've got to talk to Shannon and her grandmother to see if they'll do it."

"And keep out any information regarding the murder investigation?"

I explained my vision. "Yes, we'd keep the Stanzels and any criminal investigation out of it. But we can't have the tip line going to the police department. What I'll do is say my firm was contracted to find her, which is true, so they can only provide tips to our office. Nobody in our office is compromised by the Stanzels. Maybe anyone who knows where she is will feel more comfortable talking to one of my staff as opposed to the police."

Tippin nodded and said, "I think that could work. Make it seem unrelated, but of course, the Stanzels will know it's related."

We all sat in silence, each contemplating the risky but potentially rewarding plan. It was a gamble, but it was the best shot we had at reaching a conclusion. The stakes were high, but so was the payoff. "Yes, but if we find Victoria before they do, we can bring this whole thing down. She's the eyewitness we need to prove that Anthony Stanzel killed Nicholas Hirsch."

"Assuming your theory is correct," Special Agent Vine reminded me.

"Yes, assuming my theory is correct. But considering we already proved the theory that Victoria was at the scene, and we're pretty confident the only person who would beat her up was her pimp, who we know was Anthony Stanzel, I'm pretty confident our theory is absolutely correct. But even with DNA, I'd guess the only way we can bring down the Stanzels is if we have Victoria's eyewitness testimony."

"Sounds solid. Will the family agree?" Special Agent Vine asked.

"I think so."

Vincent chimed in. "I'll go talk to them. I'll ask them to come down here."

"Thanks, Vincent."

"Okay, so for action items. Lieutenant Tippin will have his team do a welfare check on Priscilla Keene to see if she really is gone. Then we'll move on from there. Vincent will facilitate a special news story—human-interest piece. Any tips on the whereabouts of Victoria Hightower will be directed to a tip line at Drakos Monroe," I summarized.

"I must admit, you work fast over there."

"It's easy to run when there isn't any red tape to trip over."

"Touché. Good luck, and let us know if anything comes up. We'll do the same," Special Agent Vine concluded.

With the call ended, I considered my assembled team: the FBI, Tippin of the SFPD, and Vincent. There was only one person we needed who couldn't be here for obvious reasons—Hirsch.

Vincent stood up from his chair and said, "All right, it's showtime."

"Let me know when they're here so I can be there to talk to the family."

"You got it," Vincent assured.

If this didn't work, I didn't know what would. It was our

Hail Mary to finally find out what happened to Victoria Hightower.

41

VICTORIA
PRESENT DAY

THE POPCORN POPPED, and a wave of nostalgia washed over me. Our movie nights were always a sanctuary, an echo of the peace and communal love I had found here in the convent. It was a life where everyone strived for the same goals—kindness, compassion, and service to others. I felt grateful for the makeshift family that had welcomed me so unconditionally all those years ago.

As the last kernels popped, I carried the final bowl of popcorn into the recreation room. Sisters Kate, Donna, and Suzanne were already there, eyes bright with anticipation.

"Does anybody need anything to drink? With the butter and salt on the popcorn, we might want some water," I suggested as I set the bowl down on the coffee table.

Sister Suzanne lifted her water bottle and said, "I'm all set, dear."

"Me too," Sister Donna added.

Finally, Sister Kate spoke up. "I'd love a glass."

Ah, Sister Kate—my savior. The day I met her, she saved my life. Yet, as I turned to go to the kitchen, an uneasy feeling stirred in my belly. I tried to shake it off as I filled two glasses with water and returned to the living room.

"Here you go, Sister Kate," I said, handing her the glass.

"Thank you, dear," she replied.

I was about to take my seat when something on the TV caught my eye. "What's this?" I asked.

"Looks like some sort of special-interest piece about hope. Thought it'd be great to watch before the movie," Suzanne explained.

As I stood there, my eyes glued to the screen, my heart started pounding. Displayed was a woman in her early eighties and another in her thirties. The banner at the bottom read: "Peggy and Shannon Hightower Look for Missing Woman—Thirty-five Years."

When Shannon lifted an old photograph and began speaking, my mouth dropped open. "I haven't seen my mother since I was two years old. Grandma tells me she was beautiful and smart and fun. I recently got married and decided to hire a private investigator to find my mother," Shannon said.

The reporter asked, "What do you hope they'll find?"

I felt as if time had stopped, and I stood frozen.

"We're hoping to find out what happened to her," Shannon said, staring intently at the camera. "All we know is that she was living in San Francisco thirty-five years ago. She'd been in the hospital and had called my grandmother to let her know she'd be home that day. But then, she never showed up."

Tears escaped as my mother spoke. "I believe my daughter is still out there, alive. A mother knows. That's why we agreed to come on the show. I've never given up hope that Victoria is out there. We're working with the team at Drakos Monroe Security & Investigations. They've opened up a tip line for anyone who knows or has seen Victoria to call and provide a tip. We desperately miss her and want to bring her home."

Shannon added, "Mom, if you're out there, I love you, and I miss you. The kind people at Drakos Monroe have been so great. They truly are a safe space for us, and they've said they'll do everything they can to bring you home safely." There was something in her eyes that made me believe she was sending me a message. My baby girl, all grown up and married.

My mother turned to the camera and said, "Vicky, come home."

The screen flashed my photo along with the numbers for a tip line.

Something touched my back. I dropped my glass, and it crashed to the floor, shattering into a hundred pieces. The lights hit the shards and they sparkled like glitter. I turned and stammered, "Suzanne. Oh, dear, I dropped my glass."

"Are you okay, Maisie?" Sister Suzanne asked.

Tears streaming down my cheeks, I shook my head back and forth.

"Let me help you sit down," Sister Suzanne said, taking me by the hand and guiding me to my seat.

"I need to clean up the glass."

"We can do that for you, dear," Sister Donna offered.

"Do you want to talk about what you just saw?" Sister Kate asked gently.

I glanced up at Suzanne, Donna, and Kate, then back at the television screen where they had displayed my photograph. "That's my baby. Right there on the screen," I choked out.

Sister Kate said, "Maybe it's time to tell us what happened."

I had kept my story close to my chest, but it was time to reveal the truth to the sisters who had given me a second family. I wondered if they would look at me differently once they knew, but I couldn't worry about that. It was time.

42

MARTINA

Pacing the hallway, I was tired of being cooped up inside my office and tired of the safe house. The case needed to end. I needed my life to go back to normal—whatever "normal" was anymore. When I took on Victoria's case, it never crossed my mind that my own life—and my daughter's life—would be in danger. This investigation had unraveled far more than we had bargained for. Since the garbage didn't yield any useful DNA, all we could do was wait for reliable tips from the hotline. So far, the calls had kept us busy, but as expected, most tips were dead ends.

Sometimes I wondered what motivated people to call in false tips on a missing persons case. Did they realize how much damage they were doing? Sure, some of them had mental health issues and probably thought they had seen Victoria, but the others were simply awful, thinking it was funny to play with people's emotions. My theory was these people could only commit these vile acts because they had never been through anything as traumatic as losing a loved one. Good for them.

Because of these misleading callers—whom my gut instinct and investigative skills told me were no more than time-wasters

—my role had been reduced to answering phones with erroneous tips. Not a single one had panned out, not even close. I shook my head in frustration.

Just then, my desk phone rang. I hurried back inside my office and answered, "Martina Monroe."

"Hi, dear. How are you?"

"Hi, Mom. Frustrated, impatient—the usual."

"I'm so sorry, honey. I wish there were something I could do. How's Zoey?"

"She's fine. She's probably coping a little better than I am."

"That's good. She's resilient, that one."

"How is Barney doing?"

"He's settled right in. I think he's confused, but he seems to be quite taken with Ted and follows him everywhere. I'm feeling a little jealous. I'm usually the favorite!"

I chuckled. "I know how you feel." When Zoey was little, she was enamored with Kim and talked about her nonstop. She wanted to be just like her. Over time, I came to realize that it was a good thing since Kim was a great role model and liked to do all the glittery things that Zoey enjoyed.

"Okay, well, I'm just checking in. Saying prayers the case gets solved soon and the Hirsch family can finally get some closure, or at least find out what happened to Nick and why. They deserve justice."

"Yes, they do," I agreed. And although I had my theory about Nick's murder, I needed evidence to prove it and put those responsible for his death and the subsequent cover-up behind bars.

Just then, Vincent appeared in front of my window. "I've got to go, Mom. Vincent's here."

"Okay, take care, honey. I love you."

"I love you too, Mom." I hung up and walked over to my door, opening it. "Hey, Vincent. What's up?"

"I just got a call from Tippin. He has an update."

"Is it about Priscilla Keene?"

"It is."

"Can we get the FBI and him on a call?"

"They're on the call. Tippin said he'll dial in. We just need you."

Finally, movement on the case. "All right."

We hurried back to the conference room, and I shut the door behind us. "Hi, Martina and Vincent are here." My adrenaline spiked as I waited for the update.

"Great, we have Tippin dialing in now too."

Conference calls at their best. "Hi, it's Tippin," emanated from the speaker.

"Okay, we have me, Martina, Vincent, Agent Honeycutt, and Tippin, so we can get started."

Tippin said, "I went with the team to do a welfare check at Priscilla Keene's apartment. Inside was empty; she was nowhere to be found. We also went by her office and confirmed that she hasn't shown up for work in a week. We checked registration at local hotels, travel reservations, and hospitals. No movement on her main bank account since last week. We're still diving into other possible financials like offshore accounts and investments. They'll take a little longer, but with the info we have, I'd say she's gone."

"Was there any sign of a disturbance at her apartment or in her office?"

"No, it was as if 'poof,' she vanished. While I was at her office, Maurice Stanzel showed up and said he was very concerned about his dear friend and colleague."

"Did you buy it?"

"Honestly, he looked worried. Maybe not about her welfare, but maybe about her running off or talking to the police."

Interesting. "Any rumblings about Priscilla from the FBI team?"

"Just that she's missing, and things are at a bit of a standstill with the DeMarcos and the Stanzels, which I suspect is because of your investigation."

"So, we have nothing. We have no reliable tips from the hotline. Priscilla Keene is officially missing. We're running out of options here."

The room and the call were silent.

This was frustrating. Continuing to live cooped up, surrounded by security at all times, I felt like a caged lion ready to go on the hunt. Instead, they were throwing me little bits of vegan meat via conference calls. *I don't love it.*

Tippin finally broke the silence. "What about the PI the sheriff has in custody? Is he still not talking?"

"He's not, but we could go at him again. We'll need coopera- tion from the CoCo County Sheriff's Department, but I don't think it will be a problem. I'd like to go at him hard until he breaks."

Agent Honeycutt chimed in. "You could tell him we believe they killed Priscilla Keene to keep her quiet and that he's next."

For all we knew, it was true. "I like the way you think. I'll arrange it with CoCo County."

Not to mention, I needed to update Hirsch on what was going on with his brother's case. He wasn't allowed to be involved, but he could get regular updates. They would have to escort me so that no one would see me going in and out of the building. Well, they might see me anyway, but I would be surrounded by law enforcement, making it a stupid move on any assassin's part to come after me. I could have let Vincent handle it, but I needed it. Plus, I could be a lot scarier than Vincent and planned to be. Rex Kleinman, PI, needed to know we were serious.

Special Agent Vine added, "While you try to get the PI to talk, we'll divert some resources to tracking down Priscilla. Chances are they killed her to silence her, or she's on the run. If she's alive, I bet she has a few stories she could share. And I for one would love to hear them."

Exactly. Fingers crossed they found her and made it clear it was in Ms. Keene's best interest to turn on the Stanzels. If she didn't, she would have me to contend with.

43

MARTINA

Sitting across from Hirsch, I looked into his baby blues and could feel his grief. "How is your family handling the news?"

"They're eager for those who killed Nick to be brought to justice, to go to jail—just like I am."

I could sense there was something more, something he wasn't saying. "Well, I think that will happen. It's just taking a little longer than we'd like. I think our theory is pretty sound. Stanzel killed Nick because he got in the way of him potentially killing Victoria."

Hirsch sighed. "You know, it's funny how one of Nick's greatest traits may have also been his downfall. He was always helping everyone—strangers, family, friends, people in the community. Even as young as he was, he was so incredible. Even to me, his little brother. He was never bothered when I wanted to tag along and hang out with his friends when they came over to watch movies or just hang out."

"I wish I could've known Nick," I said softly.

"You would've gotten along for sure. You both have a big, no, a *huge* heart."

With a reassuring smile, I said, "We will get justice for him. For you—for your whole family. Did you get a chance to talk to the DA about Rex Kleinman?"

"He's coordinating a deal with the FBI. If anything he tells us leads to an arrest, we'll give him a deal, even full immunity along with witness protection, if necessary," Hirsch explained.

I frowned slightly. I didn't think this guy quite deserved it, but he wasn't the big fish, and he hadn't hurt anybody that we knew of. "You're okay with this? And your family's okay with this?"

He nodded. "We all agree. We want them to pay for what they did. Nick deserved so much better than what he got."

"I know this is a lot, and probably brings up a lot of old and new feelings, but I guess I have to ask, Hirsch—is there anything else that's bothering you?"

He smirked. "I guess I've lost my poker face."

"Perhaps you got that from me."

His eyes brightened just a tad. "Perhaps. To top all this off, we didn't get great news from Kim's doctor," he said rather sadly. "It's been confirmed—secondary infertility. And due to her age, IVF is not a great option."

"I'm so sorry, Hirsch. Please tell Kim that I'm so sorry too, and as soon as all this is over, I'll tell her myself," I assured him.

The weight of our conversation hung heavy between us. With hearts full of sorrow and hope, we both wondered what the next chapter would bring.

"You know, before Kim, I never really believed I would ever have kids or a happy marriage. Then she came along and made me see all these possibilities and opened up all these new experiences—like getting married and having children. I feel selfish for being so sad that we can only have one child, and I feel terrible even saying 'only one child,' but I'm sad. I'm disappointed. It makes me think about the bigger picture. We're finally going to find out what happened to Nick, and that's a great thing. We're all so grateful. My mom and dad are ecstatic and can't wait to thank you in person. But then there's another sad thing shadowing it a bit, you know? It's almost like things always seem to even out. Something bad happens, and something good happens," Hirsch said, his voice tinged with emotion.

I felt terrible for Hirsch and Kim. There really wasn't a better couple to bring another life into this world. But they were both tough. I knew they'd get through it. "Sometimes, I think you're right," I said. "I've been to the bottom and to the top—well, not the top—but I always feel like we land somewhere in the middle. We just take the wins as they come and be grateful."

"I know, and we are. We're so grateful, but we're allowing ourselves to grieve for the future children we now know we won't have."

"That sounds like a healthy approach, Hirsch."

"Between you and me, ripping into the PI who followed Zoey would make me feel a lot better, but I know I can't," he admitted with a hint of regret.

"Well, it just so happens that I plan to rip this guy apart. So, if you want to watch from outside the room, I'll put on a great show for you," I said, wiggling my eyebrows.

"Sounds like a great plan to me."

We headed outside and down the hall, meeting up with Vincent, Ross, and Jayda.

"You ready to go get him?" Ross inquired, a look of anticipation on his face.

"I'm ready. I've been caged up and I'm ready to pounce," I confirmed.

"I can't wait to see it," Ross said, smiling with evident amusement.

Vincent and I took the lead, entering the conference room

where Rex Kleinman was looking a little worse for wear. We both sat down, and I locked eyes with him. "How's County?"

"I've had better accommodations."

"I can imagine. Working for high-rollers, I'm sure they pay a pretty penny. From one PI to another, I get why you'd want to keep your client roster quiet. I'm sure there's a big payday in it for you."

He looked away.

After a nod to Vincent, he took the cue. "So, Mr. Kleinman, we have some news for you. We're hoping it changes your mind about a few things."

Kleinman looked at Vincent and said, "I doubt it, but give it your best shot."

"I was just talking to Sergeant Hirsch. I don't know if that name sounds familiar to you?" Vincent probed.

"Should it?" Kleinman countered.

Vincent looked at me, and I took over, saying, "Well, he's the sergeant overseeing all the homicide detectives and narcotics officers here in CoCo County. He's not working the case because he's got a big interest in it, you see. We think at least one of your employers killed Sergeant Hirsch's brother thirty-five years ago, and the others covered it up. We're just waiting on the DNA."

It wasn't exactly true, but it certainly got his attention.

"As you know, while Vincent and I initially started out our investigation looking for Victoria Hightower, we've uncovered quite an interesting tale. We've learned that an innocent bystander, a Good Samaritan, was killed by Anthony Stanzel—all because this Good Samaritan was trying to protect Victoria. And that innocent bystander, that Good Samaritan, was Nicholas Hirsch. He's Sergeant Hirsch's brother. How's that for a twist? You think you're ever getting out of this? You think we'll ever stop going at you? Not only did you go after my daughter, who refers to Sergeant Hirsch as 'Uncle August,' *by the way*, but you're protecting Sergeant Hirsch's brother's killer. You're lucky you're even getting a deal at all."

Rex raised an eyebrow. Based on his reaction, I would guess the surprise wasn't the connection to Hirsch but that we were offering him a deal.

"That's right, we've been talking to the DA along with the FBI, and they're willing to give you immunity and witness protection in exchange for your testimony—if it leads to the arrest of your employer—the one who hired you to follow my daughter."

Rex leaned back, as if contemplating his options.

The last time we spoke, he seemed to be almost on the verge of telling us something. And I felt it then. The air in the room was shifting. I turned to Vincent. "I'm forgetting something, right?"

Vincent played along, feigning ignorance. "Oh, did you tell him about how Stanzel got rid of Priscilla Keene?"

That definitely got Rex's attention. He stared at me, questioning.

"That's right, Priscilla Keene is no more. Do you have any idea how easy it is to get to somebody inside County lockup? Just to shank them or pay off a guard to look the other way? If you don't cooperate with us, you're a dead man." I leaned over, practically spitting my words at Rex Kleinman.

He shifted in his seat and finally asked, "Is everything you're saying true?"

"Yes," I confirmed, locking eyes with Rex Kleinman. "But I think the real question you need to ask yourself, Rex, is this. Are you willing to die for the Stanzels? Are you willing to let them get to you in County lockup? Are you willing to take your chances with the criminal justice system when you've not only gone after one of their own—my daughter—but you're also connected to a sergeant's brother's murder? You either get protection from us and cooperate, or you're finished—never to be heard from or seen again. Do you understand that?" My voice rose, far more than I would typically allow it to.

"I want it in writing," Rex finally responded.

I leaned back and turned to Vincent, nodding. Vincent stood up and exited the room to speak with the DA about formalizing our agreement.

"To get the deal, you need to provide all the information you have, including proof that whatever you tell us is true. If you lie to us, we'll know. And if you haven't learned this about me yet, I don't give up. I will keep coming at you until you're so worn down, you won't even recognize yourself in the mirror."

"Look, lady, I hear you. Get it in writing, and I'll tell you everything I know."

"Will it lead to arrests?" I pressed.

He nodded.

With a smug smile, I said, "Was that so hard?"

"You would have done the same in my position."

"Look, I offer client confidentiality, and I'm part-owner of my own firm, which I'm sure you already know. But the difference between you and me is that I don't work for scumbags, murderers, or criminals. That's what sets us apart. It's not just a payday for me. I seek justice and do what's right. Maybe you should give it a shot," I retorted.

He let out a breath and said, "Okay, I hear you. And no, I'm not willing to die for them. But you better make sure they keep me safe because you and I both know they don't leave witnesses."

His words hung in the air, a heavy reminder of the stakes at play. I let them sink in, praying to God that Victoria wasn't lost forever—that the reason no credible tips had come in to the hotline wasn't because she was dead and buried, never to be found. Because we needed her. We needed her story to convict Anthony Stanzel for Nick's murder. And her family and Nancy deserved to know what had happened to her.

I stared at Rex Kleinman and said a small prayer that whatever information he gave us would lead us to the truth—and to Victoria Hightower.

44

MARTINA

Leaning up against the wall, I watched as Detective Ross placed the papers down in front of Rex Kleinman. Ross folded his arms across his chest and said, "You sure you don't want a lawyer?"

"I'll be fine, thank you," Kleinman responded.

"Are you sure? We can call him for you."

"I fired my legal counsel."

It was quite an interesting turn of events. Had Kleinman's attorney been paid for by the Stanzels, or whoever his client was? That was the only conceivable reason I could think of for why he would not want his lawyer present. He must have been afraid the attorney would tip off his client that he'd ratted them out. We didn't know if Priscilla Keene had been murdered by the Stanzels, but no one doubted they'd come after Kleinman if he spilled their dark family secrets.

Ross joined me against the wall and spoke quietly. "Let's hope he tells us the truth, and we can prove it."

I looked at him and said, "No kidding. This case needs to be over soon, you know what I mean?"

"On so many levels," he agreed.

It was true. I was beyond over living in a safe house. And Zoey was certainly going a little batty. She always had a lot of energy and spent most of her time at the gym in the apartment complex where we were staying. But even she had her limits, and I certainly did too. Not to mention, we both wanted to finally get justice for Hirsch's brother and find out what happened to Victoria Hightower. There were too many open questions, and I didn't like it one bit.

The burner cell phone buzzed in my pocket. It was my mom. I ignored the call and returned my focus to Rex Kleinman. If he complied with the terms of his deal, he would have immunity and a whole new identity, thanks to the federal government. That is, assuming he had enough information that would warrant such a generous offer.

What would he do with his new life? Becoming a private investigator would be a really stupid choice, considering he'd have to be licensed wherever he went. And without any investigative experience, he couldn't get a license.

Pushing the papers to the side, Kleinman finally said, "This is acceptable."

"Glad to hear it. You're probably dying to figure out what your new life is gonna look like, but first you have to tell us what you know, starting with why you were following my daughter, Zoey Monroe," I said, wanting to be clear for the recorder.

"I was hired by the Stanzel Corporation. That's who paid me. I've been working for them for several years, looking into backgrounds on potential business clients, vetting new employees, and scouting different sites for their activities," Kleinman explained.

"Activities?"

"For example, they would ask me to scout out a new hotel or a new housing development for prospective clients and employees who may need temporary housing. That's what they told me, anyhow."

I cocked my head, puzzled. "They never gave you any additional information about why they wanted you to scope out temporary housing for their employees and potential clients from out of town?"

"Let's just get this on the table. The Stanzels provide orders, they don't answer questions," Kleinman clarified.

I nodded, understanding what he was saying.

He continued, "I didn't ask questions. It would've been frowned upon."

"Okay, so you've worked for the Stanzels for several years. What is the latest job they came to you with, including dates and names of who you met with pertaining to Zoey Monroe and Martina Monroe—me?"

"Initially, I had a conversation on the phone with Priscilla Keene. She said we needed to have a meeting, and it had to be with the head guy, the big boss, Maurice Stanzel. So, I assumed it was a pretty big deal. I didn't usually work with Maurice Stanzel. Most of my interactions were between me and Priscilla Keene."

"Understood. So, what happened during that first meeting with Maurice Stanzel and Priscilla Keene?"

"First, they requested that I find out who Martina, the private investigator, was. This Martina, a PI, had visited with Anthony Stanzel, asking questions about Victoria Hightower. That same PI questioned Priscilla Keene about Victoria Hightower. They wanted to know everything I could find on Martina."

"Interesting," I commented. He eyed me, and I urged him to continue. "Go on."

"So, I took the assignment. I learned who Martina, the PI, was. It was, in fact, Martina Monroe of Drakos Monroe Security

& Investigations. I looked into her past employment, her contract with the CoCo County Sheriff's Department Cold Case Squad, and found newspaper stories about her involvement in solving high-profile cases. I also looked into her background, family members, friends, and associates," Kleinman continued. "I brought that information to Priscilla and Maurice Stanzel in a second meeting. I explained that, based on my findings about Martina Monroe, it was highly unlikely she would stop investigating."

Ross nudged me and gave me a smile. "Got to admit, he's pretty good," he said.

I shrugged. "Go on."

"Well, based on my assessment and the sensitivity around Ms. Victoria Hightower—which I did not inquire about—I provided the entire report of my findings to Priscilla Keene and Maurice Stanzel."

"And then what did they ask you to do?"

"They thanked me. I went on my way. They called me back for another meeting, and that's when they made the decision that the only way to make you stop investigating the case was to eliminate you."

Ross blurted out, "You put a hit out on Martina?"

"Yes. Maurice Stanzel and Priscilla Keene requested I find somebody to follow Martina and kill her," Kleinman admitted.

The revelation was chilling, and goose bumps went down my body. The shots fired at my house were not a warning; they really wanted to kill me. "Not to state the obvious, since I am Martina Monroe, but I was not killed. Can you explain why?"

"I talked them out of it. I explained it wouldn't be advisable because you, Martina Monroe, have friends in the police department, the sheriff's department, and at Drakos Monroe, who would likely stop at nothing to avenge your death."

It was true. Then why did they shoot up my house? "Why did you start following Zoey?"

"The theory, or the idea, was passed that maybe the best way to get to you was through your daughter. Not to kill her, but to keep her hostage until you agreed to back down and stop investigating."

He was planning to kidnap Zoey—to inflict unspeakable trauma on my baby girl. It took all of my resolve to not throttle Rex. "Doesn't sound like a very sound plan to me," I said, venom in my voice.

"No, it wasn't great, and obviously, it didn't come to fruition. But I did follow Zoey Monroe from her school through the neighborhood to the grocery store, where I spotted Martina Monroe in the parking lot and proceeded to leave. You know the rest of the story," he concluded.

"To summarize, Maurice Stanzel and Priscilla Keene hired you to investigate Martina Monroe and then to follow and kidnap her daughter until she agreed to stop investigating Victoria Hightower's disappearance?"

"Yes," he confirmed.

"It makes sense, but it doesn't answer all my questions," I said, still puzzled. "So, somebody shot at my house. That obviously wasn't you because you were already in custody. Do you know anything about that?"

"I don't, but what I can say is that I know I wasn't the only private investigator or hired gun the Stanzels employed. I'm just one of them."

"You're saying they decided to put a hit on Martina anyway, just using somebody else?" Ross asked.

"That's purely speculation, but if I had to guess, yeah, or as a warning."

"Did you know why Victoria Hightower's whereabouts were so important to protect?"

"Not at first. It was obvious she was very valuable to the Stanzels, and they asked me to find her but came up empty-handed. During my research I found the possible connection to Sergeant Hirsch's brother's murder thirty-five years ago. I put two and two together and figured it must have been Anthony who killed Nicholas Hirsch."

My body froze. If Rex was hired to find Victoria, it meant that she hadn't been killed by the Stanzels or Priscilla. "So, they believe she's still alive?"

"From what I understand, it's a possibility. But I couldn't find her or her new identity."

"Her new identity?"

"Yes, she changed her name to Maisie Ficke when she left thirty-five years earlier."

She had left on her own? And changed her name? "Any idea why she changed her name?" My mind was swirling. We expected Rex to tell us who had hired him, but the revelation that Victoria hadn't been killed was most unexpected. Her mother's intuition was correct, and my gut was telling me Victoria was out there, we just had to find her.

"No idea."

"What else do you know about Victoria?"

"Nothing. I was given the names Victoria Hightower and Maisie Ficke and the order to find her. There wasn't a whiff of her anywhere in the United States."

Where was Victoria? I turned to Ross. "Is it enough to arrest Maurice Stanzel and Priscilla Keene, if we can find her?"

"We need to prove it, first." Ross eyed Kleinman. "What do you have to prove that all of this is true?"

Kleinman smiled. "I always carry insurance. I recorded all my conversations with the Stanzels and Priscilla Keene. The recordings are in my office."

I had to admit, Rex Kleinman was thorough and seemed like

an excellent private investigator. It was too bad he chose to work for the dark side. He could've been a real asset.

Ross said, "All right, sit tight, and I'll go put together a team to retrieve them from your office. Once we hear the recordings, your duties are fulfilled, and we'll start working with the feds to get you into custody."

"I'll be waiting."

Before I walked out, I added, "It's too bad you chose to work for criminals. We could use someone with your talent."

"Sometimes life leads us down a dark path, one that doesn't seem to have any other options. And once you're on it, you're in it, and you can't leave," Kleinman explained.

Maybe he wasn't all bad or wasn't always bad. "Take care of yourself," I advised, exiting the conference room.

Outside were Vincent and Hirsch. "You catch all that?"

Vincent said, "Yeah, I hope we can find those tapes."

District Attorney Greggs walked up. "How's our guy?"

"He told us a lot. Ross is going to work with the team to retrieve some evidence he says is in his office."

"Excellent. You can escort the prisoner there to make it faster if you need to. So, does it seem like enough for an arrest?" Greggs asked.

Hirsch chimed in. "He says he recorded Priscilla Keene and Maurice Stanzel conspiring to commit murder and kidnapping."

"Now we hope the recordings are where Kleinman says they are," Vincent added.

Indeed.

"Nice work. Good to see you, Martina. You staying out of trouble?" Greggs chuckled.

"I'm trying." I smiled back.

Greggs winked and said, "All right, let me know when you need the arrest warrants. We'll get this done quickly to make sure nobody decides to flee once they realize we're coming after them."

"Will do." I nodded, turning to Hirsch. "How are you doing?"

"We're close, I can feel it." Hirsch beamed.

I patted him on the shoulder and thought to myself, *We will absolutely get them. Nobody gets away with trying to kill me and kidnap my daughter or with murdering my best friend's brother. Not while I'm still breathing.*

45

PRISCILLA

PRESENT DAY

THE REFLECTION in the mirror was a stranger to me, with its badly dyed red hair. I'm not talking about a pleasant, natural redhead orange, but red—like a clown or a shiny apple. The jeans I'd purchased at a secondhand thrift shop, along with the matching Mickey Mouse T-shirt and sweatshirt, seemed like a bizarre costume. What really pulled the whole outfit together was an Army surplus jacket riddled with tears and stains. These imperfections complemented my worn, white, generic canvas sneakers quite well.

Although the reflection looked foreign, there was something about it that rang true. I'd once been "one of them," a person you'd overlook or dismiss, and I'd sworn I'd never go back to that life. I wouldn't—at least not permanently. My mission was to blend in, and if that meant putting up with some lewd comments from the guards, it was a small price to pay for my freedom.

Going incognito was the only viable option. The stakes were high, and I couldn't risk Maurice or the DeMarcos finding out I'd requested documentation to leave the country. Not that I doubted they were searching for me—they likely were.

However, the disguise offered a layer of protection. I didn't think any of them had ever seen me in anything other than a power suit or a chic cocktail dress, my hair perfectly styled and makeup flawless, usually paired with high heels. The only person who had seen me differently was Maurice Stanzel.

Meeting Maurice was a turning point. I'd been working the streets, just like all the others, but something about him was different. I knew I could reach him. He recognized that I was more than just another drug addict seeking a fix. I wanted out, I wanted more, and I understood the business. So, yes, Maurice started as one of my johns, but with a little nudging and some incriminating photographs, I convinced him to give me a chance to prove that I was more than my physical appearance. I was more than just a body used for men's pleasure.

I'd always been more than that, and recognizing it now stung with a mix of regret and insight. I couldn't help but pity the women, men, boys, and girls who were still trapped in that life. In this world, there are winners and losers, and I refused to be a loser ever again.

Trusting in the Stanzels was a fool's game, one where I was destined to lose. And because of that, I had to win, which meant I had to leave the country. I didn't have much holding me back in the US anyway—just business associates, faux friends at the country club, Michelin-starred restaurants, and charity galas that were really just excuses to get dolled up and wear the latest Prada.

So, as I looked in the mirror at the disheveled reflection, I couldn't help but wonder if I had really clawed my way out. I thought I'd escaped, but our past has a way of reeling us back in, reminding us that we can never truly escape.

It was time to make the appropriate preparations. It should take anyone looking into my finances a while to figure out how I'd moved and protected my money.

As soon as I landed in my new sanctuary, I would have to act swiftly. I knew the system's weaknesses, and I knew how to exploit them. I had watched others try and fail to escape. I had learned from their mistakes. A lot of thought went into what I would do next. Could I truly start over with a clean slate? Was going clean even possible? Or was my soul so tarnished that no amount of polish in the world could bring it back to its original luster?

A part of me—perhaps the part that still had a sliver of a soul—wondered if I even deserved a clean slate. Was I capable of it after all the things I had done, all the things I continued to do for the last thirty-five years? If someone ever asked me if I felt guilty, what would my answer be?

Talking to myself, I pondered the question. The answer was complicated. Sometimes I did feel bad, as if I had lost some essential part of my humanity. I hadn't committed the deeds with my own hands, but I was complicit. I knew what was going on, I didn't stop it, and I profited from it. If Hell existed, I was convinced there would be a special place reserved just for me. So, yes, sometimes I felt guilty. At other times, I justified my actions, telling myself that I was just trying to survive. But maybe that was a lie I told myself in order to sleep at night.

Taking a deep breath, I tussled my hair and exited the cheap motel room, making my way to the dock. It was time to say goodbye to San Francisco once and for all. I couldn't say I'd left my heart there—just, perhaps, my soul.

46

MARTINA

IN A SMALL ROOM BY MYSELF, I called my mom back. "Hey, Mom, sorry I missed your call. I was interviewing a suspect."

"Oh, okay. Where are you?"

"I'm at the sheriff's department. Why? What's wrong?" There was worry in her voice. I feared something had happened. Was it Zoey? Barney? Ted?

"Oh, good. Something's happened, Martina. Something really bad, and I need your help."

"Mom, you're worrying me. What is it?"

My pulse quickened, and I feared the worst.

"Darren's been arrested."

Darren had been arrested several times before, so I didn't understand why this was urgent news or why she thought I could help. My brothers, Darren and Clark, were known drug dealers, in and out of jail for drugs, theft, burglary, and grand theft auto. I hadn't spoken to either of them in years, but Mom kept in touch. "I don't see how I could help."

"You don't understand. He's been arrested for murder."

"Murder?" Now, that would be a first. Was Darren really capable of murder? He did live in a world filled with drug dealers and criminals, so I supposed it wasn't too much of a leap for him to become a killer. But could a person I shared DNA with have killed someone?

Growing up, Darren and Clark were always in trouble. I was the little sister they liked to pick on when they weren't busy finding girls to take advantage of. "Hellions" was a good way to describe them. Sometimes, when I was younger, I thought they were what drove my mother to drink. It was either them or my father, who had died and, from what I understood, wasn't much better than Darren or Clark. I had kept my distance to protect my family and my sobriety, but Mom had never been able to let go completely. They were her babies.

"He called me. He was arrested just an hour ago. Some homicide detectives from the sheriff's department. He called me with his one phone call. I told him to ask for a lawyer and not to say anything. He swears he didn't do it. He said he didn't kill anyone."

"So, he's here at the CoCo County Sheriff's Department?"

"Yes."

"Did he explain to you why he was arrested? What evidence they have? Anything?"

This was literally the last thing I needed.

"They say they have fingerprints on money that was in the guy's pocket and on a bag of drugs. They think Darren sold the drugs to him. They think there was an altercation, and Darren killed him."

"If Darren killed him, why would he leave the drugs and the money?"

"See, Martina, this is why we need you. You're right. It doesn't make sense."

"Unless he panicked and fled as soon as he realized what he'd done." I wasn't jumping to the conclusion Darren was innocent. The detectives at CoCo County were smart and good police. They wouldn't have arrested him with no evidence. "Okay, Mom, do you know if he's asked for a public defender?"

"I don't know. I told him I'd call you and that you're good friends with the head of the homicide division."

Great. Here we were, trying to solve the murder of Hirsch's brother, and I had to go asking for help for my brother who might have killed someone? I supposed I shouldn't assume he did it—innocent until proven guilty and all that. But I didn't put much past Darren or my brother Clark. "I'll talk to the arresting officer and see what's going on. But he needs a lawyer ASAP. No matter what, he needs a lawyer." Everyone deserved a proper defense.

"Okay, Martina. Let me know what you find out."

"Yes, I'll call you as soon as I hear anything. But I am in the middle of something."

"Oh, sorry. I know you are, and gosh, to even ask this—I just can't believe it. Darren wouldn't kill anyone. I know my baby, I know him."

I did have a little time while Ross and the team went to retrieve the recording devices implicating Stanzel and Keene. "Okay, I'm waiting for some evidence to come back, so I'll go see what I can find out. I'll call you back."

"Thank you, Martina."

I hung up and shook my head as I walked over to Hirsch's office and knocked on the door. "Hey, Hirsch."

"What's up? Everything okay? I mean, other than the current situation in your life?"

"The plot thickens," I said and then explained my brother had been arrested for murder.

"I need to know the details of his case."

"Do you think he did it?"

"I have no idea. I haven't talked to him since I was eighteen years old, when he showed up for my high school graduation.

And then, I think he left with some friends to go get high." Not that I hadn't done the same after we took photos. The difference between my brothers and me was that I turned my life around. Saw the errors of my younger ways. They hadn't.

"Well, I can look up the arresting officer, but I can't give you the case file."

"That's fine. I just want to know if there's really anything to this."

"All right." He turned to his computer and looked up my brother in the system. "Oh, well, you know the arresting officer."

"Who is it?"

"Detective Leslie."

From the old Cold Case Squad. She probably didn't even know that Darren Kolze was my brother. Most people didn't know my maiden name. I'd kept my married name after Jared's death with no reason to change it. Plus, it was my daughter's name, and I wanted us to share it. I was her only living parent. "All right, I'll go talk to Leslie."

"Good luck," Hirsch said with a furrowed brow.

What a way to start the new year.

I knocked on Detective Leslie's cubicle wall.

"Hey, Martina. Good to see you. What's up?"

"Oh, everything. Living in a safe house, investigating Hirsch's brother's murder, looking for missing persons, powerful families putting a hit out on me—you know, the usual."

Leslie chuckled. "Well, sounds like the same old, same old for Martina Monroe."

"Not exactly. The reason I'm actually here is that my brother was arrested today. By you, for murder."

Leslie cocked her head and said, "He was?"

"Darren Kolze, K-O-L-Z-E."

She looked at me like she couldn't believe Darren Kolze was my brother.

"He's my older brother. We're not close."

"I'll say. Sounds like you've taken very different paths in life."

"We have. My mom called, wants me to figure out a way to help him. What I want to know is what you have. Did he do it?"

Leslie shrugged. "There's a lot of physical evidence against him, and an eyewitness. It looks like it'll be a slam-dunk case."

That was not the news I wanted to hear—or rather the news I wanted to deliver to my mother. "You're kidding?"

"No, he shot the man point-blank. We have an eyewitness, plus a slew of other physical evidence."

"Who's the witness?"

"I can't tell you that, Martina. Sorry. I know he's your brother and you're a friend of the department, but I can't compromise the case."

"I hear you. Did he ask for a lawyer?"

"He did."

"Good. Any way I could see him real quick, just for a few words?" It was not a privilege usually granted to just anyone. I was asking for a huge favor.

Leslie hesitated, and I understood.

"You can be there. I just want to—look, I haven't talked to him in twenty years. Please? Just give me a few minutes."

"Okay, come with me."

I followed Leslie, keenly aware that my brother was about to receive different treatment than any other prisoner—simply because he was my brother. Not that we were close, but our blood tie alone was enough for him to get special favors.

Was I any different from the Stanzels, using my position and friends to help my brother? If he really was guilty, I certainly wouldn't cover it up. But I wanted to make sure he protected himself. Even if guilty, he deserved to be treated fairly.

We waited for a few minutes while the guards retrieved my brother. It was the strangest family reunion I could never have dreamt up. "Thanks for doing this, Leslie. Let me tell you, this is not great timing, and like I said, I haven't seen my brother in twenty years. So, this is really a favor for my mom."

"Understood. If it were my brother, I'd be here too."

"Thanks for understanding."

"Plus, I know you're solid," Leslie said, nudging me with her elbow.

I was feeling more like I was going to crumble at any second, but I could fake it until I made it. "I try."

Just then, an officer appeared at the door, leading a prisoner with shackles on his ankles and wrists. His hair was a mess, and his amber eyes were bloodshot. As Darren and I locked eyes, he cocked his head, obviously surprised to see me.

"Let's go to the first conference room here," Leslie directed.

They set Darren down, and I took a seat across from him.

"Hi, Darren."

"Little sister."

Leslie gave me a look, as if she couldn't believe anyone would refer to me as "little sister" or "little" anything. "I'd ask how you're doing, but I just got a call from Mom. She says you've been arrested for murder."

"I didn't do it, Martina," he said, shaking his head in frustration. "What are you doing here, anyway?"

"Well, Mom called me because I was here on business. She asked me to check in on you." Given that our mother had married the former sergeant, it was more than likely Darren knew I had close ties to the sheriff's department.

"I see. You must have friends if they let you in here?"

"I do. So, listen, I only have a little bit of time with you, and luckily, Detective Leslie let me talk to you. I need you to listen.

First of all, do not speak to the police or anyone without a lawyer. Second of all, listen to your lawyer."

"Understood," Darren said, nodding.

I glanced over at Leslie, who smirked at me. She had to know I would advise my brother to make sure he didn't speak to the police without a lawyer present.

"But Martina, you've gotta understand. I'm no saint, and I've done some bad things, I won't lie about that. But you have to believe me when I say I did not kill that man. This is a set-up."

Could he be telling the truth? "I'm not a lawyer, but you need to get one. He or she's the one who's going to help defend you. I'm just here to check in on you and make sure you understand that and that you're being treated fairly. Are you?"

"I'm fine," Darren confirmed.

"Good. Don't say a word until your lawyer gets here."

"Understood," he repeated, as I stood up to leave. But then he stopped me. "Martina."

I glanced back at my brother, shackled, a criminal hardened by so many years of drug and alcohol use and rough living. "Yeah?"

"Thank you for coming. I'm sorry I wasn't a better brother or uncle. I hear Zoey's real smart and going to college."

I swallowed hard. "She is. She's incredible," I said softly. "You take care. I have some business to attend to, but I'll check in on you later."

I turned and exited, trying to fight the tears. But it had been a long day, a long few weeks. People were trying to kill me and kidnap my daughter, and now my brother was in jail for murder. It was too much. Tears escaped my eyes.

Leslie noticed, and in a flash, she was in the break room, returning quickly with tissues. I wiped my eyes and said, "Thanks, Leslie."

"Rough day?"

"You have no idea. Just found out there's a hit out on me from some powerful people. It's not as sexy as it sounds."

"Not to mention you had a prison reunion with your brother. I'm sorry, Martina."

"Thanks. I gotta get back to the team. We need to see if we can issue an arrest warrant for a really, really bad guy."

"Good luck," Leslie said.

I headed back over to Hirsch's office where Ross and Vincent were hanging around outside. Hirsch looked up at me and asked, "Everything okay?"

I shook my head. "A battle for another day," I replied, then looked at Vincent. "I'll tell you later." I turned to Ross. "Did we find the recordings?"

"Yep, and they're labeled—organized neatly. We listened on the drive over—we've got them."

"Everything Kleinman said is true?"

"Yep, and he has it recorded. He even claims he's got financial statements to back up that he was employed by them. This is solid ground for an arrest warrant for Maurice Stanzel and Priscilla Keene."

"Good. When we bring him in, we'll swab him for DNA. Anyone arrested on suspicion of a felony has to be tested."

Hirsch nodded as if he understood what that meant. We could be learning very soon exactly who killed his brother. "Let's get the warrant to pick him up," Ross said.

Vincent added, "I'll call Tippin from SFPD."

My body relaxed a bit with the news we were going to arrest Maurice Stanzel and Priscilla Keene and get DNA to test against the physical evidence found at Hirsch's brother's crime scene. The case could be coming to an end very soon, and I couldn't wait.

MARTINA

DARK CIRCLES RIMMED MY EYES. My skin was pasty and my hair dull. I hadn't gotten any sleep the night before and needed caffeine as if it were oxygen and I was on life support. But nothing would stop me from going in. Maurice Stanzel was at the CoCo County Sheriff's Department with his attorney, and nothing would stop me from talking to him face to face. Ross and Tippin had already tried to have a conversation with him, but he wasn't talking—not a peep. But they had managed to swab for DNA, so that was something. With a rush order at the lab, we would know within the next forty-eight hours if Anthony Stanzel was responsible for killing Nicholas Hirsch.

"Morning, Mom." Zoey looked me over. "You look terrible."

My darling teen could be so brutally honest.

"Thanks."

"Are you heading out?"

"Yes. I need to question a suspect at the police station, and then I'm going into the office."

"Sounds exciting. I think I'll go to the gym and then head back inside the apartment. Do you think Barney's forgotten us?"

"I don't think he's forgotten us. He's too clever. Grandma

says he's doing great," I reassured her. I hadn't told her that her uncle was currently incarcerated, arrested for murder. There was a solid case against him, and as much as I tried to tell myself it wasn't my problem, he was my family, and if I could help, I would try. I trusted Leslie, a twenty-five-year homicide veteran, that when she said there was a solid case against my brother, there was. But then why did he claim he was being set up? Was he lying, like most other criminals would in his situation?

Although Darren and I were practically strangers, his situation tugged at my heart, and I knew it was breaking Mom's.

"As for the case, do you think it will be over soon? I mean, what does your gut say?" Zoey asked.

"I think it will be over soon, Zoey. I can feel it."

"Thank goodness. The Sadie Hawkins dance is only two weeks away."

"Well, we couldn't miss that, could we? Let's say a little prayer that we're done before the Sadie Hawkins dance."

"Praise Jesus," Zoey exclaimed.

She attended church with me, but I wasn't sure if her faith was all that strong. Maybe it would come in time, or she could go the other way. I didn't push her one way or another—it was her heart and soul that had to believe. I gave my daughter a hug, grabbed my terrible cup of coffee, and headed out the door.

AFTER A QUICK HELLO to Hirsch and directions on where to find Maurice Stanzel, I headed back to the conference room and knocked on the door. Through the two-way glass, I could see Tippin was inside. He excused himself and met me outside. "Hey, Martina. He's not saying a word."

"Well, maybe it's time I share a few words with him."

"His bail hearing is in an hour, so you've got to be quick."

If he managed to get out on bail, I wasn't sure we'd ever see him again. Although he had several ties to the community, so the judge could make him surrender his passport. But even a mandated ankle monitor, given the severity of his crimes, seemed insufficient. I walked inside the conference room with Tippin and locked eyes with the man seated at the table. His lack of surprise made me believe he knew exactly who I was.

"Hi, there. You must be Maurice Stanzel," I said, already knowing the answer since I'd seen photographs.

"Yes, and you're Martina Monroe."

"That's correct. I'm the one you tried to have killed, after you tried to kidnap my daughter."

He sat stone-faced.

"You can stay silent all you want, but we have evidence against you."

"All circumstantial. Maybe you should leave this to actual law enforcement," his attorney said with a smirk.

"So much confidence. I wouldn't if I were in your position." Time to take the gloves off. "Listen carefully, Mr. Stanzel, because I have news for you. You're not going to get away with hiring someone to kill me, and you're not going to get away with hiring someone to follow and kidnap my daughter. There is evidence, a recording. And that's not all. You also won't be getting away with covering up Nicholas Hirsch's murder and the disappearance of Victoria Hightower."

Maurice Stanzel flinched.

"Yes, I know that Anthony Stanzel, your son, killed Nicholas Hirsch because he stepped in to save Victoria from a brutal attack. Now that we have your DNA, we can prove it. We have physical evidence from the crime scene that has a male contributor's DNA on it. All we have to do is run your DNA against the DNA at the scene and boom, your son goes to prison for murder, and you go to prison for conspiracy to commit murder, conspiracy to commit kidnapping, and I'm sure there are other charges, right?"

"That's right, Martina," Tippin added.

Maurice Stanzel leaned forward and stared into my eyes. "Listen, Miss Monroe, it sounds like you have a very vivid imagination. But rest assured, I didn't do any of the things I'm being accused of, nor did my son. And even if you have all these theories and this DNA evidence, you can't prove the DNA wasn't transferred from another person or planted."

His assurance infuriated me.

We needed to find Victoria.

"Well, if we have an eyewitness, that should do the trick, right?"

His lawyer chimed in. "Eyewitness testimony is highly unreliable. I think you should know that by now, Miss Monroe, and certainly, Lieutenant Tippin knows."

"Yes, that's true for strangers. But when the eyewitness actually knows and has lived with the perpetrator, they can easily identify them. Those types of witness are compelling in front of a jury, wouldn't you agree?"

The lawyer stiffened.

"That's right. As soon as we match your DNA to the DNA found at Nicholas Hirsch's crime scene, your son will be arrested. And when the eyewitness comes forward to testify, it's game over for the Stanzels."

"You'll never find her," Maurice Stanzel interjected.

Everyone in the room froze, and you could hear a pin drop.

I seized the moment. "Her? Who are you referring to?"

Realizing his mistake, he stammered, "The eyewitness, whoever she is. If I understand my lawyer correctly, she's probably some junkie who OD'd somewhere."

"I think orange will look good on you. But maybe you'll get black and white stripes. Tippin, do they still have those?"

"Not really. Usually orange or tan."

I turned back to Maurice Stanzel. "Tragic."

He stared me down, and I leaned in. "We will prove *all of it*. Your best bet is to strike a deal. But part of me hopes you don't, because I would prefer that you rot in prison for the rest of your life."

He looked away, and I knew my time was up.

I exited, and Tippin followed.

"What do you think of that?" he asked.

"I'd say it was an admission. He knows exactly what happened."

"And he's almost right. If we can't find the eyewitness, the case could be 50-50 for prosecuting Anthony Stanzel, assuming the DNA matches."

Frustrated, I shook my head. Not a single tip from the hotline had panned out. All were crackpots with misinformation. Just then, Hirsch approached as my phone buzzed.

Glancing at the screen, I saw it was from the office. I lifted a finger to signal to Hirsch that I had to answer. "This is Martina."

"Hi, Martina, this is Mrs. Pearson."

"What's up?"

"There's someone here to see you at the office."

"Who is it?"

"She won't say, but she insists she'll only talk to you. I think you should come down here."

My gut stirred, and I glanced over at Hirsch and the others. "I have to go." To my phone, I said, "Mrs. Pearson, I'm leaving the sheriff's department right now. I'll get my security team and head out."

"Okay. Be safe."

Tippin said, "What is it?"

"There's somebody at the office waiting for me."

"Who is it?" he asked.

"I don't know, but I've got a hunch." I looked at Tippin and Hirsch, not wanting to say the words. I didn't believe in jinxing things, but just to play it safe, I kept quiet until I could confirm what my gut was saying. "I'll call you as soon as I know anything." I waved my security team over, and we exited the sheriff's department. As we left, I prayed for a miracle.

48

MARTINA

SAFELY INSIDE DRAKOS MONROE, I rushed over to Mrs. Pearson. "Where is she?"

"She's with a friend in conference room one," Mrs. Pearson replied, giving me a look as if she already knew who it was. I returned her knowing glance and nodded.

Eager but cautious, I approached the small conference room and knocked before opening the door. Inside sat two women, one with fair skin and blue eyes, likely in her fifties, and next to her, a woman slightly older, wearing modest clothing that I recognized as a nun's habit.

I reached out my hand. "Hi, I'm Martina Monroe."

The first woman shook my hand. "My name is Victoria Hightower, and I heard you're looking for me."

"Yes, I have been," I responded, my heart pounding with anticipation.

Victoria gestured to her companion. "This is Sister Donna. A dear friend."

My heart skipped a beat. Donna was the name of my best friend who had died when we were eighteen. "It's very nice to meet you," I said, regaining my composure. "It's very good to see you, Victoria. There are a lot of people who care about you and miss you terribly."

"I saw my daughter on the news, and my mother—I couldn't believe it. I couldn't believe they're still looking for me," she said, her eyes clouded with years of unspoken pain.

"They're not the ones who hired me," I explained to her, catching the worry that clouded her face.

Victoria seemed taken aback. "Who did, then?"

"Your friend Nancy hired me to find you. She got out of that life thirty-five years ago. She's clean now and has a family of her own. She always regretted leaving you behind and tried to go back to find you but couldn't. She's the one who hired me."

Victoria's expression shifted from worry to relief and surprise. Considering what I knew of her story, she probably had feared it was the Stanzels or Priscilla Keene who were searching for her.

"Since I've been looking for you, I've uncovered quite a few things," I continued. "I understand that your personal safety is a concern, which is why we had you come to my office and not the police department."

"I appreciate that," she said, her eyes reflecting gratitude.

"Before we get into all of that, can I get you anything?" I asked, wanting to make her feel comfortable.

She shook her head, clearly eager to get to the point.

I hesitated, trying to figure out how to broach the subject delicately. "Then let's get started. Can you first explain why you decided to come in?" She'd been gone for so long she must have a compelling reason.

Victoria nodded, her eyes shining with unshed tears. "I spent a lot of time thinking about this and praying for guidance on the right path to take. I've stayed away to keep my family and myself safe. But when I saw my grown-up daughter and my mother, something inside me stirred. I knew it was time. I have faith that God will protect me and my family from those who wish us harm. And I'm ready to tell my story, but I'll need help to keep my family safe. It's not only me they've threatened. It's my entire family as well."

"We can do that," I reassured her, not surprised to hear the Stanzels had threatened her entire family. "It's our specialty at Drakos Monroe Security & Investigations."

"Thank you," she said, her relief palpable. "And that's not all. You see, I was in a very bad place once, and a very bad man tried to kill me. I'm sure of it. But another man, an angel of sorts, saved me and allowed me to escape. I came in today not just to reconnect with my family and Nancy, but also because I know I'd be dead if it weren't for that man who I believe lost his life for me. I want to know who he was, to thank his family, and to let them know I've been praying for them every day. If it weren't for him, I wouldn't be here today," she finished, her voice breaking.

I took a moment to compose myself, my eyes blurred with emotion. "We can do all of that," I assured her, fighting to keep my voice steady.

Sister Donna placed her hand gently on my shoulder. "If I didn't know better, I'd say this has been emotional for you."

Wiping my eyes, a little embarrassed at the lack of professionalism, I nodded. "Yes, it has become quite personal. And if I didn't say it before, I'm so glad you came in, Victoria. Thank you, from the bottom of my heart. And that man's family thanks you too. They have waited a long time to know the truth."

Sister Donna and Victoria both nodded, their faces a mix of relief and solemnity, as if years of unsaid words and untold stories were finally finding a place to land. And I felt the weight of the responsibility that comes with uncovering the truth but also the gratification that comes from setting it free.

49

MARTINA

With Victoria Hightower, also known as Maisie, as she had been going by for the last thirty-five years, tucked away in a safe house, I headed toward the conference room to update the team.

Victoria's story was nothing short of incredible. From her narrow escape from a man known as Blade—aka Anthony Stanzel—to spotting nuns at the bus station where Priscilla had dropped her off, it was a tale woven with surprises. The duffel bag and cash that Priscilla provided Victoria to start anew were perhaps the most startling elements.

My initial assumption had been that Priscilla was just another heartless criminal in the same vein as the Stanzels. Perhaps she was, but there was also a chance she had possessed a fragment of a soul back then. She might have wanted Victoria to have a second chance at life. This perception didn't mesh well with the mental image I had of Priscilla. Victoria conveyed that Priscilla hadn't offered an explanation for her help, she had simply told her not to ask questions and seize the opportunity to start a new life.

It was plausible that even the darkest criminals may have

shown a lighter side at some point in their lives. Maybe Priscilla still did. This theory was made even more fascinating by the fact that the convent where Victoria had taken refuge never disclosed the names of their volunteers. I had learned Victoria helped cook and clean at the convent in exchange for room and board. Since they didn't engage in financial transactions, there was no obligation for them to report employment records, thereby keeping Victoria completely off the grid.

Victoria had considered becoming a nun but felt she could better serve the Lord through other means—cooking, cleaning, and taking care of the convent's property. As a believer myself, I perceived her journey as nothing less than divine intervention. The day Nick saved her, followed by her serendipitous encounter with the nuns, were miraculous events that had undoubtedly saved her life. Without these chance meetings, I was convinced the Stanzels would have hunted her down and ended her life.

Before relocating Victoria to a safe house, we had an extensive conversation about all the events that unfolded on the day Nicholas Hirsch was killed. Now, all that remained was to obtain DNA evidence to corroborate her story so we could arrest the man responsible for Nick's murder.

As anticipated, the puzzle pieces were coming together, based on Victoria's last movements. Her assault on the street, being found passed out, and eventually ending up in the hospital. I hadn't yet disclosed that I knew the family of the man who had saved her from Blade. Given that she was already navigating through an emotional minefield and facing the adjustment to life in a safe house, I decided to hold off on revealing that information.

Happy endings were a rarity in our line of work. Outcomes were usually bittersweet. Tragedy often lingered, but justice usually prevailed.

In this case, the tragedy was Nicholas Hirsch's death. Yet it appeared that we were on course to obtain justice, and Victoria's family was likely to experience a happy conclusion. In this profession, that was about as much as one could hope for. Inside the expansive main conference room at Drakos Monroe, all the key players in the investigation gathered around the table for our call with the FBI.

I was eager to conclude the meeting and talk to Hirsch. He was the only one still left in the dark, and I hated that. However, knowing Hirsch as I did, I was certain he'd want everything done by the book. He was committed to making sure Anthony Stanzel paid for the pain and suffering inflicted upon his family —a pain embodied by the gaping hole left by Nick's absence.

Seated around the table were Lieutenant Tippin of the San Francisco Police Department, Vincent, our own rising star, and Detectives Ross and Jayda. With a sense of anticipation swirling in my stomach, I sat down. Vincent said, "I'll dial in."

Tippin raised an eyebrow and said, "Sounds like you've got some big news."

"I do."

The speakerphone emitted a ring, quickly followed by a voice answering, "Special Agent Vine and Special Agent Honeycutt here."

"Hi, there, it's Martina," I said, proceeding to list the names of everyone present.

Taking a deep breath, I began laying out our case. "Thank you all for assembling on such short notice. We have major news. As you all know, we have Maurice Stanzel in custody for conspiracy to commit murder and kidnapping. We've taken his DNA, and the lab is processing it as quickly as possible. Our plan is to match it against evidence from Nicholas Hirsch's crime scene to see if we can link Anthony Stanzel as well. There's also an open warrant for Priscilla Keene, although we haven't located her yet. As you know, if we can place Anthony Stanzel's DNA at Nicholas Hirsch's murder scene and have a key eyewitness, we'll have a slam-dunk case."

I paused for emphasis before dropping the bombshell. "Earlier today, that eyewitness walked into Drakos Monroe offices. Victoria Hightower has been living almost completely off the grid for thirty-five years—which is why neither we nor the Stanzels and Priscilla Keene could find her. She gave me a full account of what happened, including details surrounding Nicholas Hirsch's murder. She's willing to testify in open court and provide a sworn statement. Currently, we have Ms. Hightower, also known as Maisie, in a safe house. We still believe she and her family may be in danger."

The room was silent for a moment until Lieutenant Tippin broke the silence. "That's incredible. We have a team, one I trust with my life, watching Anthony Stanzel. So, once that DNA's a match, we'll pick him up."

Fingers crossed.

Everyone seemed to grasp the gravity of what I'd just shared. The pieces were coming together, and it felt like justice was finally within reach.

Nods of approval rolled around the table. From the speaker, Special Agent Vine said, "Well done. I've got to admit, the crew you have in that room right now is like a dream team. If any of you want a job at the FBI, you have our full referral."

I chuckled. It wasn't the first time the FBI had noticed the prowess of my team, whether during my tenure at CoCo County or now at Drakos Monroe. "That's very kind of you," I said. "I assembled you all for this update but also because I was hoping the FBI might have news on the whereabouts of Priscilla Keene or whispers of who shot up my house."

Special Agent Vine responded, "There's no trace of her, and given all the commotion around Maurice Stanzel's arrest, if she's out there, she's probably in hiding. But we all think she's most likely dead. We have no information on the shooting at your house, Martina. Sorry."

Ross said, "Traffic cams were a bust. The only thing we have is ballistics, but no matches to other crime scenes. If they're smart, they'll have tossed the gun."

It meant we may never know who shot at me, but we had Maurice Stanzel in custody whom we believed was responsible for the order.

The FBI continued, "Sounds like finding the actual shooter will be tricky. But we don't come empty-handed. We received some intel on movement within the DeMarco crime family. We should be getting an update from our team within the next twenty-four hours. We think we're close to bringing them in."

"Excellent," I said.

After discussing the details of Victoria's statement and fielding questions about our next steps, I said, "We'll reconvene after we get the DNA results back. And Special Agent Vine, please keep us posted if the task force uncovers anything related to the Stanzels."

Special Agent Vine affirmed, "Let's close this out before the weekend."

"My daughter, who's been in a safe house for much longer than she'd like, would prefer we resolve this before her Sadie Hawkins dance, which is in two weeks," I said, adding a touch of levity.

"Well, your daughter certainly can't miss the Sadie Hawkins dance," Special Agent Vine said in a cheery tone.

"No, she can't. Thank you, everyone."

We ended the call with the FBI. Vincent turned to me and said, "Have you told Hirsch?"

"No. I knew he'd want me to handle this by the book, so I've informed the team, and I'll let Hirsch know soon."

Vincent grinned. "Well done, everyone."

"It was the news story that did it. Thank you, Vincent. You've proved time and again it's always good to have contacts in the media."

The atmosphere was electric with the sense that we were on the brink of something monumental. We were a team united by a common mission—to deliver justice where it was long overdue. And as I looked around at the faces gathered around the table, I felt we were so close to achieving it.

50

MARTINA

Hirsch was kind enough to meet me in my office. For the time being, I still had a security detail that took me everywhere. Until we were certain the threats against me and Zoey were over, we stayed in the safe house that Zoey now referred to as the cell. But with this latest bit of news, I knew it would be over very soon. They'd have no reason to come after me now, not since the DNA came back as a match. Anthony Stanzel, or to be more specific, the male child of Maurice Stanzel, was confirmed as Nicholas Hirsch's murderer. Considering Maurice only had one son, Anthony, we were pretty sure it was him. Of course, once he was arrested, we would test Anthony's DNA to confirm it hadn't been an illegitimate child of Maurice's. But given the preliminary forensic evidence and Victoria's eyewitness statement, Lieutenant Tippin and his team were on their way to arrest Anthony Stanzel, as I waited with Hirsch.

"It's strange, Martina," Hirsch began, "but for some reason, I thought maybe we would never know what really happened to Nick. It wasn't until I met you and we worked through all those tough cases together I started to think his murder might one day be solved. And now that day is here. I'm glad there's no more wondering what happened and why, but it doesn't make me miss Nick any less."

Hirsch surely realized this was exactly what all the victims' families said to us when we caught their loved one's killer. They were happy justice was served, but it didn't bring their loved one back. The fact that we had caught Anthony Stanzel, and his father, who tried to cover up the crime, proved you can't ever give up. There's always hope until there isn't.

"Have you told your parents yet?"

He shook his head. "I'm waiting until he's in custody."

"That's probably for the best."

My phone rang at my desk, and I picked it up. "Martina Monroe."

"It's Tippin. We've got him. He's down at SFPD getting booked as we speak."

I looked over at Hirsch and nodded. "Thank you, Tippin. Excellent work."

"I'd love to say it was my team that made all the difference, but I have the feeling you know the truth. It's been a pleasure to work with you, Martina."

"You too, Lieutenant. Hopefully, this isn't the last time."

"No, I'm sure we'll cross paths again. I can feel it in my bones."

"You take care."

I ended the call and turned to Hirsch. "They have him. He's in custody." He stood there with a blank look on his face. Maybe it was more emotion than he could process. It had been a harrowing month between learning that he and Kim would only have the one child, finding his brother's killer, and now the arrest. It was a lot. He must be feeling all kinds of emotions.

"You okay?"

"Yeah, I'm okay. It's just... it's over. I mean, there's going to be the trial, I'm sure, unless he pleads out. I don't know how I feel about that. I guess it could save the taxpayers some money and not put my family through a trial. A plea deal would work for me, although it affects my parents as well."

He was always thinking one step ahead, as usual. This wasn't really the end for him. We still had to prosecute Anthony. Although we had the evidence and the statements from Victoria, it didn't look like Anthony Stanzel would ever get out of prison. At his age, twenty-five years would be a life sentence. However, that still wasn't enough to deem Zoey and me safe. We needed someone to talk because we hadn't found out who had shot at my house, and Rex Kleinman didn't know either.

"I'm going to call the FBI and let them know what we found," I said.

He nodded. "Sounds good."

Vincent walked by, and I waved him in. "They got him."

"Excellent. How are you doing, Hirsch?"

"All right. Glad my brother's murderer is in police custody."

Vincent said, "Quite a case."

"I'm about to call the FBI." I shut my door and called Special Agent Vine on the speakerphone.

"Special Agent Vine."

"Hi, this is Martina Monroe. I'm here with Hirsch and Vincent."

"How's it going? Did you get him?"

"Anthony Stanzel is in police custody at the San Francisco Police Department."

"Excellent. I've got news too. I was just about to call you."

"Oh?" Leaning over my desk, I eyed Vincent and Hirsch. "What did you find?"

"We found Priscilla Keene, but that's not all."

They didn't kill her. "Should I call Lieutenant Tippin? I just got off the phone with him."

"We'll contact him because we found Priscilla Keene in San Francisco—well, at least on a ship docked at the pier."

The three of us exchanged glances.

"She's on a ship?"

"Yep, in disguise. I'm telling you, this case just blew wide open. My team is sorting through all the charges, but as you know, we suspected the DeMarcos of human trafficking minors and young adults overseas. When my team went in for the raid, we picked up a ship full of people being held against their will—presumably to be sold into the sex trade overseas. As we were questioning them, it soon became apparent that one was not like the others. Priscilla Keene had disguised herself as one of the victims of human trafficking."

"You're kidding?"

"Nope. She was fleeing the country on a ship full of stolen children."

I could barely believe what I was hearing. How far had Priscilla fallen from grace? Thirty-five years ago, she had given money and clothes to Victoria, giving her a second chance at life away from the sex trade and the abuse of pimps and boyfriends. And now, she was buying and selling children, making her escape by pretending to be one of them.

"How did they figure out she was Priscilla Keene?"

"First of all, Priscilla Keene is in her fifties. Most of the trafficked victims are considerably younger, and that raised flags at the center. And when one of the undercover agents saw her, they knew immediately it was Priscilla."

"So, she's working with the DeMarcos, and so are the Stanzels?" I asked incredulously.

"Yep. So far, Priscilla's not talking to us, but she said she'd talk to you."

"She wants to talk to me?"

"Yep. She's obviously under arrest. There's a warrant in

CoCo County for conspiracy to commit murder and kidnapping. Based on what our undercover surveillance team has uncovered, the Stanzels are deeply involved with the DeMarcos —silent partners, if you will. Turns out, talking to some of the victims, they keep them in houses around San Francisco until they're ready to be shipped off."

"That's probably why the PI was hired to check out temporary housing for employees and visitors. If we gave Rex addresses of where the victims were being held, I bet they would match up."

"I wouldn't be surprised."

We knew the DeMarcos were bad, and we assumed the Stanzels were too, but this just confirmed it. "Do you have charges against Priscilla in addition to the conspiracy charges?"

"Oh, yeah. Tons of them. But considering she was on the run, we think maybe she'll flip. We're really interested to hear what she has to say to you."

Him and me both. "Where is she?"

"She's at a detention center in San Francisco. Can you come out here, or is that too risky?"

"It's a little tricky since I still have a security detail. Could she be transferred over here?"

"To your offices?"

"It would be the easiest."

"Sure, let me work out the details, and I'll call you back."

"Thanks, Special Agent Vine."

"You got it. It's been a pleasure, Martina."

I ended the call and turned to Hirsch and Vincent. "That's almost a wrap, guys."

Vincent shook his head. "It's crazy how all this stuff is connected. You start out investigating a missing person, an old friend, but then that person is the eyewitness to Hirsch's brother's death and is connected to a sex trafficking ring in San Francisco. It's a crazy world."

"No doubt. What do you think Priscilla wants to talk to you about?" Hirsch asked.

"I have no idea. But if what Special Agent Vine says is true, and we could flip her, I'll do my best to get as much information as possible—especially to find out who's trying to kill me."

This case couldn't be over too soon, not only for my sake, but we also couldn't reunite Victoria with her loved ones until we knew she was safe too. I hoped my meeting with Priscilla provided me with the information I needed to ensure we were all safe, so Victoria could move on and so could I. As it stood, my brother was facing life in prison, and from what I could tell, there wasn't a darn thing I could do about it. My mother was devastated and needed me. I couldn't be there for her if I was locked in a protective cage or interviewing bad guys.

51

PRISCILLA

MARTINA MONROE. The woman who took me down. Based on Rex's research, I knew she was a formidable opponent. It was unfortunate. She could have been an ally. She was attractive, but not in a pin-up girl kind of way—shoulder-length dark hair, amber eyes, clear complexion. You could tell she had been through some things, but not the kind of things I'd seen. The stuff I'd seen, the stuff I'd done, left a mark you couldn't scrub off. In another life, I would have looked up to someone like Martina Monroe, someone who fights for justice and puts her life on the line for her friends.

I was admittedly surprised to learn she had collaborated with the FBI, the sheriff's department, and the San Francisco Police Department—all to find one missing person. In the process, she unraveled three decades full of lies, deceit, and unquestionable crimes.

Martina said, "I must admit, I was surprised that you wanted to talk to me."

"I was curious about the woman who took down the Stanzels and the DeMarcos."

She sat up, took a sip of her coffee, and said, "It wasn't all me. The FBI was already hot on the DeMarcos and the Stanzels, and I was looking for Victoria, which led me to the murder she'd witnessed—the murder of my best friend's brother. But you already knew that. That's why you hired someone to kill me."

She knew more than I thought. "Are you recording this conversation?" I asked cautiously.

She shook her head. "Nope. I'm not going to say that anything you tell me I won't tell anybody else, because I most likely will. But nothing you tell me can be used in court unless, of course, you give me information that we can corroborate. And then it will be used against you. But to be honest, there's so much evidence against you, Anthony, and Maurice Stanzel—the DeMarcos, too. Sure, I found the string, and I pulled it, but there was already a whole slew of folks ready to take you apart."

"Just out of curiosity, what did you find out and how?" I pressed.

"Well, our first break, I'd say, was when I questioned the hospital staff and found that there was one who actually remembered Victoria. That brought us to you, of course, after we'd already connected her to Anthony Stanzel. From there, after somebody tried to kidnap my daughter and I caught them and had them arrested, we got insight into what was really going on. Admittedly, Kleinman wouldn't talk at first, but when we couldn't find you, and the FBI's undercover team said there were rumblings that you'd disappeared, we told him they likely killed you and that he was next. He sang like a canary," she said, rather flippantly.

"Rex was always weak—good enough as guys go, I suppose," I said. The problem with Rex was that he had a gambling problem and had gotten in heavy with the DeMarcos back in the day. We lucked out he had good investigative skills and knew how to do our dirty work, as long as we paid him and told him what to do. Who knows? Maybe there's always a defining moment in our lives that changes us, turns us into something we never thought we could be, for better or for worse.

I tried to think about what that moment was for me. I used to despise people like me—buying and selling, profiting off humans, even children. Maybe it was the loss of my daughter that broke me, or perhaps it was having to lie on my back and do other unspeakable things with men that wiped out my soul completely. I should have known better than to stand by the Stanzels. They weren't careful, even when I warned them they needed to be. I ran because I knew they wouldn't protect me.

"Yeah, actually, that broke the case pretty wide open," Martina continued. "You see, we got Maurice Stanzel's DNA and were able to match it against Nicholas Hirsch's crime scene. And wouldn't you know it, that smoking gun—along with an eyewitness that said Anthony Stanzel was at the crime scene—put him right in jail too."

"An eyewitness?"

"We found Victoria."

That was a surprise. "Really?"

"Yes," she confirmed.

Something stirred inside of me—a kinship, a shared past, I didn't know. "Is she all right?"

Martina looked puzzled. Perhaps she thought I had zero humanity left inside of me. I must admit, sometimes I wondered about that too.

"Yes, she's doing quite well. She's been clean, living a humble life. We haven't yet been able to reunite her with her family, though. Concerns over her safety and my own—like I mentioned, you hired someone to kill me, and she was threatened as well. Her family was threatened if she ever came forward about Nicholas Hirsch's murder, a murder committed by Anthony Stanzel. But you know that too, because you're the one who threatened her."

Might as well throw her a bone, right? "It's true. I hired someone to shoot up your house after Kleinman failed to kidnap your daughter."

"Are they still after me?" she asked.

I shook my head. "No, they weren't supposed to kill you. They were just supposed to scare you. Sounds like it worked."

Martina scratched the side of her face and looked me square in the eyes. "Do you enjoy scaring people? Do you get off on this? Is that why you work with the Stanzels? Why you sell babies?"

"What? I don't sell babies."

"You were involved with selling children. They're somebody's babies," she corrected.

My face flushed. She was right. I had been involved, not hands-on, of course. Being on that ship was the first time I'd seen them face-to-face, and it was revolting. I wouldn't blame them for locking me up and throwing away the key.

"Is there still a hit out on me? My daughter, Victoria, her family?" Martina asked.

I leaned back. "No, the job was finished when they shot up your house. Kleinman failed to kidnap your daughter. The only reason we did that was to get you to stop investigating. Sounds like the case is over."

"It is. The DeMarcos, the Stanzels, you—I don't think anybody's going to see the light of day in this lifetime. I hope you enjoy prison," Martina retorted.

My life was already a prison. "It's what I deserve," I admitted.

"It is. So, can you tell me who you hired to shoot at my house? That's our one missing thread."

I shrugged. "Sure, I'll give you names. I'll give you everything," I said, defeated. There was nothing left to fight for. The Stanzels wouldn't protect me, and I was going to jail for the rest of my life.

"Even your real identity?" Martina questioned.

I let out a low chuckle. "You are good, aren't you?"

"There are no records of you from more than thirty-five years ago. Why the change? What were you running from?"

I smiled. "My life. The trailer park I grew up in, the years selling my body, jerks like Stanzel, losing my child. Yeah, I had a baby girl. She died after only a few minutes. Heart defect. I don't even know who her father was. Oh, and there was that john who disappeared." After I killed him. Not that he didn't deserve it. That was self-defense, but I knew the cops would see it differently.

And then I drifted off to a different place in my mind, wondering why I was telling this woman about my past. Maybe it was just time to let it all out, to let go. Everything I'd been holding on to had swallowed me whole. Maybe I'd be free if I let it out.

"I'm sorry that happened to you," Martina said, showing a glimmer of sympathy.

"Sympathy for me?"

"I don't think we're born bad. I know what it's like growing up in a trailer. Thankfully, I never had to engage in survival sex work. I've had my share of trauma but losing a child—I can't even imagine. Is that why you helped Victoria?"

"Perhaps." I considered. "I saw something of myself in her. Even though she couldn't be with her daughter, at least she would get to start over, maybe have another one or two. Did she?"

Martina shook her head. "She never married or had more children."

"Well, still, it sounds like she took her second chance."

"Anything else you want to ask me or would like to tell me?"

"No, but you can tell the police I'll talk to them. I'll tell them anything they want to know. I'm done."

Martina looked surprised as she raised her brows. "I'll let the agent know."

"It was good to see you again, Martina," I said, feeling the weight of my choices but also the faint lightness of unburdening my soul.

She looked back at me and gave me a head nod.

I didn't think she was glad she'd met me, but it was nice to know there were good people out there. Amongst all of us rotten apples, there were a few good, sweet ones left. All this time knowing life is full of winners and losers, I had thought I was winning. Turned out, I'd been losing all along.

52

VICTORIA
PRESENT DAY

It had been thirty-five years since I stood on the porch of my childhood home. Martina, who stood by my side, assured me I was safe, and so was my family. The Stanzels, Blade, and Priscilla were all in jail. Apparently, they had done much worse things than sending me off with a duffel bag full of clothes and cash.

Martina had arranged for my friend Nancy to be there, as well as my mom and my daughter. I was nervous and excited, full of emotions I feared might burst out in heavy sobs. I had dreamed about this moment for so long. I couldn't believe it was finally happening. I knocked on the door, and my heart skipped a beat when it opened to reveal a man with dark hair and kind eyes.

"Victoria?" the man asked.

"Yes."

"My name's Kevin. I'm Shannon's husband."

My son-in-law. I had just met my son-in-law. My baby had grown up and gotten married. "It's nice to meet you."

"You too."

I continued inside. My mother was sitting in her recliner,

and my daughter—now thirty-seven years old—sat on the sofa next to her. And Nancy, oh my gosh, Nancy! I was so overwhelmed I didn't know what to say.

Martina broke the silence. "I know this can be overwhelming, but maybe we just start with a hello."

Everyone nodded, but I could only look at Shannon. She had to grow up without a mom. I stepped toward her, tears streaming down my face.

We embraced, and I never felt more complete in my whole life. We cried together, and I didn't want to let go, but I also wanted to see her lovely face.

"You're so beautiful. I thought about you every day," I said while pulling back.

Shannon whispered, "I thought about you every day too."

I turned to see my mom getting off the couch with the help of Shannon's husband. "Mama, Mama," I whispered as I stepped toward her and hugged her. She was so frail. I tried not to squeeze too hard.

She said, "I knew you were still out there, baby. In my heart, I knew."

"I'm so sorry," I cried.

"It's not your fault, honey. It's not your fault."

Overwhelmed again, I turned to Nancy. It was because of her that they found me, and we were reunited and safe. "Nancy, thank you. It's so good to see you. I don't know what else to say." We embraced, and I knew this would go down as one of the best days of my life.

After sharing many hugs and lots of tissues, we all sat down. I told them about the peaceful life I'd been living but how there had always been something missing inside me. It was them. My family and my closest friend. Nancy had been there during my hardest times, and it was her desire to find me and thank me for my friendship that brought this whole thing to an end.

That's when it hit me. "Oh my gosh, I have to thank Martina—" I stopped mid-sentence and turned to her. "Thank you so much, Martina."

She nodded with tears in her eyes. "It's nice to have a happy ending every once in a while."

As I sat and listened to Nancy talk about her life and her new grandchild, my daughter brought out her wedding album so I could look at all the pictures. Part of my heart broke that I hadn't been there, but she looked so beautiful, so happy. Her husband seemed nice too. He made sure we all had iced tea and took care of us as we cried, smiled, and laughed.

I felt both exhausted and revived at the same time. I never wanted to be apart from my daughter, my mother, and Nancy again. I knew in my heart that Nancy and I would spend the rest of our lives being friends. But there was still one thing missing. I turned to Martina Monroe and said, "Thank you so much for reuniting us. I don't mean to sound ungrateful, but it feels incomplete without being able to meet the family of the man who saved my life. Do you think you could find out if they'd like to meet me?"

Martina smiled and said, "I've already spoken with the family. They would very much like to meet you."

My eyes popped open. "You have? They don't hate me?"

She shook her head. "No, they don't hate you. They're delighted that you've been reunited with your family and that you're safe. They see you as the reason there will be justice for Nicholas. His name was Nicholas Hirsch."

"Did they say when they'd like to meet?"

"It's up to you. They're all local to the Bay Area."

I sniffled and said, "Okay." Drifting off into thought about how I would coordinate all of this—I didn't have a car or a driver's license—I was quiet until Shannon spoke up.

"Mom, if you'd like, we could go with you. Show them what their Nicholas gave us."

Martina had to sniffle away her own tears and said, "I think they would like that very much."

My mom said to Martina, "Not to call you out, but you don't usually get this emotional about your cases, do you?"

"Sometimes I do," Martina said with a chuckle. "This was a particularly special case. You see, not only did I get to reunite a family, but I haven't told you about Nicholas's family. The Hirsches are like family to me."

I gasped. "You said it was kind of emotional for you, but I guess I didn't think to ask how."

"Not to worry. This is a positive event for everyone, and I'm so glad it turned out the way it did. When your mom told me she knew you were still out there, I believed her. We weren't going to give up until we found you. A mother's intuition is real, and this just proves it."

"Yes, it is," my mom added. "That's how I knew my baby would be okay."

Just then, Shannon's husband walked in. "Should I order dinner or cook something up?" He looked down at his wife and added, "You must be starved."

Shannon seemed surprised by the comment and then smiled before she turned back to look at me. "I am pretty hungry," she admitted. Then she looked at my mom, and both of them looked at me. "We have some news."

I froze.

"Mom, you're going to be a grandma."

In that moment, I closed my eyes and prayed, thanking God for all my blessings.

53

MARTINA

AFTER I HUNG up the phone, I wanted to cry. The evidence against my brother was airtight, yet he had sworn to my mother he was innocent. His lawyer had advised him to take a deal for second-degree felony murder with a twenty-five-year sentence. He'd signed the deal. The ink was still wet, and it felt as if I was losing my brother all over again. It was strange to think you could lose something you didn't really have. Sure, he existed, but I hadn't talked to him in twenty years, and now, after briefly reconnecting, he was going to prison.

My mother was beside herself and swore her baby couldn't have done it and that there had to be a mistake, and I couldn't blame her. As a mother, you hope for the best for your children and can't imagine they could be capable of such terrible acts. You guide them, teach them, and feel delighted by their successes. But when they fail, you take it hard—part of that blame eats you up.

Biting back my feelings, I had to put on a happy face. I was about to reunite—or rather introduce—Victoria, her daughter, and son-in-law to the Hirsch family. It should have been joyous for me. I wanted to see people, who I felt were like family, get some closure—or perhaps not so much closure as an end to wondering about why Nick was killed and by whom. Those questions were answered, and now they would meet Victoria and her daughter.

Hirsch, Kim, and Audrey had already arrived. They were the first ones, which wasn't a surprise. I had opened my home to them, knowing that a warm environment would be best for the occasion. My mom was originally going to bake and bring treats, but she wasn't feeling up to it. Her son, Darren, was going to prison for twenty-five years. She said it broke her heart, and I believed her.

I gave Hirsch, Kim, and Audrey hugs as they came in. Hirsch's first question was, "Where's Zoey?"

Zoey appeared from down the hall, saying, "Hi, Audrey!" before giving her a hug.

"You're the first to arrive."

"We did that on purpose," Hirsch responded. "I want to thank you, Martina. You solved the most important case of my life."

"I didn't do it alone."

"I know, I know, but you have the entire Hirsch family's gratitude. Mom and Dad should be here soon, as well as my brother and his wife."

"That's great." I forced a smile.

Hirsch noticed and asked, "Is everything okay?"

I shook my head. "Darren just pled out to second-degree murder."

"So, he's guilty."

"Essentially. They say the evidence is irrefutable. The lawyer looked it over and said a twenty-five-year sentence for second-degree murder was the best he could get."

"That's rough. I'm so sorry. How's Betty doing?"

"Well, she's not here. She's pretty upset."

Just then, Zoey popped over, ever the curious teenager. "What's up? What's going on?"

"I was just telling Uncle August about Uncle Darren," I explained.

"Oh," she said, a hint of sadness in her voice. She'd never actually met Darren, so it wasn't as emotional for her, but she understood the weight of it for me and her grandmother.

As the other Hirsches and Victoria and her family arrived, I smiled and hugged everyone, providing plenty of tissues all around.

I stayed in the background, just there to help two families heal after so many years.

It was a beautiful thing to witness. From the tragic loss of Nicholas Hirsch emerged one of the greatest homicide detectives there ever was. Hirsch had solved countless cases for other families, and now he finally had resolution for his own. His brother's death wasn't for nothing—it wasn't a simple mugging. Nicholas Hirsch had been a good man, even in his late teens. He'd wanted to help others, and his death proved it. He had put his own safety at risk for a stranger, a woman being beaten by a terrible man—someone who thought he could own humans and sell them for profit. It was moving to see how two families, tied by the same tragedy, could heal and come out better. Although the hole in their hearts could never be filled by any number of arrests or truths known. Nicholas would never come back. But his memory would always be there.

Just then, my phone buzzed. It was a number I didn't recognize. I retreated to the kitchen and answered, "Hello?"

"Is this Martina Monroe?" a voice on the other end inquired.

"Yes," I responded, puzzled.

"Your brother Darren didn't do it."

"Who is this?"

"Look, he didn't do it," the voice insisted. The call ended abruptly. I immediately tried to call back, but there was no answer. Eventually, a message stated that the phone number was no longer working. What did they mean, Darren didn't do it? The evidence was airtight. If it was so conclusive, why would someone call me to say otherwise?

Hirsch stepped into my kitchen and asked, "Is everything okay?"

I looked up at him, still perplexed, and said, "I just got a really strange phone call."

"Oh?" he inquired.

I explained the situation to him.

"Strange. What do you think it means?"

"I don't know." But I did know that I would find out. Could it be possible that my brother really was innocent? It was hard to refute the physical evidence. And he signed a deal, proclaiming his guilt. But if he was guilty, why the strange call?

There was only one way to find the truth—and I would *most certainly* do just that.

THANK YOU!

Thank you for reading *How She Escaped* I hope you enjoyed reading it as much as I loved writing it. If you did, I would greatly appreciate if you could post a short review.

Reviews are crucial for any author and can make a huge difference in visibility of current and future works. Reviews allow us to continue doing what we love, *writing stories.* Not to mention, I would be forever grateful!

Thank you!

ALSO BY H.K. CHRISTIE

The Martina Monroe Series —a nail-biting crime thriller series starring PI Martina Monroe and her unofficial partner Detective August Hirsch of the Cold Case Squad. If you like high-stakes games, jaw-dropping twists, and suspense that will keep you on the edge of your seat, then you'll love the Martina Monroe crime thriller series.

The Selena Bailey Series (1 - 5) — a suspenseful series featuring a young Selena Bailey and her turbulent path to becoming a top-notch private investigator as led by her mentor, Martina Monroe.

The Val Costa Series —a gripping crime thriller with heart-pounding suspense. If you love Martina, you'll love Val.

The Neighbor Two Doors Down —a dark and witty psychological thriller. If you like unpredictable twists, page-turning suspense, and unreliable narrators, then you'll love *The Neighbor Two Doors Down*.

A Permanent Mark A heartless killer. Weeks without answers. Can she move on when a murderer walks free? If you like riveting suspense and gripping mysteries then you'll love *A Permanent Mark* - starring a grown up Selena Bailey.

For H.K. Christie's full catalog go to: **www.authorhkchristie.com**

At **www.authorhkchristie.com** you can also sign up for the H.K. Christie reader club where you'll be the first to hear about upcoming novels, new releases, giveaways, promotions, and a free e-copy of the prequel to the Martina Monroe Thriller Series, *Crashing Down*!

ABOUT THE AUTHOR

H. K. Christie watched horror films far too early in life. Inspired by the likes of Stephen King, Jodi Picoult, true crime podcasts, and a vivid imagination she now writes suspenseful thrillers.

She found her passion for writing when she embarked on a one-woman habit breaking experiment. Although she didn't break her habit she did discover a love of writing and has been at it ever since.

When not working on her latest novel, H.K. Christie can be found eating & drinking with friends, walking around the lakes, or playing with her favorite furry pal.

She is a native and current resident of the San Francisco Bay Area.

To learn more about H.K. Christie and her books or simply to say, "hello", go to **www.authorhkchristie.com**.

ACKNOWLEDGMENTS

Many thanks to those who helped me shape and create this story. First, many thanks to my Advanced Reader and Street Teams. These wonderful readers are invaluable in taking the first look at my stories and helping find typos and spreading awareness of my stories through their reviews and kind words. To my editor, Paula Lester, a huge thanks for your careful edit and helpful comments and proofreaders Becky Stewart and Ryan Mahan for catching those last typos. To my cover designer, Odile, thank you for your guidance and talent. Last but not least, I'd like to thank all of my readers. It's because of you I'm able to continue writing stories.

Made in the USA
Coppell, TX
09 April 2025

48095799R00162